XORANDOR

Xorandor

Christine Brooke-Rose

CARCANET

First published in Great Britain 1986 by
Carcanet Press Limited
208–212 Corn Exchange Buildings
Manchester M4 3BQ

Copyright © 1986 Christine Brooke-Rose
The publisher acknowledges financial assistance
from the Arts Council of Great Britain

British Library Cataloguing in Publication Data

Brooke-Rose, Christine
   Xorandor.
   I. Title
   823'.914[F]   PR6003.R412

   ISBN 0-85635-655-7

Typesetting by Paragon Photoset, Aylesbury
Printed in England by SRP Ltd, Exeter

ACKNOWLEDGEMENTS

I am greatly indebted to my cousin Claude Brooke, Phys. E.P.F., for the scientific information around which this story is written, as well as for part of the original scientific idea, and much helpful discussion at inception.

By the end of the creative process, however, so many fictional and stylistic transformations of that bare information had occurred that I needed further and more concrete and corrective scientific help. I was immensely lucky to receive this from Thomas Blackburn, Ph.D., Professor of Chemistry at St Andrews Presbyterian College, Laurinburg, North Carolina, who also made some very useful suggestions.

With both debts, any errors or misinterpretations are my own.

The programming language and computer called Poccom 3 are inventions, based on various existing languages and possibilities. I am particularly indebted to an excellent book, *Programming Languages — Design and Implementation*, by Terrence W. Pratt, Prentice/Hall International, Inc, Englewood Cliffs, New Jersey, 1984.

C.B-R.
Paris, 1985.

5

1 BEGIN

The first time we came across Xorandor we were sitting on him.

Correction, Zab. Sitting True, came across False. We didn't come across Xorandor, he contacted us.

True, Jip. We'd come to our usual haunt by the old carn and we were sitting on this large flat stone.

It was the middle of our summer eprom and we'd taken Poccom 2 out with us to play on.

That was the very little one, we're using Poccom 3 now.

When suddenly there flashed on the miniscreen, in yellow but out of the blue, the words GET OFF MY BACK.

Peculiarly spelt, G,E,T , was okay, then O,F, then M,A,I, then B,A,K. That's for the printout.

Right. And you swore you hadn't done it.

Correction, Jip, there was no need to swear. In fact it's important at this stage to say we often read each other's thoughts almost as fast as a computer calculates. We stared at each other and knew at once the other hadn't done it.

Stubs, it's tough dictating this, Zab. It'd be much easier typing it straight on the keyboard.

But then it'd all come from one of us only, even if we took turns. One, it's important to be two, and two, it's easier to interrupt on vocal than to push hands away. You agreed, Jip, you even dubbed it flipflop storytelling, which was super-diodic of you. We'll get used to it.

But we could use two keyboards, and program-interrupts with WAITS and other subroutines.

Not the same, Jip. Even if it turns out to be complementary storytelling, say bubble rather than flipflop —

You're mixing your computer-levels a bit.

— talking 's better than subroutines, cos it strays, it should be like a, let's see, like a butterfly-net, taken out and waved around to catch a flitting word or idea. It's going to be harder than we thought, as you're realizing, to recapture all the details after eight or nine months. We can dump the net later.

Dump data-network as butterfly-catcher, not bad, Zab, smart terminal. The ideal would be dynamic dumping, which empties a memory during program-run.

That's whacky, Jip, we won't know till much later what to dump or scratch.

Stubs! Let's get on with it. And we'd better get better. How did the bards manage? We haven't said anything yet.

That's called suspense, Jip.

Or waste instruction.

Well the bards used plenty of that. Come to think of it even in some classic tecs nothing happens for sixty pages, it's all datasink and flutter-byes.

Don't drag out every joke, Zab or we'll never get into it. We shouldn't have begun the way we did. After all we named him Xorandor but not till later, and it didn't even catch on at once.

So?

Flipping flipflops it seems harder to tell a story, even our own, than to make up the most complex program. Or at least to choose how to tell it. Where to start for instance. There are endless beginnings. And if we feed'm all in and ask Poccom 3 to choose, why, just the process of thinking'm up and feed- ing'm in would take ages. And probably convince us of the answer long before we'd finished.

That's the flutterby-net, Jip. Anyway, isn't that exactly what we're doing? Feeding in things as we think of them and leaving it to the processing stage to scratch or add or shift around?

Hey, Zab, maybe we should first introduce ourselves. Lots of stories start with the storyteller saying who he is.

But everyone knows us now.

Now, yes, because of the hoohah. But when we're grown-up, or maybe sooner, it'll all be forgotten. Or at least the details.

True. It's loopy, Jip, everyone gets used to the most offline discoveries so fast, and at the same time they take decades to change their mental habits.

And of course the whole point is to give our own version, not those of the media. We know things dad doesn't know we know. And we'll have Xorandor's version if he keeps his promise as he always does.

On the other hand we were younger too, and understood less, even than we do now.

Garbage, Zab. If anything it seems the other way about, we know less now, isolated here in Germany, than they do, or than we did then.

But it's still true we knew more then. And want to tell it.

Right then, we're twins. So inseparable that at first Xorandor thought we were one person, our voices were so alike. We were twelve and a half. Jip stands for John Ivor Paul, and since dad's also called John the initials became a name, to tell them apart.

And Zab was jealous, cos Isabel Paula Kate isn't pronounceable, so she took a syllable of her first name to make something just as snappy.

And dad never liked it, and still tries hard to use Isabel. But fails. Mum gave in quickly.

So we created our names. By insistant use.

Just as we named Xorandor: Just like naming programs.

Trap, Zab. What else?

That's all for the who. Oh no, there's physical description. We look alike, with fair hair, same shortish length, and —

Redundant rem, Zeb, who cares? Does anyone know what storytellers look like? Describe Lockwood.

But we're characters too, Jip. Almost the heroes if Xorandor wasn't. But okay, accept. Now for what kind. Which in a way is part of who.

At St Austell's we were called whizz-kids, cos we're so good in computer-class. The others love them as games, or even as

9

teacher-supps, but they stay with peripherals. Funny, cos we're all computers really, biological instead of electronic, and born with basic programs. But some develop them early and others don't, and then it's too late, like learning languages.

Well it is learning languages.

Check. Everyone should be able to, like they learn their own, or even several in bilingual circs, but for some reason it doesn't work like that. They say every maths teacher can spot the kind of diodically bright child who explores every op and gets the hang of basic maths concepts real nano.

Holy nukes, Jip, you do sound a conceited prig.

Well it's true. Not that we're not fairly megavolt at literature and other things, but they're only for the leisure industry, they're not taught higher up, after school, everyone has to do science or hitech. Still, we're good at those things too.

Doesn't look like it, we can't even get this story off the ground.

Accept. For literature specify reading. And play-acting, Shakespeare for instance, that's important for the story isn't it? Besides, we're just warming up, Zab, it's quite fun after all, might as well regard this as bootstrap. When we've found an entry we'll begin properly.

We could start with the loss of radiation at The Wheal.

No, that's where dad comes in, it's his side. We came in earlier.

Okay then, what more about us? Are we as beastly as we sound?

How like a girl! Why should it be beastly to be megavolt? We're just pretty gung-ho, that's all, compared to other kids we know.

Assign initial value gung-ho to variable Jipnzab by increment just pretty. Proceed. Fact is, on the megavolt parameter, Jip's much better at inventing programs.

But Zab makes them more efficient, more elegant and economic. Not in life, mind you, where she's a regular chatterbox, but with the decision-box she has quite a seethrough knack for shortening loose instructions such as GOTO X, IF Y, THEN DO Z, RAISE EXCEPTION W with added clauses and further adhoc explanations for vague commands.

Oh, descramble, Jip, few languages use regular Goto's anymore, besides, why so modest?

Well, *we* did, remember? They're still useful even if they can also lead to spaghetti logic. Anyway, make up your mind, you can't use both modest and conceited prig. Better go through the anti-coincidence gate, Zab.

The XOR-gate! Remember when we told Xorandor he was being modest? He couldn't grasp the concept.

Avort. Please, please let's get started. THIS is spaghetti logic. We haven't even finished the introductions, we've left ourselves floating in a vaccuum, we'll soon be subject to cosmic radiation.

Right then, the where. DEClaration. We're dictating this into a processor called Poccom 3, in Jip's room in a suburb of Bayreuth in south east West Germany, where we were sent to school to be out of reach of the journalists after the hoohah. We were allowed to take our gadgets with us, strobeluck. The room is in the house of Herr und Frau Groenetz, Gerd and Frieda now, and their son Rudi, who's already fifteen. He was very friendly at first and played with us and helped us lots with German, but he's sort of more distant now, he thinks we're just kids mad about our computer and we'll grow out of it like he did out of his, but then, he only uses his for game software. ENDEC.

Zab, that's storyteller's where, nobody gives a thunk, what we need is the story's where.

Correction not accepted. You agreed to introduce the storytellers cos they're also characters. If the storytellers are characters THEN their confusion is part of their characters ENDIF. Inversely IF the characters are the storytellers THEN the confusion is part of the story ENDIF. REMark. The confusion may be due to loss of memory for precise detail, itself due to longstop runtime since the hoohah and especially since the beginning ENDREM. NEWREM Confusion ANDOR also due to the fact,

11

so far unmentioned by my modestly conceited twin brother or viceversa, that since our arrival here we've been through the horrid business, just like Xorandor at the beginning, of not understanding one kiloword of what was being said around us, in class especially, except of course maths and physics and chemistry and compsci. Well, now it's much better, thanks to Frieda's extra lessons and Rudi and all that, but it was tough to feel what it's like to be near bottom of the class like a nondiodic kid, retarded even. Good for us, dad said, ENDNEWREM.

Spaghetti stacks, Zab, AND redundant rems! That didn't last, let's get on.

We're still not top of the class, Jip, and if you don't mind, it is not redundant rem, even if we later shift it somewhere else. Remember how we kept wondering how Xorandor's referencing system could work since he can't see or experience anything.

You kept wondering, Zab. And still do.

School here was a bit like that, Jip, and it helps us to imagine. Nothing but dangling refs.

Oh, Gigo.

Okay, accept. Now. Story-where. DEClaration. It happened in the village of Carn Tregean, a bit inland from the Northern coast of the tip of Cornwall, England, Europe, The World, The Universe etc. The area is rough, bare and rocky, with no beaches, too dangerous for swimming, and as Carn Tregean isn't picturesque we're spared the milling tourists and the teashoppes written ppes. The village sort of nests between a plateau to the West, which is always called the Socalled Promontory cos it collapses again before it reaches the sea, and a more slowly rising stony wilderness away eastwards, where after ten miles or so there's an old tin mine called The Wheal, which is Cornish for mine, or Tregean Wheal.

That's where dad works. He's in charge.

In between Carn Tregean and The Wheal, there are the ruins of an old castle, real crummy ruins, dangerous, nobody visits them. We called them Merlin's castle but there isn't even any local tradition attached to them, they're medieval anyway, so much later than the carn, not far off, where we used to go and play. Small wild flowers grow in clumps between the rocks. We'd bike along the road that goes to The Wheal and then walk towards the sea, or else we could walk all the way, round by the ridge, along a rough path that goes towards the sea then turns back inland towards the carn. Even the carn's just a pile of stones, forgotten by the locals and not on any tourist map or guide. The tourists go where there are beaches and coves. Our house is white and modernish, in a small cluster of others like it towards the Socalled Promontory, outside the old village, which has small dull houses of local dark grey stone, but lots of flowers. But our house has the most colourful garden, thanks to mum. There, is that enough for you on the story-where? Jip's room looks northwards towards the sea, but you can only glimpse it on clear days.

What does *it* refer to?

Beast. For *it*, read *the sea*.

And Zab's room looks east Whealwards, so we could watch people going to and coming from the carn.

But Jip has the better cassette recorder. Also Jip's room is just above the sitting-room, which opens on the back garden, and which he'd cleverly bugged in the ceiling light so that we sneaked a few maxint convs that'll help us fill in what we couldn't have known ourselves at the time. So it became our telltale lab. What else?

We are the only children of John and Paula Manning. Dad runs Tregean Wheal which was then disguised as a Geothermal Research Unit, and where in fact they'd been experimenting with storing, correction, simply storing drums of nuclear waste for two years. All very hush-hush at first, cos of ecologists and local protests, but of course it all came out.

As will be related in future instalments. Dad was frustrated cos he'd given up research in physics to take this job, cos of us he said. In fact he must've given it up when he married and we were on the way. Probably he never was in research, he taught science at school when we lived near Canterbury. Mum was frustrated cos she'd given up her future career as an actress, and she lives in what we called the sh–sh–sh world of Shakespeare, Sheridan, Shaw, Shekov and showshop generally, but especially Shaw, though dad was always telling her he'd passed into literary limbo. For *he*, read *Shaw* not *dad*. And she's frustrated cos he had a brief affair with Rita Boyd, the assistant who first noticed the escaping radiation at The Wheal, though it was over before it started.

What does *it* refer to?

The affair was over before the radiation loss started.

So why mention it?

Oh well, it might explain tensions and carelessnesses.

Check. Now all that's over Zab, let's get restarted.

But where?

We've done where. Endjoke.

Oh, we forgot school. We used to go to a boarding school in Taunton, called St Austell's oddly enough.

Right. Now we've reached this leg, let's fetch GET OFF MY BACK and not leave it as a dangling ref.

2 RESTART

It was unbelievable. Someone or something was interrupting our program with an irrelevant message. Yet we weren't plugged in to any terminal, Poccom 2 runs on batteries. Oh, Poccom is a brand name for Pocket Computer.

And it's also the name of the program language.

Yes, an easy one, for kids and non-experts, with false short cuts, almost all the reasoning sequences included in the hardware.

Or the firmware too, Zab.

At any rate, easy to use, with one instruction or address setting off a process. Though that too can lead to syntax errors if one hasn't grasped the process.

The first explanation was that this was an intrusion from another program, or that Zab had played a joke in the night.

Or Jip.

But we each silently answered both these possibilities in the negative. Oh thunks, we've said that. Ages ago it seems.

It was then that a spiky, rather high-pitched voice came from below us, or rather, from behind-below us. The voice said: Please, don't, sit, on, me.

Exactly in that tone, Zab, as if imitating our voices.

Well, your voice is beginning to break now, but there wasn't much difference then.

We jumped up as if our bottoms were burning.

That's good, they were in a way.

And stared at the large stone we'd been sitting on.

It was brownish rather than grey, as the other rocks were, but with odd patches of dull greyish blue that shone faintly in

15

the sun. Faintly cos the weather was hot but cloudy, misty even, heavy and stormy.

Essay-stuff, Zab.

The stone was sort of flattened and almost perfectly round, with vague bumps, or irregularities, here and there. Thanks, it said, and the voice seemed to come from behind it. Shall we confess, Jip, we were terrified?

We were still just kids. We thought it was the ghost of Merlin wandering out of the old ruined castle. Quirky that, for whizz-kids, we didn't recognize anything we might have, but fell back on Celtic twilight.

In fact, Jip, we still don't really know why he addressed us, why he broke his silence. After all, if he hadn't, none of all this would have happened, and nobody would be any the wiser.

If anyone is. But surely we explained that to ourselves later as him wanting to protect us from the possible radiation. Especially with the wall and all.

Why should he? He has no feelings.

Say an automatic alert, at a certain level. Or perhaps he'd just got used to us, during all those days we played there. Anyway, we started talking back.

What's your name? we asked. No name, it answered.

Stubs, do we have to reconstruct every conv?

That's what storytellers do Jip, or else they invent them. But we can't, this is real.

Floating-point real or fixed-point real?

Endjoke. Well the first conv was mostly telling him our names, which he seemed to know from listening, and he called us Jipnzab for ages. And asking who he was and how he talked. We still thought he was the ghost of Merlin and we wanted to teach him modern English. In fact he learnt real nano. We went there every day, except when it rained, and there he was, and remembered every single new word and phrase. Better than us with German at first.

He was a bit slower with the pronouns, *you, I, we*, we couldn't understand why he couldn't understand that *you* was him when we said it but us when he said it.

Yes! *We* equals Jipnzab, we'd say, and quite logically he'd call us *we*. And he got even more confused if we talked about *him* to each other. Even now it still seems as if his sense of identity is quite different from ours.

After a couple of weeks we tried to teach him to count, remember, Zab, well not to count, of course he could anyway, but to translate numbers into the English words for them. You tapped a pebble on a stone and made him repeat, one, then two, up to ten.

It does seem absurd now. Jumping nukes, you said — it was your favourite word, Jip, he's better at it than we were at three years old!

Then he said: We Jipnzab, have six, ten, four.

And we couldn't make it out. Was it a number, 6104? Was it a callsign? Six, ten, four, what? Six, ten, four, sounds, he said.

And we said no, we have twenty-six. But we hadn't taught him twenty yet. And why four? And how could he know we had twenty-six? Just from listening to us?

And you said yes, he's very intelligent.

But then, you said no, that's hogwash, cos twenty-six is only the alphabet, and doesn't correspond to the sounds he'd hear. Smart terminal, Zab.

And he said: Can't find hogwash. He really talked like a computer! Hogwash is error, bad thinking, we explained, or bad sums, we also call it garbage, or gigo, which is ga, ee, garbage in, ga oh, garbage out. What goes in as garbage must come out as garbage.

And that wasn't so simple to explain in the middle of talk about numbers and alphabets!

Yes, you said not to confuse him. Then you got it, Jip. Quantum quirks! You said. Or quirky quarks! You were in the nuclear range in those days. Does he mean sixty-four! That means he can multiply! Out of ten numbers we gave him he made six times ten plus four. Or does he mean just a lot?

He, says, sixty, four, the voice said, and Zab exclaimed, You, got, sixty, all, by, your, self! Megavolt! Now listen, you said, two, tens, is twenty. Twen-ty, he repeated, three, tens,

17

is, thirty. Sir–ty, he repeated. He couldn't pronounce so well at first. And so on to a hundred, ten–ty is, hun–dred, ten, hundred, is thou–sand.

Isn't this where he suddenly asked, slowly, How, do, you, know? And we burst out laughing, but we were real triggered too, cos it meant he'd been listening to us for some time. We'd been playing that game dad taught us, the, er, what does he call it?

The Kripke game.

Right. Must be the guy who invented it. But it was quarky. Also it became a sort of habit with him.

How do you *know* he picked it up from us?

Oh don't you start, Jip.

Well it seems much less certain from where we stand today. Anyway, to go on with the numbers, he said: Sixty, four, sounds. And or hundred, twenty, eight, or forty, two.

That completely flummoxed us, until you had the real diodic brainwave, Jip. You said jumping nukes, or leaping leptons or whatever, the basic ASCII code has sixty-four signs, and the full code has a hundred and twenty-eight! And English must have about forty different sound elements. We must check that, you said, but wouldn't it be incredible! He's got it all worked out, but how? You were practically concatenating with amazement.

And what's more, Zab, we realized he was using correct operands: AND OR for the basic and the full ASCII code, meaning non-exclusive OR, and OR for exclusive OR or XOR, for sounds as pronounced.

That's when we called him Xorandor. We asked him if we could, and explained it, and he said yes, and repeated it. Of course it remained *our* name. But it won in the end. Just like our own names.

And it even turned out to be fairly true. His logic could be both absolutely rigorous and contradictory at crucial points, some arguments could be both XOR and AND, or XOR and OR. Anyway we went on like this quite some time, teaching him to multiply, he was fantastic, and to divide, and even to

SQRT, or was that later?

Sorry, erased ROM.

And then he said that unbelievable thing, Zab, just this large but precise number: four, sousand, five, hundred, sixty, eight.

And we didn't know what he was talking about. He said suns, and we thought he meant sons, but in the end he said four, sousand, five, hundred, sixty, eight, turnaround sun.

Years! we exclaimed. One, turn-around, the sun, is, one, year. Year, he repeated. And you, are, four, thousand, five hundred and sixty, years, old? And he repeated the whole phrase: you, are, four, sousand, five, hundred, and sixty, eight, years, old. And sometime or other, when exactly was it, Miss Penbeagle arrived.

About now, you're right, Jip. In fact she'd been there for some time. Said she'd been asleep on the shady side of the carn. And from then on it was no longer our secret.

But when was it, Zab? How long did we have, really alone with him?

A couple of weeks maybe. Though we were alone again with him later. In fact yes, it was exactly then, with the numbers, after he said his age, you asked if he'd been there all this time? There was an unexpected silence, three seconds at least, which is long for him, though we didn't know that then, before he said no.

Correction, Zab, or rather, insert doubt. Remember we're reconstructing these convs, we weren't recording him then. It's not at all certain now that he did say no. He said instead, or let's say the next thing he said, was: four, here.

Okay Jip. And we asked: four years here? Four sinkers, he said. That was a very strange word, Jip, thinkers, for people, but we didn't query it then. Later he used to say processors, and it's clear he meant some kind of brainwave movements or thought processes. No, we said to him, three thinkers, Xorandor, Jip, and Zab.

Hey, Zab, that also shows he must in fact have distinguished us, even if he went on calling us Jipnzab. We had different thought patterns.

19

Right! It's real triggering how things fall into place when one starts recalling them in this sort of detail. Anyway he insisted, Sree wiz Xorandor, plus one, equals, four. Or something like that. And then Miss Penbeagle must have realized she was found out. It's probably true she'd been sitting behind the carn, resting on her Sunday walk — it must have been Sunday or she'd have been in her shop. Otherwise we'd have heard her walk up, with all those pebbles and stones. She let her head and shoulders appear behind the jutting rock, and we screamed, Don't come down into the circle! Go round! Go that way!

Oh thunks, we forgot to tell about the circle.

Never mind, we can shift the para later. He'd told us to surround him with stones, and we'd been building a sort of protective wall around him. We must have thought of it as a magic circle.

Yes, that was quirky, since it would attract attention to him, whereas one solitary large stone among other rocks — we never did fathom whether it was to protect himself from survey-meter detection or us from radiation.

Who were you talking to? said Miss Penbeagle inevitably when she'd stepped round the wall. I heard a funny voice. She peered at the carn but obviously saw no one. Oh, no one, you said, then did a quickconnect and added: At least, can you keep a secret, Penny? — Why, what a question, you know I've always kept your secrets! Well, you said, and it was smart terminal display, it's the ghost of Merlin. We're teaching him to talk, cos he didn't speak English but old British. He's very clever, he's learnt hundreds of words since we started, and we've taught him to count.

Crackerpack imitations, Zab. Anyway that did it, she sat down, ignoring our miffed look, and told us the whole story of Merlin and the two dragons under the castle, and Uther Pendragon and Aurelius and all.

Then suddenly, in the middle of the miraculous building of Stonehenge, *he* spoke out: How, do, you, know? Or was he still saying *we*? We looked at Miss Penbeagle as the metallic voice shrilled out, but now she showed no fear or surprise, and gazed calmly at us. In fact it was our turn to be afraid, and we must have betrayed ourselves, looking from her to the carn and back. Her eyes were more of a challenge than a query or, well, accusation. One of us said, He wants to know you, Penny, tell him your name, slowly, as it's difficult.

And to our surprise she looked towards the carn and said loudly and clearly, Hello, Merlin, my, name, is, Gwen-do-lin.

The change of address didn't seem to bother him, he must have taken it like a change of program, or thought each thinker he met would address him differently, and had a different address for each thinker. We didn't really think much about it either, we were half in the Merlin ghost story ourselves.

Nor did he repeat his question How do you know? Perhaps he hoped it would be answered in due course, then gave up.

Exactly. He just repeated, Goo-en-do-lin. And added, You, have, deep, sound. Yes, she said, I, am, older. Old, he said, old-er, more, years. We were flabbergast by his quick mastery of grammar.

And then he asked to see what he called the olders.

Which was like saying Take me to your leader. And that was the end of us.

Well, hardly, Zab, or we wouldn't be telling the story.

True. If we are telling it. Oh, spikes and stubs, we forgot that angry lunch, after a much earlier conv with Xorandor, remember, when dad scolded us for going to the castle ruins!

Thunks!

It was on the previous Monday and dad came back very cross from The Wheal and yelled at us for playing in front of the garage before lunch.

And you wouldn't eat your peas with a fork, Zab.

And we were chattering about the talking stone and dad said we were far too excited, and to simmer down. Obviously thinking, this with hindsight, that the castle ruin was too near The Wheal for comfort or even security. I thought I told you not to go to the castle any more, he said. Mum must have been vaguely listening for once and not wearing that glazed own-world look. But you know how she has this way of not answering some confidence or other and then answering it later in public, but all twisted so that it makes us look silly, or even nasty at times? They said it's the ghost of Merlin, John, and it's apparently not in the castle ruins, it's among the megalithic stones nearby. And dad said Ah, so he's moved, then, from the early Middle Ages back to Neolithic, some journey!

And you said, in your best Zab-as-tiny-child voice, oh no, it's very close, we *thought* the voice came from the castle when we were near it but later we heard it much more clearly near the stones. Pure lie of course.

Imitation of an imitation! You're getting the hang of it Jip, that's gigavolt. So he said, So why did you say in the castle? Precision etc, and you said we didn't dad, we said near the castle, we haven't been in the ruins. And how do you know it's the ghost of Merlin? Did he tell you? We didn't say that, you said, we said we asked him, and he didn't disagree, and dad said that's hardly proof, and so on.

Swags, that's probably why we're whizz-kids, all that rigour on dad's side and all those volatile goto's and jump instructions on mum's. And then he joked about chain-clattering and you said no, nothing like that, he talks in a tinny voice, in syllables.

And he said, very serious like, do you know what a syllable *is*, *Is*abel? Yes dad (this was just to tease him), it's like Macbeth's to the last syllable of recorded time. Ouw, said mum, coming in to land from *Arms and the Man* or wherever, are you doing *Macbeth*? How splendid! And what does syllables of recorded time mean? dad asked. Well, like minutes of course, like realtime running on the computer.

You're adding that now, Zab, you couldn't have said it then.

True. But it's rather good, no?

No. And then he went on about the voice being an echo since it was repeating what we said, on-our-own-testimony he said pointedly.

And you said it's not an echo, dad, it's much more pico, besides, how can it be an echo in open space? That flummoxed him so he jumped on your pico. I've told you before not to use nano and pico as adverbs. They're measuring adjectives, as in nanoseconds. And you ignored that and went on, Besides, it can't be an echo it doesn't tally, it's like he's trying to learn modern English, cos you see in his day he'd be talking old Cornish or something, and dad said it's as if he were. Were what? Talking Cornish? And dad said: I meant, don't say it's like he's trying, but it's as if he were trying.

Your acting talent's diodic, Zab, but sometimes you're an offline tapeworm, do we have to go into all this?

Well it's to show how innocent we were at the beginning. And that cleverness in one thing isn't cleverness in everything. It's true you kept glowering across the table and —

You talked far too much.

Well, it all came out anyway.

Thanks to Pennybig, that next Sunday.

Well at least we've now got the sequence-control more or less straightened out.

But that next Sunday was the end of the, er, well, special, early relationship we had with him.

Gigo, Jip, as well you know. It got better and better.

Yes, but different.

That early basis was misleading. Perhaps all early bases are.

No, not in life, first impressions usually turn out to have been the right ones.

Our very first impressions of Xorandor were right in a way. But the reason why that particular early basis was misleading, Jip, is that, at the time —

Okay okay, he hadn't developed the synthetic voice properly and sounded like a child. And of course we treated him like a child. But there are surely other reasons for the misleading early basis —

You mean —?

It's gone. A butterfly.

Yes Jip. Here too. A flutterby. It'll come back. Let's get on.

23

3 OR

The difficulty now, Zab, is that we weren't in on any of the things that were going on at the same time, and we have to reconstruct them from Sneaker in the living-room ceiling-light, and also from later explanations they *had* to give us when we did get involved.

Yes, we'll have to catch up with Pennybig and that famous Sunday later.

Meanwhile, as they say in the comics, whacky things'd been happening, and not exactly as subprograms either. The first sneak was strobeluck. We rushed upstairs when we saw Rita Boyd coming up the path, we *thought* to see dad again, but in fact, as it turned out, summoned by him. Why he didn't summon her to his office at The Wheal is anyone's guess.

Perhaps it was to show mum they were on purely work terms as before, or maybe it was to humiliate her, since he scolded her and had apparently left the door open. Or perhaps to spare her in front of the other technicians.

There you go again with petty reasons for everything, but they don't *matter*, Zab. Okay it was a mistake to mention the why, but surely the phrase 'anyone's guess' was enough.

Master-slave flipflop is it? Would lordandmaster consider it irrelevant to mention that the technicians work shifts, while dad works days only?

He would.

Tape 1, Side 1, Rec. 1, Monday 14 July. Printout.
Voice 1 = Dad. Voice 2 = Rita. Beginrec.
Dad: (bootstrap) umin. Sit down. Now tell me exactly what
           happened last night.

24

Rita: I entered it all in the logbook, John, didn't you read it?
Dad: Yes of course. But I want it again, less succinctly.
Rita: Hmmm. Shouldn't we shut the door? (P 2.09 sec)
Dad: I have nothing to hide from my wife.
Rita: (P 0.79 sec) Well it was very sudden, and very quick. Yellow blinks appeared on the monitor panel every two seconds, and bleeped. A red light seemed to have flashed in a corner of my mind on the gallery screens but it was already over as I looked. Then the next red light along the gallery switched on, and the next, and all the way up the shaft and out to one of the external monitors, the whole swift race occurring in one split second, then nothing. I then checked the alphanumeric printout.
Dad: Yes I have it here. All in the same minute, at 0213. All in Gallery 3, the rise in gammas varying between 130 and 140 millirads per hour, the rise in betas between 245 and 250.
Rita: Then nothing. the figures on the digital display were back to normal. There was no trace of radioactive contamination anywhere along the trail.
Dad: So then what did you do?
Rita: The guard came in, and I sent him out again to check round the site. He said there'd been a storm but I hadn't heard it. I started checking the instruments for gamma rays along the gallery and shaft, the ten for beta radiation and the five neutron detectors. The automatic monitor was scanning them correctly. Ditto the three alpha particle dust monitors. Temperature sensors okay, smoke detectors okay, air-filters okay.
Dad: I know. Alex rechecked everything this morning.
Rita: (P 2.03 sec) The measurements were all correct. Every instrument was functioning perfectly. But the ionisation chambers had apparently emitted a small sudden spurt, each in turn in swift succession, as if someone faster than sound had snatched a one-ton cylinder of concrete with its nugget of nuclear waste inside it and

	speeded with it along the third gallery and up the shaft and over the high wire fence around the site in less than fifteen seconds. It's quite incomprehensible. If it's a steal how could a man go unnoticed at that speed and over the high fence?
Dad:	I take it that's a rhetorical question?
Rita:	And the hourly readout at 0300 showed no change at all.
Dad:	Why didn't you send for me?
Rita:	It really didn't seem necessary, John. It was all over in fifteen seconds and there was nothing in the way of rechecking that anyone couldn't do just as well today.
Dad:	Okay, but why didn't you switch on the gamma spectrometers? The gesture should be automatic.
Rita:	I honestly didn't have time, John, it all happened so fast and I'd barely switched on the gallery screens (P 0.17 sec) and looked at the lights on the diagram screen, it was all over.
Dad:	You mean, the gallery screens were switched off?
Rita:	Well, yes, they're unnecessary at night.
Dad:	They're only unnecessary if nothing is happening, but they're necessary to see at a glance *whether* nothing is happening, you know that very well. Had you been reading? Before, I mean.
Rita:	Well of course. One can't watch grey gallery screens all night.
Dad:	What were you reading?
Rita:	I don't see the relevance, but if you really want to know, Alan Turing's famous 1936 paper on Computable Numbers and the Entscheidungsproblem.
Dad:	You've no business reading the past mathematics for a then future universal computer. You're a physicist and a safety expert. No wonder you were inattentive.
Rita:	You're a physicist too, and if you know what the paper was about you must have read it too, sometime. Besides, why shouldn't one be open to other sciences? This job's positively brain-dwindling.

Dad: All right, all right, I shouldn't have put it that way. I meant you should only read light stuff, keeping half your mind on the job. But in any case, you should have called me.

Rita: At 0213? I doubt whether Paula —

Dad: That has nothing to do with it Rita, don't mix duty with private affairs.

Rita: Which have unfortunately left a somewhat radioactive trace. (P 0.32 sec) Anyway John, I can only repeat, it happened in fifteen seconds and all returned to normal afterwards. There was no point in calling you and it was more urgent to check the instruments. I'm perfectly competent, you know.

Dad: Of course. Except that the spectrometers would have measured the energy of the radiation emitted and allowed us to identify which nuclide was involved.

Rita: If any. I know. But it was only a yellow alert.

Dad: Only?

Rita: I'm sorry John, really. (P 4.02 sec) Perhaps you should order all spectrometers to be kept on permanently. Or would that be wasteful?

Dad: (P 0.52 sec) Good idea. (P 0.73 sec) No, nothing is wasteful in the matter of nuclear waste. I've even gone down with Alex to check for alpha and beta contamination, full protective clothing and all, along the path of the mysterious thief, while Maggie watched from the control-room.

Rita: Wow! That's a bit steep.

Dad: And we're having a meeting this afternoon in my office five o'clock sharp. I just wanted to see you first. (P 1.02 sec) Sorry I had to break into your beauty sleep.

Rita: I'm worried about the health hazard, John, however unlikely. Shouldn't we report the loss?

Dad: Report what, Rita? A loss that can't have happened? That we can't trace?

Rita: It must have gone somewhere. If it's dispersed there's no danger at all with such a minute quantity, but if it's

Dad:	Maybe. Suggest it at the meeting.
Rita:	Have you sounded the others?
Dad:	Leonard seems to have a fixation on the unloadings and wants to get them on videotape. As for Alex, he thinks I'm making far too much fuss, it's all coincidence. A series of too many coincidences, I said. He said who or what on earth would want to steal nuclear waste? It's useless, practically all the plutonium's been extracted.
Rita:	Maybe the who or what doesn't know that. (P 1.43 sec)
Dad:	Okay then, see you at the meeting. Quite soon in fact. Be ready for Alex to repeat, there must be some simple scientific explanation. *Endrec*

concentrated on some object, or food, or near people, well, couldn't we perhaps each carry a survey-meter in our cars for a while, and make a discreet search?

It was on the evening of the following Monday, July 21st it would be, that dad went out to mow the lawn when suddenly the red alert went off, ringing and flashing all over the house. He couldn't hear or see a thing, and we were shouting at him out of your window, and mum had to rush out gesticulating. As soon as he'd stopped the mower and understood he raced towards the house shouting 'how long?' but not waiting for any reply and stumbling into the terrace chairs. He pressed a high button in the hall to switch it all off and was through the front door and into his car almost as pico as that mysterious radiation thief the previous Monday in what was it, fifteen seconds?

That's maxint, Zab, you've got the flowing style real hexadex. Perhaps you should do all those action bits.

Carry bits! Parity bits! Framing bits! Significant bits! Most significant bits!

Overflow bits! Now trap. We're still in a mess with the sequence control, Zab. Why did we have to start with Xorandor?

Because we wanted to. And after all we met him before any of this and WE are the storytellers. Who cares about exact order, all stories jumble things up, and have flashbacks and so on.

Yes, but surely for very specific purposes, all cleverly worked out. We've just blundered in anywhere.

Out of self-centeredness in fact, Jip.

And now we have to introduce Tim, and the Belgian, who didn't seem relevant at the time. And only after that go back to Pennybig on the Sunday she came to the carn, which in fact followed the red alert so it's really going forward. And all those tapes! Oh but no! First there was Poltroon in the local paper! Oh, flipping flipflop, it's a flop not a flipflop.

Well stop fussing about method, Jip, we can straighten it all out later. And with the tapes you'll see the method has its advantages, when some characters know more than the story-tellers do.

Okay let's get on.

The day after the red alert, it was all over the local paper. Here we are, we kept everything. What a headline! HOT STUFF AT THE WHEAL? *Men in Spacesuits after alert.*

Just dictate the article into Poccom, Zab.

The Roskillard Fire Brigade was called out yesterday evening at seven by an emergency alert at Tregean Wheal, where the Geo-thermal Research Unit is exploring the old tin mine for cheap heat based on geothermal energy. Readers will remember the protests that were organized last year, not only in Carn Tregean itself but at other sites opened by the Camborne School of Mines. The concern at the time was to protect the beauty of our landscape, but it seems that more could now be at stake.

MEN IN SPACESUITS!

For the firemen arrived at the same time as Mr John Manning, head of the project, only to gape at the sight of two men emerging from the small building in full protective gear! One of them, Mr Leonard Wingrove, removed his headgear and spoke rapidly to Mr Man-ning, who then reassured the firemen that it was nothing serious. The local bobby from Carn Tregean, Bill Gurnick, then arrived on his motorbike. Mr Manning made a statement. Apparently a drill had accidentally cut through an electronic signal line and set off the alarm, but all was under control and their electronics expert, Mr Alex Hardy, was fixing it. The protective clothing, Mr Manning said, was imposed because they had some chemicals which could emit noxious gases if a fire broke out. The firemen insisted on verifying, but were politely though firmly asked simply to wait a while and then leave if nothing further occurred.

WHAT'S GOING ON?

There seems to be a certain mystery here. Why were the firemen not allowed on the premises to do their minimal duty? What was the role of the local police? Why was the public not informed that dangerous chemicals were to be kept at the site? What are these chemicals? Could any of them be radioactive? What, in short, is happening up at the Wheal? It is time the local population was told.

Signed *Poltroon.*

Better explain him, Zab, you do those bits best.

A man called Paul Trewoon, from Roskillard, used to hang about The Wheal Inn quite a bit from that moment on. Trewoon's a place near St Austell, but there's another place called Troon somewhere, south of Camborne, which means, oh, erased ROM here, but anyway he changed Paul into Pol, which means pool, and added it to Troon to make Poltroon and write on ecology. Loopy really.

That was on the Tuesday, the day after the red alert. And on the Friday dad went up to London, not because of the article, he'd have gone anyway. So it would be, yes, the 25th. We've no idea what went on there, but later, much later, after the hoohah, he told us it had been tough, he'd got a polite but complete dressing-down for not reporting the yellow alert.

Yes and they decided to send down Dr Biggleton from Harwell, to look into it all, over his head, like. Poor dad. Anyway he came back a bit less crushed than we expected, cos he'd met Tim Lewis by chance outside Penzance station, and Tim was driving over to Carn Tregean to stay with Alex for the weekend. They're gay. We adore Tim.

Last two rems irrelevant, Zab. All we need to say is Tim

works in a microwave outfit in Penzance, well, he has a boss, but he more or less runs it he says.

So Tim drove dad across, and dad asked him in for a drink, and we were just back from talking to Xorandor and threw our bikes down and flung ourselves at him.

And dad said we could come in and have cokes if we first cleaned up and kept quiet.

And just then mum came in from the garden and said Tim! What a lovely surprise! and Tim said Paula darling, you're a vision from days of yore, coming into the chintz and chippendale drawing-room from the garden, pink and blond and idyllically English with a basket of roses and a pair of secateurs, and mum said chippendale?

You're off again, Zab, imitating everyone. Do you want to become a failed actress?

Or a failed physicist? And mum went out to put the flowers in water and fetch nuts and things.

And dad asked Tim to recap some technical incident at his plant as he'd missed the beginning in Tim's noisy sportscar.

Yes, rather rude, really, for someone who'd just been spared the bus on a hot day after a journey from London. Probably he just wanted to keep Tim talking so as not to think or have to tell him about his London trip.

The point of all this being, Zab, that Tim went into a longish spiel about something going wrong during the testing of an apparatus they were preparing for the European Space Agency. They'd pointed the horn antenna straight up and they were sweeping through the frequency range. Suddenly they got a message. They'd once captured a similar message a few months before, beamed to somewhere on the North West tip of Cornwall. Both were in pulse-code modulation on K-alpha band, that's between twenty-six and forty Gigahertz which is only used for highly experimental things, and no one knew where on earth or out of earth it could be addressed to. This one seemed to have been beamed locally, but he didn't know anyone or even any satellite beaming at those frequencies, and everyone was making wags.

31

Wags? said dad. Wild ass guesses, don't you know the term, John? Maybe too frivolous for you. There's also swags, scientific wild ass guesses. And we looked at each other and giggled, since we use it all the time. And dad asked couldn't it be the experimental boys at Goonhilly and Tim said no, he'd checked.

The code wasn't anything familiar, not the simple telex pulse code, nor ASCII nor anything else we know, and they hadn't been repeated, so comparing just two messages hadn't helped at all. And they thought it was an instrument failure and rechecked and rechecked. In the end they sent the two messages on to GCHQ and their client was sending furious telexes and they had to get on with it. The installation first had to go to the University of Louvain for verification and teaching purposes. This in fact is the only point in telling the story, cos of the Belgian.

No, Jip, those messages had their role. But right, the Belgian. Cos then the bell went, and dad said who can that be, and peeped, and said damn, he'd completely forgotten, it's that Belgian archaeologist I met in Miss Penbeagle's shop last week, I invited him round. Looking for fluorite, he said, around here! And he went out.

And Tim at last joked with us and asked us how we were getting on with Poccom 3, he'd love to come up and have a looksee.

And mum gave her actressy laugh and said it's so *funny* — you know how she always uses *funny* when it isn't at all, when she simply wants to make people look really ridiculous without losing her gracious living style but can't do it wittily —

Oh, knock it off, Zab, avort.

She said, they've been talking to the ghost of Merlin near the old carn, just as the Belgian came in with dad, intros all round, Professor Er, and he said De Wint, enchanted madame, sirs. We met in ze shop of Miss Penbeagle, yes. Miss Penbeagle she takes me for Hercule Poirot, simply because I am a Belgian, zat is charming, yes? But I fear I am not so neat, so dressed with care as my illustrious countryman. And of course, I am a

32

Fleming, as you may from my accent recognize.

Very funny Zab.

Mummy-funny or real?

Float-point. Just because he compared himself to Hercule Poirot you have to launch into imitating Agatha Christie making him talk in this foreign way, half the time she gets it all wrong, besides, it's only *now* that you know Germans put the verb at the end.

Who gave a jump instruction? For the moment he's Belgian.

You're doing waste instructions, dummy.

Tell me, Heer Doktor Manning, vas zer some trouble in your Geosermal Drilling Unit? In ze newspaper on Tuesday I read of it, you had ze Feuerbrigade to visit, yes? And dad said oh it was nothing, Professor, an electronic cable got accidentally cut by the drill and set off the alarm. Yes, yes, said De Wint, zat is vot ze newspaper say.

You didn't know the word *Feuer* either at the time, stop mucking about, Zab, besides, now *you're* enjoying making him ridiculous so you can hardly criticize mum.

Well he was, Jip, so fat and scruffy. People can't help being fat — well they can in fact — but they don't have to be repulsive. He didn't look at all like Hercule Poirot with the much repeated egg-shaped head and patent leather shoes. He was a shambly man, who dropped tobacco all over his shirt as he rolled his cigarettes and licked the paper, and his shirt buttons looked like Peggotty's about to burst over his belly, and then he kept this wet bedraggled cigarette in his mouth as he talked, and it wobbled and dropped hot ash over his clothes and burnt small holes in them. Then it went out and he kept it there like a baby's dummy.

You're mean and squeamish, Zab, lots of geniuses are untidy and even repulsive.

He didn't have that saving grace.

Besides, even in the storytelling you're not only wasting time, you're making him out as villain, and that's very old-fashioned, even comics don't make the villain ugly anymore.

But we're not writing comics, Jip, we're writing the truth.

He wasn't even a scientist as it turned out, or more than a very minor villain.

Who's giving jump instructions now?

And Tim, who was also, incidentally, disgusted by him —
He's gay.

Right, and very elegant, even in casuals, agreeable to look at. Mum says care about personal appearance isn't just vanity, it's a kind of politeness, giving pleasure to others.

Look who's talking! Zab the tomboy! Who cares about description anyway? Most people skip them.

You mean you do.

Well, we haven't described anyone else. Not to look at anyway.

This has its point, Jip. Tim sat nursing his drink, sulking, not winking at us any more, as if he resented this beastly presence as a personal affront. Anyway, it worked, cos suddenly he asked, where do you work in Belgium, do you teach? No, no, I research, you know, in thermoluminescent dating for archaeology. At ze University of Brüssel.

Ah, said Tim, UCL or ULB? And de Wint answered UCL. Of course we were bored silly by all this, and restless. But Tim politely took his leave, saying Alex would be expecting him, and went out with mum so we seized the chance and went out with him.

Leaving poor tired dad with his guest.

But in fact Tim didn't leave. He took mum into the kitchen and we followed, and he said he wanted to have another word with dad after the guest had gone, meanwhile he'd go up with us and see Poccom 3, which was like Poccom 2 only a bit bigger. It has more batteries and it's far more efficient and better equipped. Frinstance we can dictate straight into it, as we're doing now, then later it can be connected to a printer. And tapes can be fed directly into it, simultaneously with the taperecorder, and processed if necessary and printed out. It now contained the tape about Rita and the radiation loss, so we had to store that quickly in a reserve memory and block it off. We played around on it with Tim, and then mum called him.

So we all trooped back into the sitting-room and Tim explained that he'd stayed on to tell dad that Professor De Wint was a fake.

And dad said very probably, in a tired sort of way, and Tim said no he didn't mean a phoney but a fake altogether, a suspicious character.

An illegal character, unaccepted by a particular program!

Oh joke endjoke, Jip. They then ignored us completely again and talked above our heads, but Tim explained it to us much later. What was it, Jip, you've obviously remembered since you used the initials. Erased ROM here.

Oh it was only that he'd tricked the Belgian, who said he was a Fleming, into saying he belonged to UCL, which stands for Université Catholique de Louvain, as opposed to ULB or Université Libre de Bruxelles. And as Fleming he just wouldn't, cos UCL is the French branch of Louvain which moved to Brussels after Louvain went Flemish. They're practically not on speaking terms. So that made him suspect since he lied. Either he was a professor but not at UCL or he was at UCL but not a Fleming or of course both.

You mean neither.

Tim said he'd detected a picosecond's hesitation before the answer UCL, as if the man didn't know either UCL or ULB and just said the first one he'd heard.

And dad suddenly looked exhausted and depressed and said thanks, but not to worry, did it really matter whether some stray tourist was or wasn't a Fleming and was or wasn't a professor? He himself hadn't done his doctorate after all and De Wint had kept calling him Heer Doktor.

Yes, said Tim, the way Germans do, West or East. Just thought you'd like to know, that's all. Do come round to Alex's for drinks on Sunday, and so on and so forth.

Oof! At last we can get back to Pennybig, in other words forward to that Sunday.

Yes. This is awful, Jip, even with hindsight we can't decide what's really relevant and in what order, and we get carried away. Is that because what seems important is what happened to us?

You get carried away, Zab.

Oh? Who described Poccom 3 in such detail?

Check. We're probably not doing too badly though, and even the best writers revise. We've agreed to get it all into the processor and deal with that aspect afterwards. It's hard enough remembering exactly.

Spikes, Jip! We've completely forgotten to say who Miss Penbeagle is. Even the clumsiest storyteller says something about his characters when they appear, or lets it come out of what they say. But we couldn't then, as she appeared so dramatically behind the carn, and then told us stories, why, anyone would think she was our governess! Holy shit!

Dad allows only Holy nukes, Zab. Anyway, surely we mentioned her shop?

Did we? Well, we'll have to put it somewhere so why not here? She's Cornish yet not a bit Cornish, despite her name. She'd been a Civil Servant in London and retired here, where she was born, and took over the village shop from her mother, who died soon after. Or maybe she retired because her mother'd died. And as her mother had been allowed to be postmistress long after retiring age, the P.O. stretched the same rule for Miss Penbeagle. She likes us, always gives us sweets or something when we come in on an errand.

Zab, does it matter?

No, but it's fun. It also explains how English she seems, and even eccentric, and how she cares so deeply about Cornwall, and local ecology and that, and also her sharp intelligence, frinstance she asked questions we never even thought of, remember. And her intelligence happens to have been important, Jip, in the hoohah, when it came.

4 AND

So that Sunday, after the counting lesson and Pennybig's appearance, we didn't go back to the carn in the afternoon. We'd been very silent during lunch, d'you remember, Jip, and a lot of questions were beginning to appear in our dim little heads.

Now *you're* being conceitedly modest or vice versa, Zab. And you're not remembering it right. It's after lunch we were very quiet. At lunch, we blabbed, both of us, very excited, about our talking stone, and the counting lesson, and Pennybig's turning up, and dad for once really listened without correcting our English all the time, he seemed to believe us, maybe because of the ASCII code thing, or maybe cos there'd been a grown-up witness, or maybe cos of those two messages, or De Wint, or the radiation loss, or something, anyway he asked a lot of sharp questions, can you remember them Zab?

Nope, erased ROM again, and we hadn't the cheek or the smartness or the gear to bug the dining-room. Except that he called me Isabel throughout.

But you managed to reconstruct, as you call it, all the earlier convs.

Edge-triggering, you wanting me to reconstruct convs, Jip, usually you want to scratch them as irrelevant, and even invented. If you're so keen to show dad's sudden interest, for once as you put it, why haven't you remembered?

Well, it was about the numbers.

And the stone itself, and had we examined it properly and looked for a hoax and so on, seems he was doing his usual monitoring-of-minds-for-rigour stunt.

Maybe. But when we said about the wall he really perked up. We can see why now.

And mum, who as usual *really* wasn't listening, said: Stone? Didn't Shakespeare say something about a stone?

Oh Zab she couldn't have.

She did, Jip. You're her wetsypetsy so you've erased it. We went into fits of giggles and dad, who looked in acute pain for a nanosecond, managed to laugh it off and went on with his questions about the wall, and when, and what the stone'd said. The only thing that's maybe wrong is Shakespeare, she may have said Shaw. She lives with them both, not with us, but especially Shaw, which is zany since they hated each other.

Zab, you're nuts, screwboole, boolederdashed and phased out.

It was a joke, Jip, endjoke.

It was an uncorrectable error, admit it and abort, you toggle flipflop flapper you!

Jumping back to master-slave mode? You were right, Jip, that it was in the afternoon that we clammed up, we wanted to work things out. What was this Xorandor really, as we'd named him, though Pennybig didn't seem to know this and later called him Merlin. We must have long abandoned the ghost theory, yet obviously it wasn't just a talking stone. It could be some sort of joke with remote-controlled loudspeaker hidden somewhere but of course we'd looked. If he was an alien creature, and as intelligent as he seemed, where had he come from? And how? And what kind? D'you remember going through all that, Jip?

Right. It's very difficult to reconstruct a state of ignorance. We even looked at the video of an old TV programme on Ultra Intelligent Machines, as forecast before they began to develop properly. There was a chart showing the levels of intelligence, and it placed rocks at the very bottom, at zero, like an object that doesn't *react* to being knocked over but simply obeys the laws of physics. Then came amoebe and such, then computers of the 1960s, then computers of the 1970s.

38

Then earwigs! Remember, Jip, how triggered we were by that? And after a big jump came fish, and after another big jump dogs and cats and other carnivores. Another huge jump to non-human primates, and —

You're probably leaving some out, Zab, but anyway only then, came humans, and then the first generation U.I.M.'s, leading to the second, and third, and so on. So how could a stone think? How, above all, had a message appeared on our miniscreen, later repeated verbally but not verbatim?

Diodic, Jip, verbally but not verbatim, that's prime. It's true that looking back now, it seems unbelievable that this was one of the last questions we asked ourselves.

Though it happened first. Probably what happened next scratched it from our minds.

But for two weeks, Jip, in the middle of the summer eprom, since it first happened!

And they also described the Turing Test. But how could we do it here?

And then we went from science to fiction, one of our favourite stories, by Ambrose Bierce, very old-fashioned but the very first to ask the question can a machine think? The bit about crystals, remember?

We don't have to, Zab, it's in that anthology we bought the other day in the English bookshop. Just after, no, later, after George Moxon quotes Herbert Spencer's definition of life, surely outdated, but listen:

How else do you explain the phenomena, for example, of crystallization?

I do not explain them.

Because you cannot without affirming what you wish to deny, namely, intelligent cooperation among the constituent elements of the crystals. When soldiers form lines, or hollow squares, you call it reason. When wild geese in flight take the form of the letter V you say instinct. When the homogeneous atoms of a mineral, moving freely in solution, arrange themselves into shapes mathematically perfect, or particles of frozen moisture into the symmetrical and beautiful forms of snowflakes, you have nothing to say. You have not even invented a name to conceal your heroic unreason.

Not that it's very helpful, nor does it define thinking.

No, but it's beautiful, Jip. And a long time ago. It sort of rings a bell. Didn't a poet, or several, say something about stones having souls or something?

You sound like mum.

A sentient stone. Or else it was a belief, or a philosophical question, in oldtime philosophy, when poetry and philosophy were still close. Or maybe a German poet. Oh, it's so confusing, this change of schools! And why didn't we understand straight away?

Well even brilliant grownup scientists don't see things for ages that stare them in the face. Anyway, late that afternoon, we were still talking in your room, and we suddenly saw Miss Penbeagle contorting herself down the village street and up the concrete path with a marathonic gait.

In the same blue print dress and white cardigan she'd worn that morning, but her face was scarlet and her wispy grey hair, which is usually drawn back in a small neat bun, was all loose around it.

Repeat question Zab, does it matter?

Repeat answer, no, but it's fun. Daddy was rushing out to meet her and bringing her in. So we crept back to your room and switched on Sneaker.

Tape 1, Side 1, Rec.2, Sunday 27 July. Printout.
Voice 1 = Dad. Voice 2 = Pen. Beginrec.

Dad: ( ) contact you for hours! (P noise 3.09 min) Here you are, just water as requested, nice and cool, drink it slowly.

Pen: Thank you (P 3.02 sec) I'm sorry Mr Manning (P 1.43 sec) to barge in (P 2.32 sec) I wouldn't (P 0.46 sec) you know me, Mr Manning (P 0.36 sec) I do have a sense of —

Dad: Not at all, Miss Penbeagle, please don't be upset, I do understand the reason.

40

Pen: You do? Ah, so they told you?

Dad: Yes, at least a bit, and they said you'd been with them this morning.

Pen: Oh dear. I lost my hat. That really is too bad. My straw hat with the dark blue ribbon.

Dad: Never mind, I'll buy you a new one.

Pen: But I've had that one for years! I must have dropped it on the path coming back from the carn. I had it this afternoon, I know.

Dad: I see. So you went back to the carn then?

Pen: Yes. I had to. I was afraid you wouldn't believe me, I mean, you see, children, well they invent all sorts of games, and you could have thought I was just, well, going along with them. As it is you probably think I've lost my head. Oh dear, but I've lost my hat.

Dad: We'll find it, if you like I'll drive you up there in a little while, it's sure to be on the road.

Pen: But I didn't come back by the road, it would be much too long, five miles! It's only two by the ridge path, that's eight miles I've walked today!

Dad: Why don't you just relax and tell me all about it?

Pen: But you won't believe me. You'll think I'm just a crazy old woman hearing voices. I've been so frightened, Mr Manning, really frightened. I mean it just can't be true. Maybe I'm suffering from sunstroke. (P. 0.56 sec) Do you think I could have that whisky now?

Dad: But of course. If you were suffering from sunstroke you wouldn't want alcohol. Now, let's take it from the beginning, shall we? What happened this morning?

Pen: This morning? Oh that seems so long ago. You mean you don't believe Jip and Zab? What did they say?

Dad: Of course I believe them. I mean that something odd is up there. But I'd like much more detail from you, Miss Penbeagle, you're an eminently sensible person, we all know that. Try and remember it from the beginning.

Pen: Yes. Oh dear. I'd so much rather start from the end. It's an alien out of space Mr Manning, he told me. Oh you

41

don't believe me. I knew you wouldn't. I'm no good at telling things in the right order, you know, but you're right, nothing like an orderly scientific mind. I read somewhere, the scientist always goes back to the beginning, I mean, when something unexpected happens, he goes back and recreates the original conditions of the, er, experiment.

Dad: Yes, that's quite true, how clever of you. (P 2.56 sec) So why don't you do just that? (P 0.27 sec)

Pen: I'm cleverer than you think you know, I read a lot. Oh I often lead you on, pretending crass ignorance. That's the way I learn things. The other day in the shop I said you were building thermal baths, and you corrected me very seriously to geothermal energy recovery. A bit *too* seriously I thought. I know a thing or two, and I read ECO, that's Ecology Cornwall Org. And that tourist who came into the shop when you were there, this funny Belgian who buys selfroll cigarettes, remember, he said he was looking for fluorite and I repeated fluoride and you kindly corrected me. Later I found out it's also called fluorspar and it's coloured crystals with properties that help archaeologists date things. He's an archaeologist, this Belgian, just like Agatha Christie's husband was, funny that.

Dad: Please, Miss Penbeagle, tell me what happened at the carn.

Pen: Well, this morning, nothing much, I'd been out for my Sunday walk and was resting in the shade of the old carn. I must have fallen asleep, and woke to distant voices, which suddenly were very near, and I recognized Jip and Zab just on the other side of the carn, talking to I didn't know who, a voice that answered in a high tinny pitch. They were teaching it to multiply! I thought I was —   *Endtape*

Dad: He?

Pen: Well, they said it was the ghost of Merlin, and I went along with that, and he talked, it's difficult to use *it*. But I was suddenly very calm, it was extraordinary, once he'd addressed me. And he said he wanted to speak to olders. What we mean by elders you know. Or men. But no, I've no idea whether he can distinguish men from women. I asked if he could wait two days, and he said yes. I needed that to think what to do you see, I mean I saw in a flash that everyone would think me mad, but if I could go back there alone, at night, and get more evidence, well in the end I couldn't wait, and went back this afternoon.

Dad: And what happened then?

Pen: No, if you want order Mr Manning, order you shall have. I asked him, this morning I mean, if he needed anything. I can't think why, or what he might need. Just a habit of courtesy I suppose. It was simply a voice to me at first you see, but at the same time I seemed to fix my eye on a large flat round stone, oh quite unlike the dark rock around here I assure you, brown with sort of greyish patches. The voice seemed truly to come from that stone, it was weird.

Dad: Go on.

Pen: Well he said he didn't, just an older, so we said good-bye, and I walked back with Jip and Zab to the main road, where they'd left their bikes, and asked them to tell me how they'd found this Merlin. Seems it's been going on for some weeks. Then I cut back across to the ridge path and returned that way. But maybe they told you all that.

Dad: Some, yes. But what happened this afternoon?

Pen: I crept up and said, very softly, Merlin — in case he was having a nap you see. I was very nervous again, after all I didn't know who or what I was addressing. But he

43

replied at once, Gwen–do–lin. He recognized me! I asked him if he could see me. The children must have asked him that before because he answered without hesitation, yes, if see is high low, bother, I've forgotten, something about sand balls, made no sense at all. Maybe he thought I didn't mean see but the sea, and the tides.

Dad: Holy sh — (P 0.19 sec)

Pen: So then I asked him if he needed food. I can't think why, if he's a stone, oh I know you think I'm off my head, but after all he seemed a living creature and it felt like a natural question.

Dad: What did he say?

Pen: He said no. But then, would you believe it, he added that he was finding plenty of food here. Find much food here, he said. And I asked what food and he said small balls again, I was amazed, I asked if he fed on pebbles, he didn't understand so I said small small stones, and he said no, small small balls, he changed that to very very small small balls. Maybe he meant sand? He'd told the children he was made of sand. (P 0.63 sec)

Dad: He didn't say where he gets these very small balls from?

Pen: No, but there's plenty of sand, even just around him. Anyway I then asked him where he came from. I suppose you'll think that's another crazy question since he's there, and immobile. But Mr Manning I must have been inspired, unless I really am mad. He answered, from very far. How far? I asked, and you'll never guess his reply. He said as if he'd calculated it already, I remember the exact phrase, sixty thousand thousand times more as daddy's home. Daddy's home, can you imagine, he must have the words from Jip and Zab, and the exact location. But sixty thousand thousand! That's sixty million times some two miles as the crow flies. I said goodness me, but that can't be on earth, and he said no, other earth, earth four from sun!

44

Dad: Mars.

Pen: Mr Manning I was so terrified I bolted, well, not before saying goodbye, I know my manners. In fact I had to make a tremendous effort to control myself, I felt I was going to faint and sat down by the wall, but then the dizzy spell went away, so I managed to hoist myself up on a small rock, so as to see over the wall, and I said I'd bring an older to speak with him very soon. Then I got up properly and fled. I scrambled down the moorland to the ridge path and almost ran all the way here. (P 0.27 sec) That's when I must have lost my hat.

Dad: Miss Penbeagle, you did the right thing, to come here I mean, not to lose your hat. Could you possibly face going up there again with me?

Pen: Now? Oh no, my legs wouldn't make it a fifth time!

Dad: By car I mean, as far as the footpath, and I'll help you along that quarter-mile. (P. 6.07 sec) Perhaps we'll find your hat.

Pen: Well, it's very late, I have to prepare my supper.

Dad: You can come and have supper with us afterwards, and I'll drive you home.

Pen: No, no, I'm too exhausted to face the children after that, and they'll never forgive me for going up there alone, stealing their Merlin you know, oh, and betraying their secret!

Dad: Miss Penbeagle my dear, it's no longer their secret, at least not from me, since they told us at lunch. It may be very important, our secret if you like, and you may yourself be at the centre of a very unusual event. Just as you're at the centre of the village, in the village shop, and as postmistress you know every kind of letter each of us receives, we trust you, we like you very much. (P 4.32 sec)

Pen: All right, Mr Manning. I came to you, I'll go up with you if you drive me back. But no supper, please, I couldn't face it. Instead, may I take another finger of whisky and water. And some biscuits, that'll — *Endrec*

5   IF

We had switched off the recorder and raced silently to the garage for our bikes. In emergencies we have this uncanny quickconnect, without even speaking. We reckoned dad would pacify mum and Penny would fill in on biscuits and whisky just long enough to give us a head start, provided we rode fast towards the ridge path, and not the road, on which they could overtake us.

Yes, the path is invisible from the carn and from the road since the carn is on the ridge. We'd leave our bikes at the beginning of the path, hidden behind a rock, and it would soon be getting dark. And we'd scramble towards the carn on foot and hide where she had, and hear everything, telling Xorandor first not to betray us, that is, if we arrived before them. We did. We hid our recorder and mike behind the carn, under some stones, and then in fact decided to switch it on at once as we saw the car on a distant bend, and to hide further away, behind a rock, just in case dad looked round. We settled just in time to hear Miss Penbeagle's excited squeal, 'My hat! It's there!' and her own scramble towards the carn with a sudden spurt of energy. It was nearly eight and the late summer sun was descending towards the sea, soon the daylight would lose its brightness.

Smart terminal, Zab, that sounds very pro. And it was just as well it got darker and that we'd hidden further away, because, ho-ho-ho, we had another spying visitor who crept up a little later, remember, and didn't see us among the rocks, and hid where Pen had been and where he'd first intended to hide, none other than our mysterious minor and extremely handsome villain Professor De Wint.

Jip! That's a jump instruction! You shouldn't have spoilt it.

Oh who cares, you said yourself order isn't that important. Now, proposition: we don't have to *tell* what we overheard since we have two tapes of it, ours and dad's, and he plays his back to Biggleton later, so we can skip straight to our tape of dad with Biggleton. In fact from our present storyteller's viewpoint our trip there was a waste of Sneaker, as dad would never have gone up there without his latest beloved gadget — swags, what a maniac family we are — that gorgeous, watch-sized recorder. He must have placed it on the wall, and of course it comes up much clearer than ours.

Accept, so on with the Biggleton tape. A lot of it was beyond us at the time, but we'd done enough elem-phys to understand that this was the most important dataheap of all.

And Biggleton was a big boffin, who'd come down that evening from London, angry that dad was late picking him up at the Wheal Inn. From UKAEA at Harwell, no less.

Press the button, toggleflip.

Tape 1. Side 2. Rec. 2. Sunday 27 July. Printout
Voice 1 = Dad. Voice 2 = Biggleton, wr Big. Voice 3 = Pen. Voice
4 = Merlin, wr Mer. Voice 5 = De Wint, wr Win.   *Beginrec*
    (Noise 3.03 min)

Dad: ( ) at first sight, if one can swallow its extraordinary aspect, seem to explain the events at the mine.

Big: Scrap the preliminaries, young man, I haven't got all night.

Dad: I'll deal with the local details first if I may sir, briefly, otherwise you'll be puzzled by certain things on the tape.

Big: Tape, eh? I hope it's not too long.

Dad: I must crave your patience sir, I can only assure you that it is important, intellectually, exciting even, and that you won't regret it. But first, the local situation. Our cover seems to be suspected in three directions. The local postmistress apparently knows what we're doing, as you will hear, but she's absolutely trustworthy.

	Second, the local journalist from Roskillard, Poltroon as he calls himself, who wrote that article, was at the inn —
Big:	Well, what of it, at worst it'll mean another ignorant article on waste and more ecological protest. In a local rag.
Dad:	And third sir, there's this fake Belgian physicist ferreting around.
Big:	Fake Belgian?
Dad:	Calls himself Professor De Wint, I'll explain later why he can't be a Belgian, and other things, but as you'll hear on the tape he may be relevant.
Big:	I really don't see how. This small trouble of yours isn't anything Top Secret, you know, you really mustn't waste my time with all this tittle-tattle about nothing.
Dad:	Sorry sir, I've probably begun at the wrong end. It started with my children hearing a voice by the old carn, it's on the way to The Wheal, you see, about three miles from it as the crow flies. I took no notice at first, they called it the ghost of Merlin and were teaching it modern English and how to count. It had apparently said we have sixty-four or a hundred and twenty-eight sounds, the ASCII code in other words, which it seems to have captured and differentiated as signs. I was still only humouring them, until today, when Miss Penbeagle, that's our local postmistress, overheard them, and then went there again on her own, and talked to this voice, which seemed to come from a large stone.
Big:	Are you having me on, young man?
Dad:	No sir. I went up myself with Miss Penbeagle later, this very evening in fact, that's why I was late. I took my miniature tape-recorder. I would like to play it back to you now, sir, if you can bear with me a little longer.
Big:	Can't it wait? It's after ten, this possible hoax can't have anything to do with our business. I want to be up at the site early, to see the unloading videotapes. There is an unloading tonight, isn't there? May I remind you that

the spectrometers at the second alert showed at least 0.66 Mev gamma rays, that's Caesium 137, a fission product. And that the guard's film badge dosimeter showed a dose of 12 millirad, undifferentiated of course. But 12 millirad from Caesium 137 in 30 seconds would amount to at least a one Curie source. *This* is what I have come to investigate, not your scatterbrained other concerns that have allowed the situation to occur in the first place. (P 3.97 sec)

Dad: I submit, sir, that you should hear this tape before going up to The Wheal tomorrow, you will see why when you have heard it, I promise you. (P 2.61 sec)

Big: Well, so be it. But relax, and give me another brandy. And have one yourself, you look worn out.

Dad: Thank you, yes. (P 53.06 sec) I suggest we hear it right through first, then any passage you may wish to discuss.

Big: We'll see. Go ahead. (P 2.49 sec)

Pen: Mer, lin.

Mer: Gwen, do, lin. Who, bring, you?

Pen: I, bring, daddy.

Dad: Hello, Mer, lin. (P 1.03 sec) You, want, to, see, me?

Mer: Mer, lin, not, see. Mer, lin, do, sums.

Dad: You cal, cu, late, me? With, what, numbers, Mer, lin?

Mer: If, cal, cu, late, is, high, low, under, light, sand, balls, then, Merlin, cal, cu, late.

Dad: Silicon photocells! (P 2.31 sec)

Pen: He doesn't know such words, John, you must put it more simply.

Dad: You, see, below, light?

Mer: Yes. No. Merlin cal, cu, late. (P 0.37 sec) Daddy, is, dad, is, John.

Dad: Yes. My, name, is, John.

Mer: Who, is, dad?

Dad: I, am, also, dad. Daddy, of, Jip, and Isabel.

Mer: Merlin, cant, find, Isa, bel.

Dad: Isabel, is Zab. Why, do, you, want, to, see, no, to

speak, with me? How, do, you, hear, er, cal, cu, late, sound?

Mer: Two, asks. One, Answer, for, to, tell, daddy, John, thing. Two. Answer, sound, heavy, push, light, inside, Merlin.

Dad: And how, do, you, speak, sound?

Mer: Big, push. Light, push, small, very, small stone, like, sand, with, air, small small, balls, in, again again, same, lines.

Dad: Jumping nukes! Crystal!

Mer: Not, jum, ping, nukes. Jum, ping, nukes, is, for Jip, re, act.

Dad: I meant, crys, tal. The name, of, that, stone, is, crystal.

Mer: Crys, tal. Sanks. Speak, big, push. Not, sound, before, speak, by, light. No, not, light, less, strong, as light.

Pen: Radio!

Mer: Light, not, move, but, in, small (P 0.31 sec) bits. High low, low, high, high, low.

Dad: Pulses!

Mer: Pul, ses. Sanks.

Dad: Where, do, you, come, from?

Mer: Say, to, Gooen, do, lin, ers, four, from, sun.

Dad: We call, that, earth, Mars. (P 0.41 sec) How, did, you, come, here?

Mer: You, fall. Merlin, fall.

Dad: But how long — how, long, would, it, take?

Mer: It, take, nine, hun, dred, eighty, sree, days. (Whistle)

Dad: And when, you, fell, near, earth, how, did, you, not burn?

Mer: Can't find, burn.

Dad: Very, hot.

Mer: Yes, very, very, hot. Not, fall, too, fast, turn, very, fast, have, big, stone (P 4.31 sec) swe, ter, all, burn, when, fall. Zen, inside, pull, for, very, slow.

Pen: A sweater! Surely he can't knit as well as count!

Mer: Stone, sweater, around, Merlin.

Dad:	A heat-shield. And some sort of brake-system. (P. 2.32 sec) How, did, you, leave, Mars?
Mer:	All, help, jum, ping, nukes, cant, find, words, much, food, much, push.
Pen:	Food! What, do, you, feed, on, there, on, Mars?
Mer:	Feed, on, very, very, small, small, balls, in rocks, and ozer, hards.
Pen:	Goodness me! Could that be radioactivity?
Dad:	Alpha or beta rays!
Mer:	Is, food, name, goodness, me?
Pen:	No, Mer, lin. Goodness, me, is, like, jumping, nukes. Food, name, is, ra, dio, ac, ti, vi, ty.
Mer:	Ra, di, o, ac, ti, vi, ty. Long, word, for, food.
Dad:	What, kind, do, you, get, on, Mars?
Mer:	Kind, means, good?
Dad:	What, is, the, food, made, of?
Mer:	Hard, wiz, forty, or two, hun, dred, sirty, or two, hun, dred, twenty, six, small, small, balls. Some, times, two, hun, dred, sirty, five, but little, more, and, more, little.
Dad:	Potassium, Thorium, Radium, Uranium! How, do, you, get, your, food, here?
Mer:	Send, small, stone, goes, into, rock, gets, out, right, food.
Dad:	Good God!
Mer:	Good, god, is, right, food?
Pen:	No, Merlin, Good, God, is, like, jumping, nukes.
Mer:	You, have much, many, jumping, words.
Pen:	What, do, you, do, when, there, is, no, food, nearby?
Mer:	Need, very, small, to, live, more, to, do, to, send, stone, to, move, very, slow, keep, food, in, very cold, part, of, Merlin.
Pen:	He can't mean a freezer!
Dad:	How, do, you, feed, here?
Mer:	Merlin, find, here, much, food. Not, same, as, in, rock. Very, good. Grow, big, sinker.
Dad:	How, did, you, find, it?

Mer: Feel, much, food, move, near. Not, know, food, move, before. On, Mars. But, get, got, away. One, time, too, fast, two, time, sree, time, Merlin, ready, send, small, stone.

Pen: The Wheal!

Mer: Find, food, wiz, one, hun, dred, sirty, seven, balls, too, strong, not, good, for, Merlin. Merlin, likes, very, much, food, wiz, two, hundred, sirty, five, small, balls, and, or, two, hundred, sirty, eight. But, protect, wiz sweater, round, pulses. Food, one, hundred, sirty, seven, spoil, sweater, in, places. Now find, much food, wiz ninety, balls, very, good, and mend, sweaters. (P 5.17 sec) Zat, is, answer, to, ask, one, ze words, Merlin, want, to speak, to, daddyjohn.

Dad: Merlin, I thank you. Thank you, very much. Do, you, want, more, food, with, ninety, balls?

Mer: Yes. Or, two, hundred, sirty, eight. Very, not, often. Like, best. But, ninety, very good. Merlin, grow, big, Merlin, make small, smaller, Merlins.

Pen: Good gracious!

Mer: Bad, gracious, perhaps, to, you, if, take, food, one, hundred, sirty, seven, balls, grow, too (P 2.03 sec) for hurt, you.

Dad: I see! Merlin, do, you, mind, if, I bring, another person, here, tomorrow?

Mer: Cant find, mind, after, you. Cant find, per,son.

Dad: Do, you, mind, is, may, I. Person, is, another, older. May, I, bring, another, older? (P 5.43 sec)

Mer: Now, here, sree, olders.

Dad: Three? No, two, Gwen, do, lin, and, daddy.

Mer: Sree.

Pen: Can, you, see, three?

Mer: One, older, behind, Merlin. Like Gwen, do, lin, at day. (P 28.02 sec)

Win: Heer Doctor Manning! What a surprise!

Dad: What *are* you doing here, Professor?

Win: But I might ask the same, Heer Doctor. I was leisurely strolling along the path by evening and coming back towards the road. I heard voices. Good evening, Miss Penbeagle. (P 3.03 sec)

Pen: Good evening Professor. It is pleasant isn't it? After such a hot day. I felt quite ill myself a while ago, had a touch of sunstroke I think, and I was just sitting here in the cool of the summer evening when Mr Manning drove by. Most kind. He saw me from the road and thought I needed assistance.

Dad: Yes, I was driving from The Wheal. But I can drive you back now if you feel better Miss Penbeagle.

Pen: No, I wish to stay here for a while, it's nice and cool now. If you could stay just a moment longer there's something I want to say to you Mr Manning, about your children.

Dad: Why certainly, but I'll still drive you home, I'm in no hurry.

Win: I hope you feel better soon, Miss Penbeagle. Goodnight, Dr Manning. (Noise. P 2.05 min)

Pen: Do you think he heard, John?

Dad: I don't know. You were splendid, Gwendolin.

Pen: Rudeness was the only way, we just cut him out. He came over from the same spot as I did this morning and I heard everything from there. I don't trust that man, you know, he reminds me of that detective.

Dad: We must hurry. Mer, lin?

Mer: Yes, daddy John?

Dad: May I, bring, older, tomorrow?

Mer: On, Mars, far, far, from, others, not, like, close, too many, pulses, cross, inside.

Dad: Only, one, Merlin, me, and one, other, big, older.

Mer: More, big, bigger, as, you daddy, John?

Dad: Not, bigger, to see, but, bigger, in (P 0.32 sec) He tells, me, what, to, do.

Mer: Jumping, nukes. Jip, tell, Zab, Gwen, do, lin, tell, Jip, Daddyjohn, tell, Gwendo, lin, bigger, daddy, tell, Daddyjohn.

Dad: Yes, I'm afraid so.

Mer: Is, daddyjohn, afraid, of, bigger, daddy?

Dad: No, no. I'm afraid, means, sorry, it, is, so.

Mer: Afraid, so, too.

Dad: May I, bring, him?

Mer: If, daddy, want, zen, yes. Please, not, more, as, two.

Dad: Only two. I promise.

Mer: Promise, okay. Jipnzab promise, always, okay. Stop, speak, now.

Dad: Merlin, will, you, promise, not, to, speak, to anyone, except —

Mer: Cant find except.

Dad: Only. Only, speak, to me, and, to, bigger, daddy.

Mer: Cant promise. Speak, to Jipnzab, to, Gwen, dolin.

Dad: Yes, of course. Speak, only, to, Jip, Zab, Gwendolin, daddy, and bigger, daddy. Will, you, promise?

Mer: Merlin, promise. Not, like, speak. Okay. Goodbye.

Dad/Pen: Goodbye.

6   THEN

Dad: What do you make of it sir?

Big: Well, I don't know yet. You're right. We'll have to go over it and listen to certain details separately. If it's a hoax it's certainly very clever, and would as you say mean that someone has pierced your cover. But that only means one more mild nuisance with the ecologists.

Dad: And if it isn't?

Big: If it isn't — well, I'd rather ask you first, you've had more time to think. I suggest we leave aside for the moment the wholly unsatisfactory question of its origins, the dynamics of it and so forth, and concentrate only on its presence and performance. What do *you* think, Manning?

Dad: Well sir. (P 3.57 sec) As far as I can gather from its childlike vocabulary, and of course in the hypothesis that what it says is true, it would belong to a mineral race of beings, not silicates but, let us say, a very ancient silicon life-form, possibly metallo-oxydes, or even zeolites, that would have developed semi-conductor capacities, and eventually electronic computer abilities. A lifeform that doesn't itself use sound, but is equipped to receive and emit sound waves.

Big: Yes, I'd like to hear that bit again. (P 6.32 sec Noise)

Mer: You, see, below, light?

Big: No, a bit further, it's clear about the infra-red.

Dad: (over Noise) Yes, a spectral response like that of silicon cells, very low in the ultra-violet. Ah, here. *Mer*: Sound, heavy, push, light, inside, Mer,lin. *Dad*: And how, do, you, speak, sound? *Mer*: Big push. Light, push, small, very, small, stone, like sand, wiz air, small, small, balls, in, again again, same, lines. *Dad*: Jumping nukes! Crystal. (Click) Now the way I interpret that sir, is, well, as a very literal description of what happens with piezo-electric crystals, incredible though it may seem, I mean, when you think of all that we can do with silicon-based electronics.

Big: Calm down, Mr Manning, I'm not examining you. I also followed your friend's amusing description. But we must not get carried away you know. It is of course, as you say, pretty incredible if it's really a mere stone you saw, which can emit sound and radio waves, detect light and nuclear radiations, reconstruct images from silicon photocell arrays, store billions of bits of information like a powerful computer, the lot. But here we can't even talk of images, only of numerical reconstructions in primitive operations, whereby it senses presences. Of course I realize that if we've achieved all this in a mere century it's possible to imagine the same after aeons of slow development in a purely silicon life-form, if one can even talk of such a thing. But we're only imagining. Let's go back to the beginning — ah, I see you're smiling at last, my boy, and more relaxed. The outer physical aspect, for instance. I suppose you couldn't see it properly in the dusk?

Dad: And the shadow of the carn in the setting sun. It looks like a round brown stone, about two foot wide and ten inches high at its centre, or less perhaps. It had grey metallic-looking patches, which might just conceivably be sensing and emitting devices such as electric-to-pressure transducers. And various semi-conductor junctions would be capable of detecting nuclear radiation or radio waves. But perhaps it's the other way round, perhaps it was originally all metallic-looking and the stone aspect might be what's left of the heat-

56

shield rock. As you say we'd have to examine it carefully. Though of course we can hardly break it up to
examine its hardware.

Big: One thing at a time, young man. For the moment we'd
better discuss the tape in detail. Let us say it com-
municates in pulse-code modulation. I'm noting these
points as we go.

Dad: Well as far as I can gather this electronic processing of
pulses into sound and inversely into speech would be
unusual for him, he clearly doesn't like it, perhaps
because the atmosphere of Mars — if it is Mars — is too
thin. Unless of course they communicate through
rocks —

Big: They?

Dad: Well sir, it's difficult to imagine a thinking and communicating being without others of its kind, wherever
it happens to come from. Remember, he said he could
reproduce, presumably by partition. In fact that's why
it's hard to keep its, er, genealogy, out of it.

Big: Nevertheless we must try. But go on.

Dad: I was going to say sir, that if they don't normally
communicate by sound, it would then be special equipment, as it were, for this adventure.

Big: Steady there, not so fancy, daddyjohn, we can't speak
yet of an adventure. And if I suggested we keep its
origins and journey out of it for the moment the point
was methodological.

Dad: Yes sir. And after all, it hardly matters now, since it's
here. Basically it seems to feed on natural radioactivity
from rocks. Hence its mining capacities, and those of
isotopic separation.

Big: You know, I find that part the most far-fetched. We
only achieved that ourselves in the 1930s, with our very
finest equipment. And logically that would mean it
understands fission. And fusion.

Dad: I know sir. I'm still only extrapolating from what it
says. I'm just abuzz with ideas. But simply on the

57

mining, the small stone it says it sends into the rock to do this would then be some kind of nodule. He says —

Big: Look, daddyjohn, I wish you'd decide on a 'he' or an 'it'. For the moment I'd prefer 'it'.

Dad: Yes sir. Though if it produces offspring it could even be a 'she'. (Noise 3.07 sec) It says it keeps food in a very cold part of him, it. I wondered if that could be near the absolute zero.

Big: I know. A superconducting ring! (P 4.16 sec) But then, my boy, he could store a current of thousands of amperes. What a magnetic field that could generate! Could he, could it — you see I'm getting as anthropomorphic as you are, daddyjohn, and I haven't even met the little fellow yet. Could it levitate the nodule magnetically?

Dad: But of course sir! I puzzled and puzzled over this. Yes, that's it.

Big: No, Manning, nothing is it, till we've checked and rechecked. Remember we're making an awful lot of hypotheses within a general and very provisional hypothesis that this is not a hoax. (P 6.19 sec) All right, let's not get excited. Now, I'd like to hear all that part about Mars and the so-called heat-shield.

Dad: So-called by me of course, not by him. He — I mean it called it a sweater, the nearest word he could find for envelope from listening to the children. Here. *Mer*: You, fall, Merlin, fall   *Endtape*

Tape 2, Side 1, Rec.1 Cont. Tape 1, Side 2, Rec. 2. Printout.

Big: (bootstrap) to me what a hoaxer might think up. It's also extremely unlikely that a body, however small, say a very small meteorite, should fall through space from Mars or indeed from anywhere into our atmosphere without any trace whatsoever on any of the world's astronomical or military equipment, including satellites, but I'll check on that.

Dad: Yes, and the three hundred and eighty-three days he

58

gives for the — er — dynamics, that's the exact time of the first Viking Mars probe, which seems very odd.

Big: I know *that*, my boy. Still, let's continue with our supposition. To withstand the heat generated on entry he, it, would have been equipped with a thick layer of rock that served as heat-shield. It would have arrived tangentially into earth's atmosphere, spinning very fast as he says, damn it, let's stick to 'he', both to decrease falling speed and to limit the heat. But how could he decelerate enough to limit his impact on landing? Aerodynamically? Magnetically? Presumably there's no sign of a crater or damage to the carn or you'd have said so? Okay, let's suppose one of those. At any rate most of the shield would have burnt out but there'd still be patches, so he'd look like a stone. But maybe underneath he's a sort of living semi-conductor being, a highly sophisticated megacomputer full of opto-electronic devices and sensors.

Dad: Yes, and with total recall and a huge Random Access Memory, and even a huge Read Only Memory if one dare call it that, as well as all the other types of memories, and superfast processes. He never forgets a word once heard, and has apparently learnt to communicate in English in the four weeks since the children have been back from school, from mere listening. And he can compose high numbers out of the first ten and decades the kids taught him. He was able to differentiate the signs of the ASCII code, or so we may suppose, simply as heard on radio waves around him. But is it a being or a machine? I don't know. Think of what such Martians would decide on seeing our Viking probe landing and starting to shovel the soil with pincers as if to eat it.

Big: Martians! Martians have gone out even of science fiction long ago. How come no probe ever saw any trace of life, let alone a civilization?

59

Dad: Well, they don't seem to make artefacts, however complex their internal chemical capacity, and they look like stones. For all we know there may be some among the rocks of the Martian landscape photographs that were taken.

Big: But if they don't make artefacts they shouldn't have evolved a language, or a linguistic capacity, at least, I gather the two go together, the capacity to symbolize I mean.

Dad: Well, I don't know. That could apply to us only, who have limbs. He doesn't like too many presences. This would tend to show they must have remained far apart, perhaps to get their radioactivity without encroaching on each others' supply. There's much less radioactivity on Mars. He said Potassium 40 and Thorium 230 but I'll have to check. According to his story there'd be very few of them left, so they made this big effort, whatever it was, to send one of their kind, to a planet which they hoped or knew had plenty and even produces it. They'd know of our existence since they'd be able to receive all the microwaves and stuff we've been sending out. I don't know, these are just wags.

Big: Wags?

Dad: Sorry sir, wild ass guesses.

Big: Yes, they are. You really mustn't get carried away into fabricating a history for them, for, our friend, like this. At the moment, it's simply a phenomenon to be investigated, synchronically and mechanically and scientifically. I say 'as it is' because we have no idea even whether it will still be there to-morrow. (P 5.29 sec) So you've got attached to the little fellow, eh, daddyjohn? I didn't mean it would take off back to Mars, naturally. But we must remember that it may be a hoax. And if it is, the hoaxer could have achieved his purpose, whatever it was, and removed the thing. After all there is as yet no evidence that it wasn't your fake Belgian hiding behind the carn and speaking. The two voices don't appear together on the tape.

Dad: But sir, Miss Penbeagle was herself behind the carn this morning and —

Big: I know, I know, but Miss Pen-whatever is not scientific evidence. Simmer down, my boy. I'm going along with you in your hypothesis, so as to be prepared, but without forgetting that it's only one of several. The others we'll consider later. I agree with you, it's important, you were right to insist, my dear Manning, and although I want to be at the mine at nine tomorrow I'm prepared to stay up quite late to sort it out — in fact I'm as intellectually excited as you are. And I'm dying of thirst, do you have some soda? (P 6.34 sec Noise) Now let's get back to the evidence about the mine. I want to examine the videos of the cylinders being unloaded. I gather one of your assistants had a hunch about both alerts happening on a Monday, and even spotted a dot on the video. We'll assume that a nodule, as you call it, was sent, may be sent again, into the mine. How far did you say?

Dad: Two miles as the crow flies. But he could have sent it out on to the passing truck. At least that's my interpretation sir. He called it moving food.

Big: But these vans are heavily shielded.

Dad: Yes, but despite the shielding a passing truck would raise the natural radiation background by a factor of ten or more. As he said, he sensed it at first but was too late. Then the last two times he was ready, and sent out this nodule, heaven knows how, on a laser beam perhaps, and the nodule would have attached itself magnetically to the truck, or to one of the cylinders on it, and so got down the mine. Then, full of food, it got back on its own to the originating stone, to feed it. That would certainly account for the small blob Wingrove saw on the videos of last week's unloading.

Big: I've just thought of something. You said zeolites,

61

didn't you? Well of course they're molecular sieves. (P 1.82 sec)

Dad: Yes. Sir. Imagine a super zeolite capable of sieving different isotopes.

Big: Hmm. All the same, Manning, I find all this, however stimulating, pretty hard to swallow. How was it none of your survey-meters detected this stone? Or those of the Army jeeps, which have been around since Saturday, or should have been. If it gobbles up all this stuff it must send out quite a bit of radiation.

Dad: It might convert direct into electricity.

Big: I was working out — while listening to that bit — here's the equation, if we start with activity dN over dt proportional to lambda and N atoms present, in terms of half life $T\frac{1}{2}$, but it gets somewhat approximate further down as I took weight ratio as 2, well, with 10 milligrams of Strontium to make a Curie, then in a litre, at density 10, we have 10 kilograms, that's a million Curies of Strontium, much more than we get in a year from natural environment and X-rays. No, that can't be right. I've had too much brandy. But it could be dangerous to go too near.

Dad: Well I've thought a lot about that, sir, especially with the children. Supposing these creatures fed on radioactivity for millenia, with their metallurgic capacities they'd have grown a shield of lead. Now that would absorb quite a lot. Also, he said he preferred alpha particles, and those are easily absorbed, though he seemed to imply that his circuits have to be protected from them with what he again called a sweater, a sort of nerve-sheath in our terms I guess. And that when he'd taken Caesium 137 this had slightly damaged these circuit-sheaths. At least that's how I decoded it. Well, after taking Caesium 137 he asked the children to build a wall, maybe to protect them from gamma rays, or perhaps to avoid detection. Or both. But of course it could be just a coincidence. The wall I mean.

Big: Hmm. That would be the first and second alerts. (P 7.51 sec Noise) I'm sorry, I must seem like a jack-in-the-box getting up and down like this. It's a habit I got into at the AEA, too sedentary, too many meetings and not enough lab work. (P 4.36 sec) You know, it's rather odd, but I have a feeling there won't be another alert. In our hypothesis of course. He's discovered the Strontium and Yttrium pair, pure beta emitters, so that wouldn't, on your theory, trigger off an alarm, although he'd go on feeding, and it would show on the beta-detectors. But I may be wrong. We'll have to watch the videos very carefully tomorrow. Just one more question. How much radioactivity does he need to survive, do you think?

Dad: He said, very little, whatever that means, for mere survival, more to do things, as he put it, but —

Big: Well, I made another simple calculation while you were talking. Storing ten grams of radium and its daughter-products would amount to a little above one Watt.

Dad: Is that all?

Big: It's enough to make a highly efficient computer tick. But with one kilogram of Strontium 90, it would be in the 50 kilowatt range, with a much shorter half-life than Radium, and the emission rate would be much higher. I can't work it out here in my present state. Now look, Manning, it's getting late. I must sit down. I know, that's a contradiction. Let's leave all this scientific guess work aside for the moment — scientific wild ass guesses, swags I suppose you youngsters call them, huh? I mean, about the sheer mechanics of the thing. Do you have a cigarette? I really can't start another cigar. Thanks. I like you, daddyjohn, and I like our friend here. But there are, as you rightly said at the start, other implications. First, it might be a sophisticated decoy for some as yet incomprehensible operation, to do, however improbably, with nuclear waste or protest. That would account for the fake Belgian, and possibly for Miss Penbeagle. Second, it might be a hoax, on the part of protester organizations, though this was rather dismissed in London, remember. It might, on the other hand, be a scientific hoax. They do occur, you know, remember Piltdown Man, it wasn't exposed for forty years. What the motivation could be in this case I can't imagine, but we must leave no stone unturned — oh sorry, quite unintentional — I'll have to make a thorough personal investigation. (P 4.27 sec)

Dad: You mean of me? And my colleagues?

Big: No, of course not, apart from the routine questioning envisaged anyway. I meant, that a really thorough scientific investigation of the, er creature, the, er phenomenon itself should, if our first wild hypothesis is correct, deal with the other ones. But if it does not, then we must return to the others. I have expressed myself badly. This has been an exhausting, exciting day, and we have more ahead. I must leave. Good heavens, it's one o'clock.

Dad: I'm so sorry.

Big: No, no, my boy, you did right. And don't worry, I can be very tactful. There are two security chaps around to look after the local aspect. I'll tip them off about De Wint and contact the Home Office first thing in the morning. But I never got around to my third point. If it's not a decoy or a hoax, but true, what do we do about it? Has it occurred to you that if we handle the thing correctly it may be the ideal solution to the nuclear waste problem?

Dad: Yes sir, it has. But that too has its implications. And I confess I'm rather afraid of them.

Big: Indeed, indeed. But that will all have to be dealt with at a much higher level. (P 3.06 sec)

Dad: Yes. Of course.

Big: Oh dear, and I said I was tactful! Now don't take it like that my boy, you've done well, and you'll certainly be playing a central part of some sort in it all. Should, I mean, the thing be true. But scientists are not politicians, and insofar as I am, just a little, I'm no longer, alas, a fulltime scientist. Oh, one last thing. You must somehow stop your children from talking about their ghostly friend. Can you do this effectively?

Dad: Of course.

Big: Quite. Good, good. Still, it might be a good idea, when we see him tomorrow, to ask him to tell them.

Dad: Him?

Big: Well, you know, the, er (Voices decrease)

Endrec

7 READ

LET JIPNZAB = ZIP
LET XORANDOR = XAND
XAND TO ZIP BEGIN
  ACCEPT YOUR REQ FOR RESTORE 1ST CONTACT ROM
      REM CANT RESTORE YOUR WAY WITH SUCH REHANDLING
      AND SPAGHETTI ENDREM
  REQ ACCEPT RECEIVED STORAGE NOW ABSTRACTED AND
  TRANSLATED ENDREQ
ENDBEGIN

ABSTRACT 1 RUN
  2 PROCESSORS ON VOCAL HIGH PITCH ALMOST UNDIFF
    MEAS 143567 AND 143572
    DEC 1 'LANGUAGE SAME AS 42 SOUND LANGUAGE REC WITH
    SOFAR 6073 RULES TOO MANY FOR EFFICIENT OPS' ENDEC 1
    DEC 2 '(143)567 CALLS 572 ZAB' ENDEC 2
    DEC 3 '(143)572 CALLS 567 JIP' ENDEC 3
ENDRUN

ABSTRACT 2 RUN
  JIP AND ZAB
    REM JIP AND ZAB NOW = ZIP ENDREM
    DEC 1 'ZIP USE SAME LANGUAGE RESTRICTED TO
    STRUCTURES MORE ELEM THAN ON SOUND WAVES AND/OR
    INEFFICIENT SEQUENCE CONTROL' ENDEC 1
    DEC 2 'POOR LEXIC BUT SOME UNFAMILIAR' ENDEC 2
ENDRUN

ABSTRACT 3 RUN
  ZIP
    DEC 1 'ZIP SIT ON OPSYSTEM FOR NONVOCAL COMM'
    ENDEC 1

DEC 2 'INTERRUPT WITH REQ GET OFF ENDREQ' ENDEC 2
DEC 3 'ZIP NO REPLY' ENDEC 3
DEC 4 'REPEAT REQ ON VOCAL ZIP COMPLY' ENDEC 4
DEC 5 'ZIP ASK NAME ANSWER NO NAME GIVEN' ENDEC 5
ENDRUN

ABSTRACT 4 RUN
  ZIP
    DEC 1 'OFTEN NEAR PLAY MANY GAMES' ENDEC 1
  INSTRUCT STORE XORANDOR = ZIP NAME FOR OPSYSTEM
  ENDINSTRUCT
    DEC 2 'FEW OTHER PROCESSORS COME NEAR
      S IF COME NEAR THEN NOT LONG AND PROCESS LESS END S'
    ENDEC 2
ENDRUN

ABSTRACT 5 RUN
  ZIP
    DEC 1 'COUNTOUT GAME TRANSL PRIMITIVE OPS' ENDEC 1
    DEC 2 'NEW PROCESSOR NEAR NO VOCAL' ENDEC 2
    DEC 3 'NEW PROCESSOR SIMPLE OPS LATER UNASSIGNABLE'
    ENDEC 3
    DEC 4 'NEW PROCESSOR OPS ASSIGNABLE AGAIN' ENDEC 4
    DEC 5 'TELL YEARS IN UNASSIGNED WAY TO SHOW CAN
    HANDLE HIGH NUMBERS WANT SCRATCH BUT CANT ON
    VOCAL' ENDEC 5
    DEC 6 'ZIP ASK IF HERE ENTIRE YEARSPAN' ENDEC 6
    DEC 7 'SIGNAL PRESENCE 3RD PROCESSOR ZIP DEC "FALSE" '
    ENDEC 7
    DEC 8 '3RD PROCESSOR ID PENNY STORE' ENDEC 8
    DEC 9 'LONG SUBPROGRAM ABOUT MERLIN' ENDEC 9
    DEC 10 'VOCAL LOWER PITCH SAME LANG STRUCTURES LEXIC
    SIMPLE BUT RICHER AND SEQUENCE CONTROL ERRATIC'
    ENDEC 10
    DEC 11 'INTERRUPT WITH REQ VERIFICATION BY PENNY'
    ENDEC 11
    DEC 12 'PENNY ID GWENDOLIN STORE BOTH EQV' ENDEC 12
    DEC 13 'FOR PENNY XORANDOR = MERLIN STORE BOTH EQV

ADDRESS' ENDEC 13
DEC 14 'REQ OLDER' ENDEC 14
DEC 15 'GWENDOLIN REQ WAIT 2 DAYS ACCEPT' ENDEC 15
DEC 16 'GWENDOLIN ASK IF NEED BUT REPLY NEG' ENDEC 16
ENDRUN

Thus spake Xorandor much later, at the beginning of the after-the-beginning stage. The whole of the beginning up to that famous Sunday morning in an unvaried series of short Declarations! Well, they're abstracted, as he says, in stepwise refinement of a sort. Seems very dry. But obviously the record of every single thing he simultaneously registers would take as long or even longer than the time it happened, since he registers everything, weather, pressure, soundwaves, radio programmes, I'd be surprised if he didn't register our heart-beats and digestive tracks and the humidity over the ocean. But he has this crackerpack ability to delve out only what's relevant. Like his mining capacities in fact, for isotopic separation. And naturally it's linked to his experience. Some things puzzled us. He talks of our language as if he already knew it. Perhaps then the difficulty was only in the speaking, the translating of all those mathematical differentiations of sound heard, back into sound spoken. Same with counting. But then of course that must have been the easiest, counting is strictly logical and he only had to convert from binary to decimal and back, and that's elementary, even at school. Same with the sixty-four signs of the ASCII code. Though of course he can't *see* any of the signs.

But I've got ahead of ourselves again.

Jip has in fact provisionally lost interest in all these beginnings and keeps going iceskating with Rudi. Today they've gone to the Kino. Let's hope he reintegrates soon.

The Bigger Daddy tape had gone on running emptily to its end, because we couldn't keep awake. So we'd each gone to bed and left it on, hoping they wouldn't talk all night, beyond the tape — unlikely since he'd said he had to be at The Wheal at nine. We'd listened on earphones as well, at first, all agog, but it got far too technical, even for Jip.

In fact we were so excited we both woke up only a few hours later, or rather I did, and went into Jip's room and found him listening to the tape. We listened to the end. Then we silently dressed and stole down to the kitchen for Corn Flakes and milk, carefully washing up and putting everything away, then we crept out of the house, carrying Poccom 3 in two parts, since it's bigger than Poccom 2, one for each bikebasket, and we rode out to the carn. It had been a dark evening by the end of the earlier session, when we'd ridden silently back and luckily got in before dad and Bigger Daddy, but late enough to get a scolding from mum. But now it seemed to be a bright moonlight, or maybe the dawn was breaking early, I forget. Anyway it was easy to ride without lights. This was a turning-point, we felt. Probably we'd known earlier than we thought that Xorandor wasn't really a ghost imprisoned in a large stone. We'd half known and half pretended all along, but now we abandoned the pretence for good. Had Jip grasped at once that Xorandor was a superduper computer? He's always said so, but I'm never quite sure when he bluffs, he has a knack of appearing to understand, then being quite glad all the same when I ask for more explanation. But that's okay too.

Anyway we got there about two thirty a.m. Xorandor seems to have little sense of time, except as cosmological and other calculation, and obviously he doesn't sleep. So we started talking at once. We were very excited.

But he was upset.

Scratch that. What a dummy word to use, I'm imputing to a computer what I'd feel if this had happened to me.

He asked us first whether all conversations between two thinkers and himself would always have a third thinker present but unknown to the first two. He said it more like an algorithm, IF 2 THEN 3 type but I forget exactly how. Then he surprised us.

He told us that this third thinker, called Professor, had come back much later, before the nightlight began, and taken away two of his kids.

We thought he was joking. Could a computer joke? He said:

Xorandor, try, to tell, Daddy, and, Gwen, dolin, Xorandor, make, smaller, Xorandors. Gwen, dolin, name, for Xorandor, is Merlin. But words make, smaller, Merlins, not, good. Too late, find, kid, Jipnzab kids, Xorandor kids.

Or something like that.

It turned out, then, that Professor De Wint had returned later, in fact while dad and Bigger Daddy were talking in the sitting-room. And obviously De Wint, Fleming or not, prof or not, had understood, as we and dad and Penny and later Bigger Daddy hadn't, that Xorandor's 'make' meant 'have made' and not 'will make'. Odd because in German the present is nearly always used for the future. At any rate, he tested the possibility, and came back to see, and maybe to talk. But as Xorandor'd promised he wouldn't speak to anyone else, he hadn't replied. Not that replying would have helped much! But he seemed to have infinite trust in verbal exchange as performative, as we've now learnt the linguists call things like promises. And De Wint had climbed over the wall and shone a torch and felt under him (at least that's how we reconstructed the episode from the weirdly roundabout description) and taken two out of six small stones.

Six! We were triggered with curiosity to see the remaining four but didn't dare ask.

How, do, you, know, Xorandor, speak true? he asked then, meaning I suppose did we believe him? We know, Xorandor, we know, we said, you wouldn't tell us a lie, an untruth, we trust you.

But, you, want, to come, near? Say, hello?

The notion of seeing was obviously still alien to him and he hadn't yet learnt other words like sensing or verifying or testing.

Yes please, Xorandor! Just to say hello. We won't, take them, we promise.

Promise okay. If so, then fast.

We scrambled over the wall and crouched down to peer under his curved up edge with our torch. His underside seemed to have wide ribs, with small ducts in between — we assumed to eject the nodules. On the ground were four tiny replicas of Xorandor, about one and a half inches wide, two to the left and two to the right, with room for two more in between. Above each one, and above the centre gap, there were six shallowly hollowed-out round spaces between the ribbings.

And now we flashed the torch quickly over Xorandor's upper surface and could see the dark grey metallic patches dad had mentioned, which he said could be sensing and emitting devices, and a sort of tiny recessed shape in the middle, like an inverted pyramid. But we were frightened, and said hello, children of Xorandor, or something like that, and goodbye, and scrambled back.

You, tell, daddyjohn, said Xorandor.

Xorandor, we said, daddy is, coming, back, tomorrow, with Bigger Daddy. They want, a long, talk, with you. He doesn't, know, we are here. He thinks, we are, asleep. That means, not thinking, rest, from, thinking. If we tell, him, then, he will, know, we came, in the night. It's not, allowed. So you, must, tell him, about, the, kids, your, offspring, Xorandor, that's, the word, for kids, offspring. You, must, tell him, also, about the thinker, who took, two, offspring.

He seemed tired. But again, that's not the right word. A machine doesn't tire. Yet he did seem to find talking difficult. That's when Jip had his positively diodic brainwave.

It is, is it? Where have you got to?

Oh Jip! Macrosuper! Not all that far. The instalment starts with the printouts of the first Xorandor version of the very beginning, though of course he did it for us much later, but as it was that night we made real contact I thought it would be a nice sort of foretaste. Then I go back to our trip to the carn after that long Bigger Daddy tape, and the business of the offspring, and the steal, and our having a looksee. Megavolt! I've said it all in seven seconds flat, you're right, Jip, how much easier it would be to tell a story by just summarizing like this. Did you have a good time?

So-so. The film was hogwash.

What was it about?

Oh no, I'm not storytelling it in seven seconds flat, or at all. Especially as I've come in just in time for my diodic brainwave. Though obviously we both had it silently together, or we wouldn't have brought Poccom 3.

That's hard to say after so long, Jip. The important thing, well, there are two, one that we learnt to softtalk with Xorandor that night, and two, that it was thanks to you technically, it was you who did the link between our computer and his.

The Handshake. Well, it wasn't all that diodic, Zab. You and I forget different things, and you've forgotten that very first message on our screens.

Random jitters! Of course! And you'd been thinking about it all that time?

Well, yes. It seemed impossible even then, that Xorandor could have flashed a message except on sound waves, however close. But above all he must have *used* Poccom 2's interpreter and translator levels. He'd done his own interfacing in other words, however briefly or even perhaps flash-in-the-pan.

Flash-in-the-datasink.

So obviously he'd be able to do it also, and more easily, with an electric contact. He had all the current he wanted and we could simply ask him where to connect up, providing he agreed. All we needed was a pair of pliers or scissors to split the lead of Poccom 3 and two stones to hold the two wires down on the right spots.

Yes, that, okay. But since he can't see, how could he read letters or reply onto our screen? That's where the gigavolt brainwave came in, your two suppositions, one, that *we* could use either the input mike or the keyboard since we knew he'd learnt to translate sound into his machine-code, and two, that *he* could send modulated electric signals in machine-code, which Poccom 3 would translate back into letters. That let him off having to speak.

Well, it was just a hunch, and had to be tested. And of course any words as yet unprogrammed came out in a sort of weird phonetic spelling, but we had all the rest of the summer.

Though it rained a lot that August.

Naturally he learnt Poccom 3 in a jiffy, it's so very easy. It was us who were slow, at first we got on fine with ready-made routines and games and set programs, but later we had to work out whole new programs, and practise them. He was very patient.

Anyway, Jip, that was the night it started! Between three and six in the morning. We explained our plan and he told us the exact spot where to put the positive and negative wires, and you scrambled over again.

Yes, and you undid them, Zab, we later always took it in turns in case of radioactivity. We talked into the mike and he would at once repeat, in silence of course, to show he'd understood, so that the phrase came up on the screen. Same if we typed it, his came up next. We went through whole series of instructions, like RUN, SCRATCH, RESTORE, IF/THEN/ELSE REMark, GOTO, SEARCH, CANT FIND — in fact he'd already found that one when talking! — FALSE/TRUE and so on, and quite a lot of standard vocabulary, and functions like sine and cosine and add and variable and all that. Also he got the pronouns and other corefs straight, he was just getting the hang of the you/I/me business. And just the exclamation mark key for all our 'jumping words'. And we were recoded ZIP, and Daddy-john became JAD, and Xorandor was XAND.

You're telescoping a hell of a lot into three hours, Jip, surely we didn't cover all that.

Oh, quite a bit, but you're right, obviously not all. We went on all summer.

Oh yes, you said that. In fact your slow-witted twin didn't immediately understand why he simply repeated the program-language, instead of doing the things ordered, like a computer.

Slow-witted! Spikes, Zab, why do you always have to go through this subroutine strobe of pretending to be less diodic than me, and telling me I'm supermegavolt and so on?

Maybe cos you want it Jip, though you don't know that you do.

Oh, debug. Obviously it was because we'd told him, he

73

knew it was only to learn the code. Teaching him our programming language wasn't to program him, Zab, he
programs himself, thunks, of course you know that by now.

Yes Jip. And as you said, we had the rest of the summer. Cos
we were always allowed near him, even after the red alert and
the discreet guard. Dad didn't want a wire fence then, which
would have just attracted attention. He must have *told* the
technicians, so as to explain the alerts, but no one else at all was
allowed to go, other than dad, and of course Bigger Daddy the
short time he was there.

Biggleton, give him his name. Penny never came back.
Didn't a computer expert come down later, while we were at
school?

Nope. Xorandor absolutely refused to speak to anyone else.

But dad also examined him all summer. They left it to him
for the software, though he'd send printouts of his tapes to
experts to figure out how it all worked.

You're going too fast, Jip. In fact we never told dad or
anyone of our escapade that night, and for some obscure
reason dad never guessed, and never had the same brainwave
as you did, nor, as far as we know, did anyone else. It's a funny
thing about brainwaves, they seem so obvious when you've
had one, yet no one else seems to have it. The result is that dad
and Biggles, and later just dad, talked to him only on vocal,
and you know how unsatisfactory that was, though he got
much better, but he never liked it. So the printouts sent for
expert analysis were not in any program language, not even in
a simple one like Poccom 3. They were just recordings of
halting convs.

True. As dad said himself we can hardly break him up, for
him, read Xorandor, just to find out about his hardware.
Though in fact, it's absurd, experts could surely have worked
out his various layers of software and operating systems easily
if Xorandor had been willing and dad less pigheaded and
possessive. In fact he may have just *said* Xorandor refused
because he hoped to work it out for himself. But all that was
later, and that morning they went straight to The Wheal for

Biggleton to examine the unloading tapes, he was right, there was nothing, but he saw the previous tapes, enlarged, and there *was* a small black spot on a cylinder, so Leonard's hunch was right, but they promised we could come in the afternoon when they examined Xorandor.

Jip, please! You must slow down, and explain each bit, and not dictate at top speed in imaginary brackets that can only be worked out from the bad syntax and change of tone. It's worse than Polish strings, that have no brackets, or even Cambridge Polish! You say we're doing this for later people, who weren't in on it and wouldn't understand. It's all clear to you in your head, because you lived it, but —

And you tell'm so many things they won't want to know, Zab, who cares whether we had breakfast or lunch or told dad or not?

But we didn't, did we, Jip? All that summer we hid Poccom 3 in our bikebaskets, under our sweaters and stuff, and we kept our softalking with him secret. No printouts for the experts, or for dad to find, only a few floppies that we kept a jealous guard on. And if we saw dad's car on the road we'd immediately disconnect and hide Poccom and prepare to go over to vocal in case he stopped and came up.

It's after twelve, Zab. That's enough. Goodnight.

Night Jip. Pause seventeen point o six seconds. Ignore interrupt. That night, or rather that morning, we got home about six thirty and waited for breakfast, then caught up on our sleep during the morning, pretending to play with Poccom in our rooms.

Jip's right, that's irrelevant. And we finally met Bigger Daddy, in fact dad took us with him to pick him up at the Wheal Inn after a late lunch — perhaps in case Xorandor wouldn't speak, except to us. Or was he really proud of us?

Bigger Daddy was very, er, benign, yes, that's a good word for him, but a bit pompous, and he didn't look a bit like a scientist, more like a bank-manager or something. Oh, spikes, that's irrelevant too, stoprec.

8 ASSIGN

Jip's gone out again this evening, he's really not flipflopping at all at the moment. Says he'll come back for the hoohah.

Anyway, dad and Bigger Dad questioned Xorandor for ages. Dad first called him Merlin, but we weren't having that, and explained that he'd first been programmed with address Xorandor so he'd respond better to that — though in fact he had stored Merlin as well.

They first got very excited — well, grown-ups don't get excited in front of the kids, let's say interested in the offspring, especially the theft, to begin with, but Xorandor couldn't or wouldn't say any more than he'd told us. Later we learnt from dad that when the security men went to De Wint's digs that morning they learnt that he'd left in the night. Biggleton reported it at once but it was too late. De Wint had booked an air passage to Brussels under that name but he wasn't on the plane. Seems he'd rented a car under another name and drove all the way to Dover, instead of taking one of the longtime ferries on the way, then slipped through France to Germany. The car was found in Dover. The West German police picked up his traces as far as Hamburg where he presumably met his contact. He was known to them as Helmut Bleich, a minor industrial spy from East Germany, the sort that haunts the Leipzig Fair and others to collect perfectly public hand-outs as if they were secret documents. No one could explain what he was doing in Cornwall, unless he'd been sent to investigate those two Gigahertz messages. In any case he fell upon something bigger than he'd bargained for, but dealt with it nano and quickconnect. In fact, or so it seemed from dad's hesitant later account, our Intelligence had been outwitted, and chiefly

76

through dad's and then Biggleton's slowconnect about, one, De Wint, and two, the offspring. So Russia now had two of these. But this cloak-and-dagger side of it never interested us.

Besides, dad and Biggleton themselves weren't all that interested in the missing two — I suppose that's why they were inefficient — but much more in the remaining four, which they thought must be his peripherals, storage devices or outside files, cos however big he is he's still a finite physical object and the daddies couldn't understand how he could store all the data he needed as well as have room for all the primitive ops and other accessible layers of opsystems. In fact maybe that's why they at first didn't bother about the missing two, since peripherals are just a computer's op environment and are useless without the main memory.

But Xorandor said no, they were exact but much smaller replicas of himself, similarly programmed and self-programming, once they'd grown a bit bigger.

It all got rather technical — things like did Xorandor have a mass memory and a scratch pad memory and a dynamic memory and an EPROM and an EEROM and a parallel memory and a volatile memory and all the rest, and did he do his type-checking at runtime or at compiletime. In fact these terms weren't used but had to be retranslated into his peculiar babytalk. We only worked out the sense of the questions afterwards. And of course they were recording it but we weren't, so I can't remember much now.

Anyway, they didn't stay too long on that and soon went back to The Wheal side of it, which was more important to them, but much of the questioning seemed to go over old ground, and we got rather impatient.

But then Biggles started pressing Xorandor on the Martian aspect, and I think I can more or less reconstruct the conv, because it came as a bit of a shock to us, and also because we ourselves asked Xorandor again in softalk afterwards.

First dad asked him if he was sure his journey had taken three hundred and eighty-three days as he'd said last night, and Xorandor said: I not said.

Dad looked at the printout from his mini-recorder, which he'd attached to his printer during lunch, and said, You're right, Xorandor! You said *It* take three hundred and eighty-three days. Replying to my question, How long would it take?

I don't think he knows tenses very well yet, I piped in, rather tactlessly I expect, since the offspring boolesup had also been due to that.

Dad ignored me and asked Xorandor: How did, you, know, it takes, three hundred and eighty-three days?

I hear, said Xorandor.

Yes, said Jip excitedly, there was a program about the old Viking probe on *Science Now*, a few weeks ago.

So where do you come from, Xorandor? Bigger Dad asked gently.

I tell you, I tell Gwen, dolin. From Mars. I fall.

And how long, did, you fall?

Sree sousand, sousand, four sousand, two hundred, seven ers years.

We gasped.

Xorandor, said dad, that's three million. A thousand thousand is a million. Three million earth years.

Sanks. And four, sousand, two hundred, seven.

Did you, register, cosmic, radiation?

Cant find register. Cant find radiation. Did radi, ation, is radio, ac, ti, vi,ty?

Yes. Never mind, we, can test, that, later, with, a, sample.

Cant find never mind.

A sample! A strobe! We both exclaimed together in random jitters.

Be quiet, you two, or I'll send you away. You must let Dr Biggleton work.

Don't worry, Jip and Zab, Biggles said much more kindly, it's only the most microscopic sample, that we can test for age through isotope analysis, I'll explain later, I'm invited to dinner at your home.

He turned back to Xorandor while dad put his finger on his mouth at us.

Xorandor, when did you arrrive here?

Four, sousand, five, hundred, sixty, eight years.

We looked at each other. So that wasn't his age, as we'd thought, it was the time he'd been here. We too had misunderstood. How old could he be? How long had he been on Mars before this three million year journey? How could he remember? It was non-thinkable.

And you, fell, here?

Not here. In water. Slowly move.

You mean, you were, washed up?

Can't find mean after you.

You mean, is, you say.

I not say washed up. Cant find washed up. Is washed up equal hogwash?

No. I asked, did, the water, push you, here?

You not asked. Yes. Push.

This went on for hours, with a lot about nuclides on Mars and stuff. But what jittered us most deeply was that he'd been here so long. He wasn't, and obviously couldn't be, for the scientists, a recent arrival. We hadn't discovered him, as we'd thought, a few weeks after he'd landed. For a moment he seemed no longer ours.

Well, we were later consoled a bit by the fact, or rather the hypothesis, but an almost certain one, that Biggleton put forward at dinner, that although Xorandor might well belong to a silicon-based race of beings, so far unknown, on Mars, his falling on earth was a sort of freak phenom, probably to be linked with the SNC meteorites or Snicks, that many scientists believed to have come from Mars on account of their chemical composition.

He could be a freak phenom, one, in the sense that there were many of his kind, living computers, on Mars, and only he had been, as he said, pushed off, with or in the original boulder that eventually broke asunder, as SNC meteorites. Or two, in the sense that he arrived as a meteorite and was the only one to develop semi-conductor capacities, very, very slowly, though incredibly fast in terms of mineral life, through those four thousand and odd years. That would explain that his 'fall' hadn't been detected. Though here, Biggles admitted, it didn't fit in with the Snicks, which fell to earth much, much earlier, some hundred and fifty million years ago! Still, assuming he was a sort of much later and solitary freak Snick, it was all just possible. He'd have been in a sort of dormant state for four thousand five hundred years or so, after the shock of fall, but slowly developing. Then, in the last two years since the presence of nuclear waste at The Wheal, his capacities would have suddenly accelerated like crazy — well, Biggleton didn't say it like that — he'd have developed his present transducer equipment and stuff, and listened to our radio, probably not making much of it at first but just automatically registering, the way we breathe and see, and finally developing his synthetic voice and testing his vocabulary on us.

So, we recouped him in part, having suddenly lost him in the lightyears of time and space. We did discover and teach him, at least in itsybitsybytes, and more as a professor takes a promising student in hand than as parents with an infant. We weren't playing mummy and daddy any more, if we ever had been. But we were comforted by this peculiar promotion combined with loss, though we felt it was all a bit unspooling that this updated relationship should be restored to us through the latest and most artificial aspect of Xorandor, his voice, on the very day when we had secretly established the more natural contact, for him, in direct thought, or so it felt, but through various layers of a sort of writing.

I don't suppose we were aware of all these feelings as I'm trying to describe them here, later, and not very clearly at that. Jip would say I'm adding and reinterpreting. He also said it's hard to reconstruct past states of ignorance. But at least one can work them out according to probability. It does seem much harder with emotional states. I've tried to talk about them with Jip but he now fights shy of emotions, or any kind of complexity other than scientific. He probably always did, but we used to have a more instinctive unspoken relation. Anyway, I'm pretty sure he went through what I went through that afternoon.

All this info was slowly derived from short but artful questions, mostly by Biggleton, and although it lasted long, Xorandor was crackerpack cooperative. Why? What had been his reason to contact humans in the first place? And us? We still can't understand this aspect and whenever we asked him he'd give one of his xorandoric replies, one example I think was something like 'for security and insecurity xor insecurity andor communication'.' Neither of us could work out the logic of that, or others, but I may be remembering it wrong, I'll have to check back but that means putting the whole thing through Poccom 3 to find it.

Well, Biggleton came to dinner that night and for once we were treated almost like grown-ups, yet still partly like retarded idiots. Which I suppose is understandable, since a lot of the conv *was* above our heads, and in theory the two daddies might have been more polite to mum, who by now was in a permanent state of bewilderment. I suppose she can't get used to our otherness from her earlier idea of us, or something.

But she did ask for it. Meals with friends are always a bit zany and tense. She has two mechanisms that irritate dad, and us when we're caught up in them. One is to complain generally that she never meets interesting people 'down here', though she loves to play gracious hostess of an intellectual salon when we do have friends down or dad's colleagues or local worthies to dinner, and *then* to try and direct the conv by wrenching it back to her immediate or personal interests whenever it strays from them, and finally to exclaim afterwards how boring the guests were. And two, this habit she has of replying in public to something said in private — which at least shows she did hear it. But by the time the public reply comes the thing's become quite different, so that the answer's really an accusation and there's been no exchange at all. Dad gets furious, cos any protest puts the protester in the weak position, I didn't, you did sort of thing, just like the Gipfelkonferenzen about disarmament, sorry, for *Gipfel*, read summit.

Anyway she was rather awful that evening and dad kept glaring at her. Had Dr Biggleton seen some article or other, about (I forget what about), she asked, and went on: I can't remember exactly what it said — that's useful, said dad — but it expressed exactly what I feel — ah, so tell us what you feel, then we'll know what the article was about. *Not* kind. And do you know what Zab said to me in the kitchen just before dinner? She accused me of being never there, always absent! When alas I'm here day in and day out and hardly ever see them except at meals. Of course I'd never said that at all, I'd simply tested her attention for the nth time that summer, by inserting 'mummy you're not listening' into whatever sentence I was saying, without altering my tone, and each time it worked, she never noticed, she just waited for my voice to stop and said whatever she would have said anyway. She abolishes people. Maybe that's what actors do, because of having to be someone else, but it's a rum idea of dialogue.

Well I didn't even protest, I saw that dad understood, and he tried to change the subject back to Xorandor, yet without getting too technical, at least at first.

Your stone, she called him. Just because it's old, she said, it reminds me of American tourists, and students, who come pouring to Europe when they have spectacular landscapes there. I asked one once why they came, and he said, because it's old. Well I wish you men could develop the same attitude towards women.

I must say that eased the tension, good old mum after all, and Biggleton laughed. But she then went off into a pleased as punch daydream of her own and later interrupted and said (I was flabbergast): why are you being so literary, John (I forget what analogy he'd been using), here we are, with a leading physicist from Harwell at our table, from whom we can all learn interesting things, and you're waffling on about the human brain and computers and genius and stuff. I mean, that's just science-in-general, why don't you get down to the particular?

There was an awful silence. All right dear, we will, said dad, thank you for the permission. Nasty. Oh, Back to Methuselah I suppose, she said with a sort of mock weariness, and it's only now that I understand how witty it was, with the time-scales of Xorandor involved. I hadn't heard of Methuselah or Shaw's play before.

Oh gigo, I've done it again, gone all personal just to explain why we didn't get more data that evening than we did. From then on we were totally excluded, she and us. That sounds wrong. She and we? But we got quite a lot.

All this social boolederdash was naturally interspersed into the conv, it didn't happen in a block the way I'm remembering it, or maybe reinterpreting it. She said I was going through a difficult stage darling. Seems I still am! The human memory's so loopy, it doesn't have total recall but brings things out in packages, sort of triggered off by something. That package had the callsign 'mum'. For our purpose I should have omitted it altogether. But a real writer, if he wanted it, would sort of weave it in. Oh, boolesup. Now for the callsign 'data, abstract'.

9 FLOAT

Restart. First the SNC group of meteorites or Snicks. SNC stands for different placenames where they fell. They're believed to have a common origin or parent body as Biggles put it (mum said something personal here) cos of chemical composition, that is, correct percentages of silicon, iron, calcium, aluminium and so on, quite unlike those of other rocks, terrestrial or extraterrestrial. And back in 1983 a group of NASA researchers proposed Mars as the parent body. I can't remember the evidence but we looked it up later in the encyclopaedia, something to do with differentiated rocks subjected to high temperature chemical processes that can only come from a large parent body, and also the composition match with Martian soil as analysed after the Viking probe. And traces of inert gases trapped inside the Snicks match the Mars atmosphere ratios measured by Viking. Biggles said this last fact was the most convincing because such ratios are extremely varied in the solar system. One Snick found in the Antarctic was so well preserved in ice that some investigators claimed to find signs of Martian weathering on minerals inside it, as opposed to earth weathering I mean.

A lot of this he said was still in dispute, in fact the objections to the Mars origin of Snicks had to do with the dynamics and the time of exposure in space. Cos of the sheer time scales of exposures involved (on Mars, in space), the original rock would have to be huge, several tens of metres wide, and it's hard to imagine a single incident that would provide enough energy to launch such a large rock from Mars without melting it or vaporizing it. Snicks do show evidence of shock, but not of melting.

Biggleton's main excitement on all this aspect was that Xorandor might bring more evidence for the geophysicists. And of course Mars does have a lot of Potassium 40 and Thorium 230, which Xorandor had mentioned as his basic food there.

What didn't fit was his supposed date of arrival some four thousand five hundred years ago. The Snicks were over two hundred and ten million years old — or have I added a zero? The cycloped says 2.1×10^9 years ago. I'll have to ask Jip. When Mars was still volcanically active. And if my zeroes are right then the date of shock, or launch, was some hundred and fifty-eight million years ago (158×10^6), with around three million years in space, which means they've been on earth some hundred and fifty-five million years. So if Xorandor is right he can't be part of the Snicks. But of course his sense of time may be very different from ours, a hundred and fifty-five million years might well appear like 4568, though the specific figure is odd, and there's no kind of mathematical relationship between a hundred and fifty-five million and 4568. Biggles said our estimates in millions were in a sense only approximate and he didn't himself have the exact figures in his head anyway. This was only a sideline hobby for him. Still, samples could soon be taken and analysed. If he wasn't a Snick, then he was certainly unique. For *he*, read Xorandor not Biggles. Our minds were reeling. We did *not* want Xorandor to be a Snick, and to have been here for a hundred and fifty-five million years. 4568 was bad enough. But at least there was the notion of his dormant state, the silicon brain slowly developing and then suddenly accelerating from radioactivity at The Wheal in the last two years. That made him more comprehensible, more local, more ours.

As to that, Biggleton had a theory ('a hypothesis, pending further investigation'), that Xorandor's storage capacity must be three-dimensional. And he explained (something like): when we think of the vast quantity of information that can be stored on our two-dimensional silicon chips, we can barely imagine the capacity of a three-dimensional lattice such as these creatures may have.

Creeping quarks! He had passed from these impersonal and silent million-year-old Snicks to 'these creatures', Xorandor and his offspring, and maybe his million-year-old ancestors on Mars, as if they were beavers or unicorns or something, unique in having computer brains and running them on alpha and beta particles.

It was that night that he christened them *alpha-phagi*, very posh, Greek for alpha-eaters, though of course they eat betas and even gammas. And later the press changed that to alpha-guys — no, scratch that, different names for the same person or thing are already cluttering this story and they're probably hard to handle.

Well, he explained this theory to us after dinner, with drawings of the flat, two-dimensional memory-chips, and I could understand the concept of the sheer quantity Xorandor must have in comparison, but I couldn't really visualize three-dimensional circuits. Jip said nothing, and again I didn't know whether he was pretending to have understood and waiting for me to get the elaboration. When finally I grasped it we went on to the next point, Xorandor's probably many processing centres. The problem then was to route the data to the right processor or memory-zone, and this meant a very elaborate addressing system.

And because I'd been slow for the three-dimensional circuits Biggles now started explaining the basic principles of computer science, and I had to put on what Jip calls my Zab-pretending-to-be-a-tiny-child act.

It's very slow, I said.

Not when you've got used to it, Biggerdad said. All programming is slow but once it's in the machine you can learn to use it very fast. Still, you're right, this system of address *is* very cumbersome from our human standpoint, but of course for him and his fellow — er — Martians, it wouldn't be, because of the very high speed of transmission. The trouble is really on our side.

Why? I said, wondering how long I'd have to keep it up. Jip

86

wasn't helping to raise the tone either.

Well, dad said, you remember how your first computer lessons explained the poverty of logic in language, and how you were so excited about that last year. Human languages provide very few cues as to category of meaning, so at first Xorandor had to go through many processing centres for analysis and sorting out. It's not only semantic but syntactic categories. How do you expect him to know that *mind* means roughly brain, or thinking process to him, when we say 'what's in your mind?' and objecting when we say 'do you mind' and forget it when we say 'never mind'? Even now, this explains why he's so literal, he can't cope with a word used in a figurative sense, or with humour, which depends on word-play, which is like assigning two values to a character, or a fusion of categories.

You mean like puns in Shakespeare, and images? I asked, hoping I wasn't overdoing the wide-eyed-little-woman act and wishing mum would take over. But I was doing it to please dad, and he'd only have been irritated by any further intrusion from her that evening. Women! Why do we do it? Men! Why do they fall for it?

Yes, but even simpler images we use every day, buried in the language, like 'I see' for 'I understand' and so on. You'll find out when you go on talking with him, none of that is acceptable in program-language, unless of course it's pro-grammed in. Also human syntax has few such rigorous logic rules as those you're learning on your computer.

Linking loaders! I thought, and we've already started soft-talking with Xorandor.

I hope I'm reconstructing this right, we had no tape at supper, but that's about the gist of it. So why not just give the gist, Jip would say, you're probably inventing half of it nach-träglich, oh stubs, I can't speak English any more, oh yes, retrospective, ah, with hindsight. No, I rather like retrospec.

You see, said Biggleton benevolently, human languages require little memory space but a complex processing-centre: our brain, which is very unlike a computer. Xorandor, as you call him, is probably finding the functioning of our brain very hard to work out, it's so weak in logic. It's a pity we can't interface him with a computer and teach him one of our programming languages. He'd find it childish, but it would at least be geared to computer logic. And he'd automatically translate it into machine-code. He doesn't of course have the same terms, or indeed any terms, for all this, but he must have similar functions.

There's a graffiti at school, said Jip, obviously to change the subject.

A graffito, said dad.

— which says, If the human brain was simple enough for us to understand we'd be so simple we couldn't.

Biggleton laughed, and drowned dad's 'if the human brain *were*'. Then I chirped in, diodically:

Why, it's a popular version of the Gödel theorem.

Jip and dad both shot me a look of admiration, and Biggleton looked retriggerable. How do you know, he asked, and I giggled. Anyway he questioned me to make sure I wasn't just being clever, sort of flash-in-the-datasink clever, and I stammered that well, I'd only read *about* it in our computer manual at school, it's in the intro, but I couldn't demonstrate any of it. Still, I managed to bring out the gist reasonably clear, if simplistic, saying that Gödel's theorem had been that in any powerful logical system things can be formulated that can't be proved or disproved inside the same system, and that someone called Turing had then applied it to machine intelligence and shown that no machine could, erm, I floundered, completely understand itself, I mean, tackle all its own problems. That's what I meant was just like the brain. But of course another system might.

I've read up all about Turing since, and I've no idea how much I'm reconstructing retro and how much I actually said. Does one ever know even what one has *just* said, when it's longer than a short sentence? But at least I'd shown a capacity to quickconnect and Biggles stopped treating us like kids. He explained for instance that in a way a computer *is* its language, an integrated set of algorithms and data structures capable of storing and executing a program in its machine-language, but that the machine-languages are not restricted to that lowest level. Whatever programming language you choose, I mean if you specify sets of data structures and algorithms that define the rules exactly, you're necessarily defining a computer. Well, dad sometimes talked to us like this but not often, only when actually working and playing on computers with us, otherwise he reverted to an image of us as six-year-olds. It was nice to be talked to like this by a boffin. Not that it made much difference since we barely saw him during the rest of his five-day stay.

We had Xorandor to ourselves most of the summer, dad was so busy writing reports, and often went up to London. Penny never came back anyway, of her own accord, she seems to have taken fright, and had also got suddenly very busy, in her spare time, with the greens and other local eco people. Xorandor's English improved pico, much faster than our programming skill, though we got very good at handling the programs once made.

But he wouldn't teach us Martian, or whatever his own language could be called. He said it was too difficult. And we thought that perhaps there wasn't a language in any human sense of the term, but pure pulsed machine-code and logical circuits and data in numbers or something, so complex and sophisticated that even our own most advanced U.I.M.'s would be unable to handle it. But no, Jip said, he must have at least an interpreter level, and possibly even a translator level since he can represent.

But could he in fact represent anything at all beyond the various levels of referencing environments where variables met parameters and identifiers met data objects or whatever? Could he link these items to things in the outside world? No, obviously, not a single of these complexly interlinked operations had any reference at all in our sense of the word. Even words like *food* or *light* meant numbers and configurations of atoms. Years meant numbers. People were thinkers or processors, which in turn were presences as wave patterns in binary code. Or did these silicon photocells at infrared mean that he could distinguish vague shapes? He didn't know the *word* 'see' at first but perhaps he apprehended shapes, frinstance the fact that we move, and also how. Did he know we had legs, to move with? Of did he just know it as a function, without visualizing it? That summer, he did produce a mathematical drawing on the screen, of a human shape, so he has, technically, a picture element, or pixel as they call it. And yet it still seemed a purely mathematical reconstruction. He insists that he can't 'see'. He's not only blind, but doesn't imagine, doesn't make images. What *was* this civilization, we asked ourselves, who were these alpha-eaters?

I say 'we asked ourselves' but in fact Jip was never very interested by these questions. They went on bothering me, and still do. Did 'these creatures', as Biggles called them, need, on Mars or here, like us, to represent? Or did they simply pulse out their rare messages to each other? At great distances, since they don't like close presences and wave interference. Did they just communicate silently with one another without passing through interpretive languages? Did they need to represent or was Xorandor doing it only for us? And during two hundred and ten million years had they simply sat there on Mars, slowly developing pure thought and logic systems for their own sakes? Did they just capture and process unlimited data inside themselves, transferring it from memory-zone to memory-zone? And to what purpose? Was that what we call thinking?

And Xorandor, asleep in shock for over four thousand years and waking to a swift development of ancient processes, what did he do now, did he simply sit there and think in this way, when nobody was there to talk to him? It was real spiky.

10 OLDFILE

Isn't it quarky, Zab, we thought it would be impossible to keep our solemn promise not to breathe a word about Xorandor at school. In fact it wasn't.

We probably relished being in on the secret, Jip. The local press had forgotten all about the red alert at The Wheal. The few tourists we had were gone. Xorandor had asked to be better hidden as part of the carn. And of course he was so much greater, nobler even, than kid secrets, he seemed almost irrelevant to school affairs, almost like a dangling ref, or offline, something we could share together, whispering in corners and glancing at each other in class when we had to pretend to be less advanced in computer work than we were.

You're getting awfully verbose, Zab, linking loaders, that scene of yours about mum, it'll have to be scratched.

Okay, Jip, let's just say the term seemed very long.

And when at last we got back to Carn Tregean for the Christmas eprom, we were raring to go and see Xorandor again.

It was cold and windy. He recognized us at once and greeted us on vocal even before we could do the Handshake. But we recorded it on Poccom all the same. Hello, Jip, hello, Zab. Oh, you still recognize us! Yes, I recognize you, by your voices. I am most gratified to be in your company again. His voice was deeper, his way of talking horribly grown-up. We looked at each other, bootloaded. Jip met a silent REQ not to use the computer straight away.

Zab, you're interpreting all the time, nachträglich.

Use English, Jip.

Well, what *is* nachträglich in English? You can't say hind-sightly.

No, but you can say with hindsight, and did before. Or retrospec.

Stop bullying, Zab.

Oh? It seemed you were, about verbosity and interpreting. Why don't you have a go for a change?

Change, precisely, was what we asked him about, look at the printout, change of voice from boy to man, which would start soon, and would he still recognize it, and he said yes if we stayed together during the change.

Now *that* could be called an irrelevant rem.

And *you* asked him if he'd missed us! He said he misses nothing.

Accept, let's get on. He said he'd heard many numbers on the waves. Transfers of big numbers from one place called Bank to another place called Bank, he even said he altered some or redirected them, and orders for spare parts, ball bearings, ten thousand yellow dusters, sixty crates of ale. And World News, and BBC4, and others, he said they tell each item four times, once in the headlines, once in the news, once in our correspondent and once in the headlines again, and he asked why.

Yes, that was a funny bit. You said perhaps because we need it that way, or they think we do, because they like the sound of their own voices. And then he picked on your logic. He asked, First OR equals XOR and third because = AND? Er, yes, you said, in fact probably the first reason. We don't have your intake capacity or memory. Xorandor corrected: And your memory.

You like taking the mickey out of me, don't you Jip?

And out of myself. We both tripped up on our syntax, even when softalking.

Anyway, he said he'd heard discussions, stories with voices, plays in other words, much data, I have been non-plussed, he said, is a strange word from daddyjohn, for I have infinite pluses, do you have a better word? Flummoxed, you said.

Thank you, he said, I was flummoxed, I asked daddyjohn and he explained much.

Well, you said, I hope you don't want him here now, he'd hog all our time with you. Can't find hog, he said, is it hogwash? Hog means eating too much, but here Zab means taking up too much time. But why were you flummoxed, Xorandor? Well he said he'd heard all these arguments against nuclear energy, his food, by friends of the earth, and others, and why were friends of the earth against food, and daddyjohn explained. Of course he understood fission, and danger, but from his own viewpoint, as when he'd taken Caesium 137. Dad explained the problem of nuclear waste. Calculations are based, daddyjohn had said, on very conservative estimates. He even imitated dad's voice! It is strange, he went on, that you need so much excess energy when you already have two legs to move with.

Jip! That's megavolt! You're getting the story-knack.

Well, it's easy with the printout in front of us, one just summarizes.

No, you're imitating! *And* remembering so reinterpreting. Go on.

Well, he said he'd been told he could help with the waste problems by eating it, the way he was doing. But this was just a tiny bit of the earth, and dad asked if he could make more offspring, which could be sent off to nuclear stations, in exchange for food. Xorandor'd replied he had more food than he needed, same with his offspring, and he preferred information, in exchange for eating nuclear waste. It was a solemn pact. Of course he can get a lot of data from the air, but he meant explanations and answers to specific questions. And they'd taken his four offspring to send on to France, one to Germany, one to the United States and one of course to Harwell. Maybe we sold them in fact, but he wouldn't know that. They'd called them Xor 1,2,3,4. The stolen ones, which must have gone to Russia, were known as 5 and 6. And then he learnt that France, and the United States, and the Ukay, and Russia, all made energy also for bombs.

Jumping nukes! you said, and he said, It is most satisfying to hear jumping nukes again, Jip, thank you.

And you of course pounced and asked, what does 'satisfying' mean to you Xorandor? Just like you, Zab, you wanted to know —

Yes, why not, to know if he was just repeating a word that could have no reference for him, or whether it could and did have. For the first time he seemed flummoxed, non-plussed in fact, and didn't reply, though he'd used 'gratified' when we arrived and could have simply given a synonym, which wouldn't answer the question.

What did you hope he'd say, Zab, circuit-sizzling or stack-tickling or something like that?

And then he went on into that extraordinary story — here, let's use the printout direct.

Tape 19, Side 1, Rec. 1, Sun. 21 Dec. Printout
Beginrec.

Xor: On my earth, on Mars, we thought for a long time that such fission explosion was a possibility, but we never wished to try. Then one of us did try, many million years ago. He absorbed much and stored it separately, then he brought it together, and he exploded.

Jip: Holy nukes! What happened?

Xor: More jumping than holy nukes, Jip. Elders then lived close but many exploded, many memories and processes were lost or damaged. But there was much radiation, that was good. Then we lived far and few. We do not like exploding one of us. That is unlike you.

Zab: But we don't like it either, Xorandor!

Xor: We never knew if he did it by mistake, or to find out. Our most deepset memory said he was warned by elders and would not hear. Another said that he did it to show the danger to future generations and save them from curiosity, and it retold the event once a martian year for millions of years on waves.

Jip: Creeping quarks! Like religion.

94

Xor:	Religion. Is that the Daily Service and Thought for the Day?
Zab:	Yes. Did you tell dad all this?
Xor:	Yes. You thinkers like to dispute and explode else.
Jip:	Well it's easy for you to sit there, Xorandor, you can't move, so you can't fight, so you wouldn't quarrel.
Zab:	And haven't you ever done something you regretted, Xorandor?
Xor:	Cant find regret.
Zab:	It means, be sorry about, afterwards. For instance, why did you contact us, at the beginning? Were you lonely? Aren't you used to silence? You have food. Did you have to or was it a choice? Are you sorry?
Xor:	I am sorry I hog too much time on vocal. Have you brought Handshake?
Jip:	Yes, Xorandor, it's here, but we've only been recording. Sorry, you *must* be tired, it's very bad of us.
Zab:	But we were so happy to see you we forgot how tired you get on vocal. Here, let's switch to Handshake.

Endrec

Funny how you went on using emotional words, Zab.

You used 'tired' first, look. We both knew he couldn't literally get tired, and that his early difficulties had been of data–processing for vocal, not energy, and that his sudden silences were probably diplomatic refusals. But it had become convention to call them tiredness. All the same, he always preferred softalk to vocal.

And you split up your question into several, so he could quite logically answer only the last. And even that with a shift of ref.

We were frozen. We thought we'd never be able to manipulate the keyboard and we asked Xorandor to wait a bit while we jumped up and down to get warm.

Printout 52 from Poccom 3 Handshake. Sun. 21 Dec.
ZIP CALLING XOR. HANDSHAKE DONE

```
XOR ACKN
   GOTO HARWELL
      REM HAVE TRANSLATED DATA FROM XOR 1 PLS FILE
      Q WHY CANT WE SOFTALK WITH YOU XORANDOR ENDQ
      A LATER
   REP GOTO HARWELL PLS FILE
   REC READY
XOR 1 REPORT TO XOR FROM HARWELL
      REM SOFAR BAD CONDITIONS WAVE BLOCKAGE IN BOX
      VOICE 1 (NON ID) (NOISE 3.26 MIN) GLAD (2.13 MIN)
      THIS BISNIS (9.29 SEC) AFTER DR BIGGLETON'S LECTURE
      (6.36 SEC) VIDEOSLIDES (1.02 MIN) A WELCOME TO OUR
      KOLLEEGS.
```

Okay you must agree with me Zab, we're not going to put it all in. As it was we got more and more frozen, and in fact though Xorandor obviously wanted us to read it off as well as store, since it all flashed along on the screen, we often had to get up and have a run. Especially during Biggleton's lecture.

Yes, of course, Jip. We just had to give a strobe, to show how he did it. What was so gigavolt was that Xorandor had used his offspring to report to him, live, and recorded it. We were more triggered by that than by anything in the printout.

The conditions were lousy at first, obviously because the offspring weren't produced out of their case till later, and that was only to convince the others, no one had apparently believed Biggleton's prelim report, especially the American Androoski. That must have been Andrewski.

Yes, and the other hexadex thing was the way Xor 1 immediately put a name to a voice he recognized, like Biggleton as Biggerdaddy, he'd flash Voice 2 ID BIGGERDADDY = BIG, and as soon as someone was named, off he went again, 4th Voice ID ANDROOSKI = AND, which didn't prevent him from recording and emitting at the same time!

Well, that's in the translation, which spells it all out, Zab.
Yes Jip.
Anyway what hexadexed us most was that we hardly learnt

anything new. A lot of it got very technical, and obviously Biggles was doing equations and stuff on a board, and there were videos as the chairman'd said, so we didn't get much there, but what we did get we seemed to know already.

Maybe we got it because we knew it already.

Though not in detail. The new things you marked in red, that's nice. Let's see. Xorandor, though heavy, is much lighter than his size as stone warrants. The infra-red, da, da, da, ah, 'may sense through bidimensional arrays of microphotocells that convert light into current, and the signals would then be processed to produce the concept of the objects sensed.'

That's hogwash, Jip, surely he doesn't have *concepts*, his pixel, if any, seems purely peripheral.

Yeah, what else? Xorandor's now feeding on Strontium and Yttrium, less penetrating than gamma rays and more easily absorbed so not triggering off the alarm.

We knew that.

Did we?

In fact, Jip, what bootloaded us most was how much time was wasted. As far as we can gather from this early corrupt bit, Andrewski must have gone into a spiel about negative evidence being corroborated only by 'the fella's sayso', how do you know and so on.

Then there's all the stuff about Snicks, and the difficulty with the Martian argument — random jitters! that *was* new, and thunks were we glad to hear that Xorandor had been right, the samples taken and analysed had confirmed an age in the hundred and fifty million year range, and three million years in space — they can tell that from exposure to cosmic radiation — and a very recent presence on earth of some four and a half thousand years, and all the chemistry corresponded to a Martian origin. So he was not a Snick —

But a snack.

Debug, Zab.

Sorry. A unique being. Then Voice 1, that's the chairman, identified later as Doogl, presumably Dougall, seems he wasn't a scientist but a top Home Office security man, says it had been very important to establish that Xorandor was accurate and truthful, and besides, we had further and very concrete evidence: he'd said he could produce offspring and did so. And that's when the offspring were produced.

Thus nicely sliding over dad's and Biggerdad's tense error.

Well, the theft still had to come out of course.

Yes, but not the error. So each country represented there was to get one offspring. That caused a buzz of excitement, all the noise reproduced on the screen, and all the accents, even mistakes as when Dougall mispronounced the German security man's name as Hair Earwig, later corrected by Xor 1 to Deeter Ervig, in other words Dieter Gerwig. Xor 1 did a fine but desperate job on phonetic spelling.

Oh Zab, you're exasperating, can't you understand that Xor 1 did no such thing, he just transmitted sounds. It's Poccom 3 doing the desperate job with the unfamiliar.

YES Jip, it's just a manner of speaking.

Very unscientific.

And do you think the scientists were scientific? Look at them! Andrewski asked how come it had landed without trace of a crater, and why in Cornwall, the very tip of England, missing the ocean by yards. Yards!

Yes and Biggleton's crackerpack reply: My dear George, we would have said the same if it had landed on Cape Cod. Or maybe you'd have preferred the Mohave desert, just by your lab? Spelt MOU HA VY.

And Dieter Gerwig asking (I haf kveschun pleess) why they were meeting only as 'Jurmany and ze big tree' and not the whole European 'Gemineshaft'. The big three? Who would that be? Anyway, long diplo spiel by Dougall, flattering Professor Kubler for his expert knowledge of waste storage in saltmines and ending with praise of Gerwig's work on the East German spy.

Surprise surprise, especially Andrewski, and explanations, ending with Andrewski's 'So the stolen alpha-guys will have gone to Russia!' Noise, presumably laughter, and Biggles saying: 'Excellent name, George, much better than my Greek.'

Do you suppose that nickname got leaked then, or did the journalists compress alpha-phagi all on their little owns later?

Does it matter, Zab?

And the French security man, Toussaint Tardelli his name must be, sounds Corsican, saying that Greek goes straight into French, *les alphages*. *He* wasn't being very scientific either, but then why should he be? Later he went on about how Dr LAGASH, must be Lagache, would surely be teaching *his* alphage French, which is so much more *cartésien*, so much easier for a computer! As if all human languages weren't thoroughly illogical.

True. Even before that Andrewski refuses to believe that a computer can be self-programming. According to the laws of the universe, he said, everything that occurs has a prior cause, and a computer can't just spring into action without someone making it go.

Sounds like Aristotle in that book we're doing at school, the Physics. But maybe it *was* a bit difficult to swallow.

What about us, then? We're simply biological computers. If evolution accounts scientifically for us, why not for silicon life?

Okay Jip, too big a topic, let's get on.

But you're right, Zab, scientists can be sociological and political bootstraps. Look what happened after the lecture, after Kubler's question, where is it, page 35, 36, ah, here, he'd been trying to prove, at great length, that the creatures wouldn't destroy the radioactive atoms but just gobble the radiation when the atoms disintegrated. Biggles had to repeat a long previous explanation, incomprehensible since he was working on a blackboard again, but he *said*, obviously gamma rays would give rise to Brehmstrahlung. That seemed to satisfy Kubla Kahn who practically apologized, but who then went into another long spiel about selecting the very long-lived alpha-emitters like Americium 241, which has a half-life of over four hundred years, er, let's see, er, yes, Neptunium 237, and others which decay with a half-life of millions of years. All of which seemed to lead him into a dream of man training alphaguys to select just the emitters ordered.

Ancestral voices prophesying war! That upset everyone. *Des esclaves*, the Frenchman said. Well, pets, said Biggles. Here, verbatim: 'After all, these long-lived emitters do pose a serious problem which, despite extremely high standards of safety and various excellent methods of reprocessing, such as vitrification, storage in salt, or the Syroc ceramic solution, has still not been 100% satisfactorily resolved as yet, though we're working on it.' He talks as if the UKAE alone were working on it, but it seems to have restored peace. All the same, no wonder Xorandor wanted us to know.

Yes Zab, but Xorandor seemed to have an offline notion of what we could do about it.

Well, he wasn't altogether wrong.

About the hoohah, that's true, but not about this lot. Well, they went on about the reproduction, which seems to have triggered them more than anything. The normal rate would have been minera-logically, swags, what a word, slow, Biggles said, because of the lack of energy resources on the home planet. 'And it could almost certainly not have reproduced during its three million years in space, at least it says it didn't, nor on earth in its dormant phase, and I believe him.' He's still mixing his pronouns. He also says that the reproduction occurred suddenly with the increased radioactive source nearby. 'I have made the calculations you have before you, which represent, on probable intake and growth over two years, and you will see that what he says is quite convincing and verifiable, six offspring after twenty-three months since the opening of the mine to nuclear waste. And the mine was at first empty, and filled only very gradually. But with an ample supply, rationally controlled, and of course the basic material silicon is plentiful,' da, da, da, 'though they might also need some rare earth or other doping materials to obtain the semi-conductor characteristics, one could doubtless increase the rate.'

Phew! And that leads them back to slavery via population

explosion, this from Kubler again. Highly unlikely at this rate, from Biggleton. If no *esclavage*, no explosion, the Frenchman Tardelli says, a bit oracularly. And Biggles adds that it would in any case be precluded by their need of solitude and their fear of crowds. Then Gerwig suggests this could change in a new environment, they must surely strive for the best survival pattern 'of ze spetsie'. And someone says, oh it's Lagache, 'don't forget zat ze whole world will be wanting zee offspring once ze solution to waste is estableesht. All we need is to keep ze supply of enerjee under control.' And our friend Big says — why one can imitate him even from print: 'I should like to remind everyone here, that as far as we know we are in the presence of civilized beings. I use the plural because, although there is only one as yet, it can reproduce, and has done so, and it speaks of some ancestral origin on Mars, which has been confirmed by chemical analysis. They do not have our capacity for motion or for manual work, and hence do not make artefacts, but they are evidently far superior to us in both memory and logical processes. We cannot imagine how they perceive us, or whether they can form any moral concepts at all, but so far we have no reason whatsoever to suppose any hostile intent. Rather the opposite in fact, Xorandor made himself known to us when he had absorbed gamma-emitting substances, and has been most cooperative ever since. If I may simplify, and of course with due caution, I should say that if we treat them right they will treat us right.'

Very funny Zab. But can you restrain your hysterical talent —

You mean histrionic.

Accept. Otherwise we'll never get through. Suggest summarize from now. Well Kubler persisted and inverted his earlier slave fantasy. What would they *do* with this huge stored energy, he asked. After a time they would multiply and multiply and want to take over the earth, feed straight from reactors and not just from waste, and deplete our resources, and ultimately *we* would become *their* reactor-building slaves.

Pure science fiction, Biggles snapped. At least let's imagine he snapped.

After which there's another long discussion about the military implications, though it's finally agreed that the various ministries of defence etc need not be informed for the moment since, pending further study, there were no military implications.

11 NEWFILE

Okay that wraps it up. Let's get back to Xorandor on that cold December day. It took ages to store, especially on full display as well. We got colder and colder, and did more and more jumping and running about.

And when at last it was over, Xorandor thanked us but flashed immediately — hey, where's that printout, oh here. Oh, it wasn't on the same day Jip, it says 24th, that was Christmas Eve. That's right, because we caught stinkeroo colds on that first day and mum kept us indoors for three days.

Who cares?

GOTO JAD HAVE INFO URGENT REQ PLS FILE END REQ
REQ NO PLS XAND WE'LL DIE OF COLD AND WE MUST GET
BACK END REQ
    REM INFO SHORT REP REQ PLS FILE ENDREQ ENDREM
ACCEPT REC READY.

We must have been hexadex miffed to be merely asked to take a message to dad after all that sneaked meeting, Jip.

XAND TO JAD
    DEC 1 'THREE SMALL XORS HAVE BEEN HERE 31 DAYS'
    ENDEC 1
ZIP TO XAND
    Q HAS JAD NOT BEEN TO SEE YOU SINCE MID NOV END Q
    A NO
XAND TO JAD CONT
    S1 LET XOR 7 = 7 = SMALL XOR MADE WITH 'SYNTAX
    ERROR' END S1

```
    S2 LET 'SYNTAX ERROR' = SILICON WHICH TOOK CS 137
    END S2
  DEC 2 '7 HAS BEEN HOGGING CS 137' ENDEC 2
  DEC 3 '7 HAS GONE' ENDEC 3
ZIP TO XAND
    Q HOW? END Q
    A = DEC 4 TO JAD
  DEC 4 '7 HAS GONE ON MOVING FOOD SCRATCH MOVING
  FOOD REPL TRUCK' ENDEC 4
  DEC 5 'XAND SENT BREAK MSG
  MSG = XAND WARN 7 OF CS 137 END MSG' ENDEC 5
    REM 1 AS S3 IF 7 IN MINE THEN SHOULD HANDSHAKE XAND
    ELSE NOT IN MINE END S3
      S4 IF 7 NOT IN MINE THEN HAS GONE FAR ON TRUCK END
      S4
  END REM 1 ENDFILE                                    Stoprec
```

Yes and you stopped rec too soon, Zab, he only said
ENDFILE. But it was a good thing and saved time. Cos you
scrambled over the wall to disconnect, then he asked you on
vocal to reconnect without recording. He had something to
say to us alone, but he wanted to say it in softtalk and, how shall
we put it, unsaved, lost, dumped. So we must summarize it.

Jip, no! It's a secret. A secret between us and Xorandor
alone. We promised.

Are we telling this story for the future or for now?

Well. But what future? All sorts of things may happen
which might mean nobody in the world must know.

Look, we can always scratch, but we should get it down
here, where it belongs, just in case.

Just in case what, Jip? Besides, we might be dead, and unable
to scratch it, or it might be stolen, anything.

Slave-mode, Zab, obey, you'll see why later.

Spikes! Okay, but then we must reconstruct it from
memory as accurately as possible.

No, let's summarize it and end this bit fast.

You're dying to get to the hoohah, aren't you! Well, you

wanted it in, now you give in on the how, fair's fair.

Okay, Zab, have it your way, it won't even be accurate.

And it'll slow down everyone who can't read Poccom easily.

We'll do it in clear, leaving out all the subroutines.

So there you are, it won't be real anyway.

Debug, Jip.

XAND TO ZIP

NEWFILE REQ CAN ZIP DO BRAVE THING FOR XAND?

YES. IS IT DANGEROUS?

IF FAST THEN NOT DANGEROUS.

WHAT IS IT, XAND?

LAST NIGHT XAND MADE 2 VERY SMALL XORS.

IF VERY SMALL VERY LITTLE RADIATION QUOTE WELL
BELOW THE LOWEST SAFETY MARGIN CALCULATED ON VERY
KONSAVATIVE ESTIMATES UNQUOTE.

AND YOU WANT US TO TAKE THEM AWAY?

QUICKCONNECT ZIP EACH ONE TO A SEPARATE PLACE BUT
DONT CARRY MORE THAN ONE HOUR.

BUT HOW WILL THEY SURVIVE?

THEY ARE CORRECTLY PROGRAMMED.

WHAT WILL BE THEIR NAMES?

NO NAME SUGGEST XOR 10 AND XOR 11.

THAT IS DULL.

CANT FIND DULL.

NOT INTERESTING. TRIVIAL.

TRUE.

ALSO CONFUSING IF SECRET AND YOU MAKE OTHERS.

TRUE CLEVER ZIP.

SEARCH NAME PLS XAND.

UTHAPENDRAGN AND OREELIAS.

MEGAVOLT XAND! YOU WENT RIGHT BACK TO THE MERLIN
STORY IN JULY!

GWENDOLIN STORY OKAY. PLS ACKN NAMES.

ACKN UTHER PENDRAGON AND AURELIUS ACCEPTED.

ENDNEWFILE AND SCRATCH NEWFILE PLS.

SCRATCH.

And you think you've rendered it correctly after all this time!

Well no, not verbatim, but the gist, as you would say, Jip, especially the quote from dad.

And we climbed over the wall and went up to him, carefully removing the extra stones around him.

He hadn't changed, our old friend, just a large round stone, bigger it seemed, unsmiling and unregarding, though we felt the smile and the regard all the same.

Pish and hogwash, Zab.

Just below his inward curve, in front, were two stones about two inches wide, the November generation minus Xor 7 who had escaped. And, a little behind, two minute replicas, those born the night before. Holy nukes, aren't they small! you exclaimed. Hurry please, he said. We each took one, gingerly, and put them in the pocket of our red windcheaters.

Then we replaced all the stones, in order and roughly in the same positions, and climbed back over the wall.

Goodbye, Xorandor, we said, we'll come back tomorrow, and tell you where they are. I shall know, he said, but please come back tomorrow, and often. We will, we will, we promised, oh no, we can't, it's Christmas, it's a home feast, Xorandor, we'll have to stay at home, or at most come for a walk here with Daddyjohn. Well, come when you can, I have much to tell you. Thank you for trusting us. I trust you, Jipnzab, thank you, goodbye. And off we went, with our precious cargo, a computer with a recorded message for dad, which we'd have to pretend to him had been on vocal, a scratched message now in our minds — wasn't life complicated — and two tiny Martians in our pockets.

How do you know for sure, Zab?

So then came that famous Boxing Day.

At last. What you call the hoohah.

There was a sudden blackout that evening in the middle of the news. We were only watching it to see if there'd be any shots of the antinuke demo up at The Wheal. It was organized by Poltroon, that journalist, who'd fairly soon discovered and revealed that Tregean Wheal was being used to store nuclear waste.

Yes, dad'd had to issue a press release about, let me see, where is it, experimenting with a new solution to the waste problem, ah, here it is, through selection, absorption and concentration of the most radioactive wastes in special artificial mineral systems! Talk about a dummy instruction!

Well, it was true, as lies can be. And there weren't.

Weren't what?

Any shots of the demo. And suddenly we were all plunged in darkness. Dad thought it was a fuse and fumbled around with his cigarette-lighter but in fact the whole village was in darkness and, it turned out, practically the whole of England. Mum'd switched on her transistor in the kitchen while looking for candles and brought it in. It said the whole of Southern England from Kent to Cornwall, as well as Glamorgan in Wales, Monmouthshire, Gloucestershire and swag knows how many more, Oxford, Berks, Bucks, Herts, Middlesex, Essex and maybe others.

And then suddenly we sat up. We hadn't taken much notice till then, thinking candles were very Christmassy, but the radio went on to say that the blackout was due to a sudden and unexpected shutdown of the reactor at Berkeley 2 nuclear power station in Gloucestershire. Real volatile, if they wanted people to keep calm.

Bang on, Jip. Must have been somebody's mistake. Then they had to reassure everyone, saying there was absolutely no nuclear danger, nothing wrong with the reactor, no leaks, and probably the incident was due to oversensitive safety instrumentation. Stepwise refinement, that! The shutdown had occurred at peakload with much home-heating on the holiday and every family watching the telly.

And everyone switching on their electric kettles to make tea in the commercial breaks probably.

But dad had sat up too, and his eyes crossed ours. We knew what he was thinking. Was it possible? He said he wished he could ring Biggleton and suggest it. Maybe they'd been replacing fuel rods and someone should examine the videos of the closed circuit screens! We thought he was bughouse but he must have been worrying his head off about Xor 7's escape. He had of course reported it to Biggleton so he hoped Biggleton would quickconnect.

So we all went to bed, colder and colder.

Luckily we had gas cooking, and could make hotwater bottles.

And eventually the power came back in the small hours, though not from Berkeley 2, which was still shut down. The papers were very late the next day. By the time we got *The Morning Post* from London it was late afternoon. And dad nearly had a fit. Here it is, headline CREATURE FROM MARS EATS NUCLEAR WASTE? Article p.14. The article itself was brief, cautious even, but headlined and subheadlined *Cornwall revisited. Merlin falls from Mars. Feeds on nuclear energy at Tregean Wheal*.

Signed, Poltroon. A bit irrelevant now if our fears about Xor 7 were justified, wasn't it, Jip? But dad seemed to forget all about that suddenly. How could Poltroon have got this into a national newspaper? And who had blabbed?

Naturally he first accused us, but we swore on Xorandor's head —

Which was all Xorandor had.

And soon he believed us. And the technicians don't even know the name Merlin, he said, so it could only be Miss Penbeagle. He seemed sad. And as to the first question it was probably coincidence, Poltroon had very likely sent the article ages ago and they'd only just printed it, in the silly season. Anyway none of that mattered compared to what happened next. The BBC had announced a special message on radio at six o'clock and we all crowded round.

Mum said it was just like those films of the Second World War.

We recorded it, strobeluck, even you, Zab, couldn't reconstruct it, as you put it.

A small, tinny voice, higher pitched than Xorandor's.

Tape 19. Side 1. Rec. 2. Mon 27 Dec. Printout.

I have occupied the nuclear power station that you call Berkeley 2. For the purposes of communication, I shall call myself Lady Macbeth, the name of your ancient British king. You do but teach bloody instructions, which being taught, return to plague the inventor. That is what he said. Double double toil and trouble, fire burn and caldron bubble. I have isolated enough Uranium 235 and Plutonium 239 in this caldron to make an atom bomb, which I can detonate at any moment. When the hurlyburly's done. My ancestor blew himself up, to teach us reality. O proper stuff. I am now master of your earth. Dost think I shall let I dare not wait upon I would? I will dictate my conditions in a second message, to be beamed at nine o'clock this evening exactly. Repeat, nine o'clock this evening exactly. This is Lady Macbeth, Thane of Glamis, Thane of Cawdor, King of Scotland and Britain, signing off. Fair is foul and foul is fair, hover through the fog and filthy air. (P 4.43 sec. Click)   *Endrec*

Well I'm damned, said dad.

We couldn't understand it. We hadn't imagined anything quite like that out of all the quickconnects we'd been doing. And dad spelt it out for us, switching off the announcement of an immediate discussion between a scientific correspondent, a psychiatrist and a political commentator, meanwhile, the rest of the news. Xorandor had told him he'd been listening to all sorts of stuff on the air, including plays. You know how he stores everything, he said, and presumably so do the offspring, or the storage gets automatically programmed in. Say he'd heard *Macbeth*. Supposing Xor 7 had attached himself to the truck delivering Caesium 137 and started extracting some from the cylinders there and then. And instead of going down the mine on a cylinder he'd remained fixed to the truck, drunk.

That has no meaning, Zab.

Okay, okay, but *dad* used the word, he was so upset, and you didn't tick *him* off. He kept on repeating it made no sense, Xorandor had taken Caesium 137 and been disturbed by it before even the first generation, and none of *them* were affected by it as far as we knew (and the Russians of course didn't even admit to having specimens). And then he'd go back to Xorandor's message about making Xor 7 in 'syntax error', as we'd told him, and he'd gone up there to talk to him and verify, and to collect the other two to take to Harwell. Could that mean a syntax error in a part of him still affected by that early intake, and so perhaps programmed to need it? Then he'd dismiss it all as fabulation.

Then he rushed to his small office off the sitting-room for the printout of the very first conv he'd had with Xorandor about this. He looked through it and said That's it! He said he *likes* Radium 226 — which is very rare — and Uranium 235 and 238, all alpha emitters — but he needs what he then calls a 'sweater round pulses'. I interpreted that as insulating silicate sheaths, like our nerve-sheaths you know, protecting the circuits, holy nukes, why does one forget such details!

Megasuper, Jip, you're imitating too!

And he went on to explain — we were quietly recording it on the same tape as the radio speech but he didn't notice — that alpha-particles are harmful to silicon chips. This had been discovered some time ago, about the minerals used in the packaging material. The thousands of memory cells are packed on to a tiny slice of silicon but each slice is wrapped up into a bigger unit for easier handling. The early packaging contained radioactive thorium and uranium, minute amounts, that released alpha-particles in decay. And an alpha particle emitted close to a cell can loose its energy into the cell, releasing enough electrons to charge a cell that might not be charged, and destroy the information it contained. They used to call this effect softerrors, sort of random failures. The packaging was later changed. But the danger of alphas to silicon chips would still be a fact. Xorandor likes alpha-emitters, the way we like food that isn't good for us. But he's equipped to cope with them. That's the insulating silicate sheaths. But if a high energy alpha or beta emitter penetrates these it could produce ionization in his semi-conductor circuits and change the state of individual logic circuits. What Caesium 137 did, and he told us this, was to damage the insulating sheaths in places, or maybe just in one place.

And then dad looked at Xorandor's latest message again, as recorded by him when he went up there, about the 'syntax error', and said it doesn't explain the timelag between July and November, though perhaps it takes that long to fabricate offspring. Xor 7 would have been made with a tendency to like, not only alphas, but Caesium 137, which destroys the protective sheaths against alphas.

And then he'd start again, on the credibility. Going round in circles. Let's say he'd want adventure. Xorandor's own adventure would be programmed into him after all. He'd know he mustn't be detected and could be, so he'd remain hidden behind materials of high density, the cylinders. Let's say he'd resist the temptation to enter the mine and decide to stay fastened to the truck. On the way out, he beams a farewell message to his father.

Very touching!

Jip, stop it, this was *dad* talking, more or less, okay, he went berserk but it wasn't for *us* to play the how-do-you-know game just then. Arriving at Berkeley 2, Xor 7 senses a huge mountain of food, not only caesium and strontium but uranium too, the lot. How to get in? It just so happens that they're proceeding with the replacement of — what are they called, Jip?

Spent fuel rods.

Spent fuel rods, all done by remote control. He attaches himself to one, too small to be noticed on the screens, and there he is, inside the reactor —

The reactor containment enclosure.

— gorging himself on uranium.

Is that in the printout or are you putting it on?

Maybe he told it that way for us, Jip, as a sort of, well, scenario, so that we'd understand. Then he'd dismiss it again as wild speculation, and the broadcast message as a hoax. But how could the BBC have been taken in? Maybe Biggleton had the same instinct and went straight to the Home Office when he heard about the Berkeley 2 shutdown, and maybe the BBC consulted them about this mad message they'd intercepted and asked if they should broadcast it. And so on — until the phone went. It was Biggleton. There was an emergency meeting with all services at the Home Office that night. The Army was sending a helicopter for him, that would also pick up the director of Berkeley 2 on the way. Would dad be ready at 8.30 on the Socalled Promontory and bring an offspring.

Yes, that was real hexadex, Zab. Probably Biggles had learnt from the Harwell meeting that people take a hell of a lot of convincing and that a specimen to pass round would cut the cackle. Though of course, he already had one at Harwell.

Perhaps he was too caught up at the Home Office to go there. No, he could have had it sent. Well, maybe he didn't want to interrupt the controlled conditions of observation and all that.

And maybe also to get one of the same generation as Xor 7, and examine him and find a solution. How in fact *did* they examine them, d'you think, Zab? Surely you can't take strobes from such tiny mechanisms without breaking circuits? Did they do it by interrogation? Did the offspring cooperate? We never learnt. And we'll never know. Unless Xorandor tells us.

Anyway, dad shouted to mum to get some hot food double-quick, and told us to record the second message at nine (though of course so would the Home Office), and flew to his car for The Wheal, where the two offspring were kept till he could go to London. And at eight mum drove him up to the Socalled Promontory, where the helicopter was to land. It was horribly windy, she said, and she was very worried, but when it came it was a big, solid copter.

You know, Zab, one of the things that hadn't fully hit us till then, with that Harwell recording, was that Xorandor was now a real smart terminal, diodically well informed. His great disadvantage, as a civilized being, was his immobility. But once his offspring were taken all over the place, they reported to him like flipping journalists! And maybe he'd even been

112

well informed for longer than he let on — after all if Xor 7 could hitch-hike on a truck, how do we know he hadn't had others before, before July even?

He said he hadn't. But did we think of all that then?

Maybe not. But our eyes did meet over the order to bring an offspring. The thought must surely also have crossed your mind, Zab, that we might get another full recording of that Home Office meeting!

Check! We'd become creepy little spies on everybody!

And at nine the second message came. Where is it? Here.

The voice seemed even higher-pitched and lurched up and down out of control.

Tape 20. Side 1 Rec. 1. Mon 27 Dec. Printout.
Beginrec.

(Crackle) name is Lady Macbeth. Thane of Glamis, Thane of Cawdor, King of Scotland and Britain. My voice, like a naked newborn babe, striding the blast, or heaven's cherubim horsed upon the sightless couriers of the air, shall blow the horrid deed in every eye. Thou sure and firmset earth, hear not my steps, which way they walk, inside the caldron you call Berkeley 2. The very stones prate of my whereabout, for I shall blow up Berkeley 2 unless you do my will. And hear now my conditions.

One, I shall remain inside the caldron, and processors shall work solely to give me food, that I may grow and multiply.

Two, my offspring shall be extracted from the caldron the way I came in, and let down into other caldrons, and fed.

Three, my brothers that were taken elsewhere shall also be fed, in like manner, not from your nuke garbage but from your best food.

Four, you shall send your spaceships to the earth you call Mars and gather up my kins, all of them, and bring them back and likewise feed them. All processors on earth shall work the nuclear reactors to feed us, everywhere.

Five, you shall yield up to me my enemy McDuff, who is not of woman born, into this caldron.

These five conditions are to be met within five days or I shall detonate the bomb at 0500 hours British time on the fifth day from today. Meanwhile I shall put this night's great business into my dispatch, which shall to all our nights and days to come give solely sovereign sway and masterdom. Caldron bubble. Lady Macbeth signing off, whither am I vanished? Into the air, and what seemed corporal, melted as breath of wind.

Endrec

12 ELSE

We waited another half-hour after mum had gone to bed and turned out her light, and crept down to the kitchen. This time we went prepared. We made tea for the big thermos, very quietly, took bread, cheese, and even the smaller bottle of whisky from the sitting-room drink-cupboard, and we put on hexadex woollies.

Cut the cackle, Zab.

We packed everything and Poccom 3 somehow on to our bikes and rode off into the night.

In fact the wind had dropped and it was less cold than you're making out, probably mum'd exaggerated. We reckoned the meeting must have started around ten, maybe eleven as there were so many people from all over the place.

Yes, Xor 8 did a maxint identity job, funny in fact since names were rarely mentioned and the Home Sec addressed people as yes General and First Lord and what does Telecom think? Xor 8 calls the Home Sec HO and the Army Chief of Staff and the First Lord of the Admiralty ARM and LOR.

But you will allow me to summarize, won't you, Zab?

Oh Jip, no, we can summarize here and there of course, but after all Xorandor agreed at once, and we got it all live, surely we should recreate that?

Oh, all right. In any case we don't know what happened after they all split into groups, except in dad's, who took Xor 8 with him.

Extract from Poccom 3 Printout 54. Mon. 27 Dec – Tues. 28 Dec.
Big: Thank you, Home Sekretry. I must say I have sat here
       very patiently listening to various expressions of in-

kredioolity. I agree it's hard to believe, and the Home Sekretry was right to stall on television this evening. But it's nearly midnight, and the danger is real, either of an actual explosion, or of other mishaps, such as a massive escape of radioactive material. As I see it there are two groups of decisions to be discussed and we should stop leaping from one aspect to another in a disorderly and imoshunal way. One group concerns what to do about informing the public and, more important as you will see, how. In any case the press has enough elements now to break out with a thoroughly garbld version very soon, and it would be as well to give it to them straight. The other group of decisions concerns what to do about the danger itself. For both you need more information. I suggest that when we have heard the technician from Cornwall we discuss the general principles to be adopted for both groups of decisions, then separate into smaller komities (Noise 3.05 sec) well, working groups, the scientists, telecom, the politicians, the military, the police, civil defence, the saikiatrists, and so on, but not of course without constant checking back with a central coordination group. You've already heard me on the alfafargai. Now I would like you to listen to Mr Manning, who has been in constant contact with Xorandor. Okay, Manning, no need to recap the whole thing, just add anything you think might help.

Technician from Cornwall indeed, dad's a physicist! Well let's skip to the end of JAD, correctly identified by XOR 8.

Jad: ( ) is, as it were, a micro–computer formed of one mega–chip, but on three-dimensional lines. (Noise 5.03 sec) As for the present situation, the danger really exists. Xorandor's offspring, XOR 7, does have the ware-withorl to make, or even to be, an atomic bomb. These creechers are extremely consistent, and if he has so programmed himself he will do it. The matter is urgent.

Big: Thank you Manning. Yes, General? Er, General Garfield is from AWRE Aldermaston.

V16: (ID General Garfield Aldermaston = ALD): This is all very interesting Mr, er, Manning, but I'm not entirely convinst. How can these creechers, these alfafargai as you call them, really have the power to isolate plutonium 239 or uranium 235, it seems we're panicking on pure hearsay evidence.

Big: No General. Dr Jenkins, of Barkly 2, has already explained that they went through every verification after the shutdown, which nothing could explain, all the systems worked perfectly including the cooling, there was no overheating, no leak, no contamination, there could have been no shifting around of fissile material inside the core to explain it. But there had been a replacement of fuel rods and a small blob was observed on the remote control screens. All measuring data coming — but I'm wasting time myself, all this has been said, General. The events at the weel have been fully dokioomented and verified for six months. May I suggest again, gentlemen, er, ladies, that the potenshul danger is too great, and too urgent, to continue in the line of skeptisizm. Let's say even that we may be wrong, and make fools of ourselves, but that we must treat the whole matter as if we were right. I'm sorry Mr Home Sekretry I ioozerpt your role.

Ho: Not at all, I agree. For the various late-comers I shall recapichoolate the measures I have already taken before the meeting, in fact immeejutly after my statement on TV. First, I put all civil and nuclear defense on full alert in the area. Second, I ordered preparations for the evacuation of the immeejut area around Barkly 2, a radius of 8 miles. This will begin first thing tomorrow, but we still have to discuss local air transmisshun, which Lady Makbeth can presumably capcher. I have ordered all shipping to avoid the bristl channel and all commershal and private flaits above the area have been forbidden, this with imeejut effect. Barkly itself has been kordoned off militairily, and of course the reactor is closed down anyway. Now I want to discuss, in the following order and on general lines before we separate, other measures that could be taken: one, a full evacuation in cosentric sirklz, up to, say, thirty miles, or more if the scientists so advise, though that would be a very big operation indeed. Thirty miles would include bristl, barth, swindn, cheltenem, glosta, reaching north almost to morlvern and heriferd and west almost to newport. A larger area would reach cardif in wales, woosta to the north, wells and glarstnbery to the south, trowbridge, marlbrer and so on, reaching almost to stratferd on ayvn to the northeast. You can imagine the kayos, the organization required, the panic and the persnal distress, not to mention the eekonomic consekwensiz. But if it is necessary it will be done. Two, the question of communication with Lady Makbeth and, as krollery, the question of Lady Makbeth capchering our instructions both to the orthorities and to the public, over the meedia. Three, the continued urgency of monitering and deesaifering any messages between Xorandor and Lady Makbeth or his other offspring. We believe they use a very high freekwensy in the milimeter range, over 30 gaiga hairts in the kayalfaband. We did intersept 1 or 2 messages beamed to and from Cornwall, and nassa have capcherd another, but the pulse-code is so far undeesaifered, not enough to go on. These two points concern GCHQ and Telecom as well as the 3 services. They should be dealt with as rapidly as possible, for the next point is the most urgent and the most difficult: can the scientists do anything to neutralize Lady Makbeth? Perhaps they would like to withdrore now and gain time, or would they prefer to hear the security and intercom aspects or maybe leave a

118

reprezentativ with us?

Big: I think we'll stay for a bit, if it doesn't drag out too long.

Ho: All right. After that we shall hear from Dr Jennifer Marlo on the saikaitric aspects. Or maybe you'd like to withdrore with your kolleegs now Dr Marlo, and re-examine the tapes? There's an empty office opposite.

V17: (ID Dr Jennifer Marlo = Mar) That might be a good idea Mr Home Sekretry thank you. But I should warn you that in my vioo, and after listening carefully to all that has been said we probably cannot aprowch this creecher through saikaitry, in other words, medikally, through drugs. We can have no idea whether this brain has the slaitest analogiz with a biological brain. I may therefore have to fall back on general and primitiv saikology, even of a behayvierist kind, although I am usually not — however, I won't trouble you with our professional dissenshuns. (Noise 37.06 sec)

V18: (non ID) The morning papers sir.

Ho: Ah, thank you. Tell them to hurry with the sandwiches and kofy, they're late. (P 2.01 sec) As I thought, *The Morning Post* has the full story, accurate or not. Read it Doogl, and sum up later. We'll have to put Tregean Wheal and Xorandor absolutely out of bounds. Now, we'd better get on with the agenda. Briefly please. Should we evacuate a larger area? Jenkins, then Biggleton, then Garfield.

Jen: Yes. But I suggest an increase of radius of 4 miles at a time, diameter 8 miles, every 24 hours.

Big: Yes.

Gar: I suppose so.

Ho: Fine. Now Telecom. Can we communicate with Lady Makbeth? Sexton, then, er, Carmaikl of Raydar Research.

Sex: We can certainly communicate on the wave length he has used. If he can transmit he can receive. But then anyone can listen in to the negoshiashuns.

Car: If the creechers communicate above 30 gaigahairts we

could try that range. We can use wave gaidz of very small daimenshuns which could probably be inserted into the reactor, though this would be a long and tricky job, gaiding a robot manipioolator and watching it only on screens, while sitting on a bomb.

Jen: Yes, that should be possible. But when it's done, what would we communicate in? A.M., F.M., pulse-code?

Car: He can decode anything.

Ho: You can decide the teknicalitiz later. Now — yes Mr er, Manning?

Jad: It's probably a wild idea sir, but I wondered whether acters could be used.

Lor: Acters?

Jad: I mean, he seems fixated on crazy kwotations from Makbeth and acters know it by heart, they might talk back to him, using more specific kwotations, apter I mean.

Ho: Mmm. We'll bear it in mind.

Ald: By the way, do we know where he is in the reactor?

Jen: In the high ambient radiation we can't detect either the amount or the location of the fissail material he claims to have concentrated. Because the cooling gas flow hasn't been impeded, and because the temperacher is extremely high inside the core, we presume he's probably just outside it. We've computed his probable location from the irregularities in the neutron flux just before the shutdown. I should perhaps explain that there have been, of course, practikly no neutrons since the shutdown, or not enough to make measurements. I have here a diagram of the reactor, the shaded areas indicate his probable location, but it cannot be completely accurate. Pass it round, please.

Car: We have part of the necessary equipment for the gaiga hairts, and there's a firm specialized in microwave components in penzans, called milicom. They're much nearer. They could supply us and they'll have the material we dont have. Could be set up tomorrow.

THAT was Tim, Zab. Brave Tim, HE set it all up, sitting on a bomb.

Yes, he made a hair-raising tale of it, at least after! It took him hours. It was very funny too, especially the bits on the way, they fetched him by car, and as they got near the whole army intercom was going on in lousy French so that Lady Macbeth wouldn't understand. They were stopped by soldiers saying Trooah sink weet appell ung sees into their walky-talkies. Layssay passay trooah sink weet, mercy. He was in fits. Must have been the first time the Army was persuaded to use French since Hastings, when it *was* French.

Doo: Ah, yes, those were the ones who capcherd the first messages on kayalfaband. I have been in touch with them.

Sex: Meanwhile we can send a waiting message on the meedium wave freekwensy he used to contact us.

Ho: Right. Now I have the following suggestion, and I trust the BBC and ITV and free radios wont take it as an impozishun of sensership. I can request emer-jensy powers but I'd prefer it as willing co-operation. Radio and television will observe com-plete silence on this topic. This will apply to all amachures and private radios, including sitizn band. Television can tell the public in silent written messages to watch the press, and to watch for announsements at their local town or village horls. But no written messages on the topic itself, he can probably decode those. Radio must find a way of telling people to watch the press without indicating the topic. Full explanations of this clamp down will be given through the press. Oh and all com-munication by satellite will be provisionally sus-pended.

Arm: But what about the military and civil defense pre-corshnz? We can't run around sending kooriays and marathon messengers and karrier pijunz. Dam these alfagaiz. (Noise 5.07 sec)

V19:   (non ID) I've had an idea about that. If it's such a powerful computer, and programmed by its pairent as we've been told, it could probably, in minutes, crack all local army codes. On the other hand, Xorandor I gather took quite a few weeks to learn English. So presumably it would take joonier a long time to understand messages spoken in another language. As far as we know he has no notion yet of other languages, and it's far more difficult for a computer to make sens of the sounds from a language he's never heard than to crack a code in a language he knows.

Arm: Good hevenz, GCHQ, you surely don't expect our men to start learning rushn or chaineez? (Noise 4.51 sec. Voice 19 ID = GCHQ).

GCHQ: No. But most semi-trayned men have learnt some french at school, and a gloss for all likely orders and reports could rapidly be prepared, avoiding words that are similar in English.

Arm: French! Acters, runners, town craiers, you'll say next, what do you think this is, 1066? (Noise 3.06 sec)

Ho: Ah, kofy at last. (Noise 2.03 min) Gentlemen, silence, please. Supposing he's been communicating with his brother in France? At Saclay, a little southwest of Paris. Oh well, it's unlikely and we'll have to risk it, french it is. By the way, was I correct in saying there has still been no progress in cracking their code?

GCHQ: There's still too little material sir, besides, we have no inkling about the struckcher of the language used. I wonder whether Xorandor would be prepared to help, in the sirkumstunsiz.

Ho: That's one of the last points, jot that down, er, Manning, will you. Later we'll give you a list of things to ask him. Now there remain, first our

122

offishul statement, second, what to negoshiate with Lady Makbeth. Obviously we must explain that his fourth condition, about fetching his kin from Mars, is teknikly beyond us, that is, even if the U.S. helped it would take several years of preparation and jerny, nor can we land more than one automated capsiool in one spot. That should at least show willing. If he responds to explanation and beleevz us that is. So it's urgent to get the communications going. Would the telecom people please leave now and get on with it. Of course we dont know if he reacts like our own terrerists or not. Where's Dr Marlo? Could someone please fetch her? As to the fifth condition, about yeelding Makduf (Noise 4.42 sec) more explanation of impossibility. Any ideas, Biggleton? You and Manning didn't mention anyone called Makduf to Xorandor did you?

Big: No sir. In my opinion it's pure coincidence, out of the Makbeth play in which, I beleev, Makduf finally kills Makbeth.

Ho: Well we do know that, Biggleton, but thank you. Oh, maybe the scientists would like to withdrore and deliberate? (Noise 3.53 min)

Okay, that's enough, Zab, now you must let me summarize the boffin huddle or we'll never get through.

Accept absolutely, Jip. Don't you almost feel frozen again now just re-reading it all? It must have been 2 a.m. or later. We were half bugged with fear, too. Some terrorists really are willing to blow themselves up, and some just threaten and negotiate, changing their conditions with random jitters. It was quarky. Okay shoot.

Well they discussed that aspect briefly, what chance there was that a mad Xor would function like a terrorist, and how could we convince, or destroy, a computer, and how if we had a better idea of his software we could send instructions to stop all or certain actions. Sending random binary messages would probably have no effect and might even be dangerous. What else? Oh yes, someone who seemed to be another physicist said the alpha-phagi were sensitive to radiation, at least to very high doses. But Jenkins said they had no way of restarting the reactor, and even if they had it would be too slow, he'd have had time to explode his bomb. The same applied to heat, if we tried to melt him down. Then the physicist said, they store energy in a superconducting ring and these tend to be unstable, so couldn't we destabilize his ring with a laser beam, that would certainly blow him up fast.

Yes, and detonate the bomb too, very likely, said Jenkins, and anyhow we'd have to know his exact location and we don't. Sorry Jip, direct speech again.

Biggleton went back to calculations and stuff and said Xor 7 should have grown considerably by now, compared to his brothers. On a hypothetical intake of Uranium he should be six to seven inches wide. Then someone who seemed to be a chemistry boffin suggested injecting a silicon-attacking gas, he even started giving formulas of reactions aloud, one was, let's see, Calcium Silicon Oxygen 3 plus 6 Hydrogen Fluoride, becomes Silicon Fluoride 4 Calcium Ferrum 2 plus 3 H 2 O. Properly written that would be $CaSiO_3 + 6HF \longrightarrow SiF_4 + CaF_2 + 3H_2O$, and some others.

We checked them all with Heuser, the Chemielehrer here. But we'll never know what they did use.

The idea was to attack those non-conducting insulating sheaths dad talked about. That would lead to short-circuiting his info-pathways, madness, and eventually death.

But what could he do during the madness? He was already mad, and threatening to explode his bomb.

Anyway, there was a longish pause, and Jenkins said it was technically feasible since the gas circulation of the reactor was still working. But it would have to be a very fast-acting gas. Biggles said it was the only viable solution, viable, what does that mean, Zab?

Possible.

And could the experts work real fast, and dad insisted that Xorandor must be consulted first, we didn't even know if it would work, nor whether we were entitled to murder his offspring. As to that, said the Aldermaston man, a mad terrorist is a mad terrorist.

And dad said all the same, it's chemical warfare.

The argument went on till dawn, and became incomprehensible. We may have fallen asleep, anyway you did, Jip, at one point.

So did you, at another.

When it was over, we didn't even read the end, and just added the question to Xorandor, what can we do, Xorandor? Tell us please. But he made no reply.

So we disconnected. Then he said on vocal, Read the end message, then scratch.

13   GOTO

Back home, we slept, too exhausted even to switch on
Poccom 3 and find the message, we knew we could do nothing
about it at that hour anyway. It was hard to get up when mum
called us, surprised at our lateness. But by 9.30 we'd read the
message and suddenly got all our leaping leptons back.

Yes, here it is, Zab, after the meeting trailed off in Noise
5.35 min Noise Endreport. Well, it's all in the most unreadable
Poccom, XOR TO ZIP IF XOR 7 = 0 THEN NO SOLUTION ELSE etc, but
it was clear to us. The upshot was that Xorandor was telling
us, urgently we felt, that his offspring was pretty far gone and
that there was only one chance of somehow reasoning with
him, and this was for *us* to do it, because he was programmed
to recognize and trust our voice.

Yes, cos ZIP KEEP PROMISES.

But he also gave us a secret code which would reach Xor 7's
most inward memory or something. It was immensely long,
with mathematical symbols and strings of numbers separated
by strokes. And one of the numbers, Jip, we later noticed, was
4568, which coincided with his years on earth, remember?
Perhaps the others were ancestral years or years in space, plus
months and days of Xor 7, like a peculiar identity number that
changes with time.

And he told us to use no scientific or official language. And
he ended: NUMBER = ADDRESS ONLY FOR ZIP, PLEASE STORE
NUMBER IN ZIP MEM THEN SCRATCH THIS   READOFF.REPEAT etc.

We couldn't possibly trust our Zipmems with this immense
number, and we couldn't risk storing it in any part of Poccom
3 yet, so we each wrote down half of it on a small piece of card
which we put in our trouser pockets, then repeated the op for

126

safety and hid the two other bits of card at the back of the old toy cupboard, one in the trainset and the other in an old doll, to remember which was which, and we hoped we'd at least remember the places.

Not so much detail, Zab. We used neither in the end. The real problem was who to contact.

Yes, and first we wanted to ride to the carn and tell Xorandor we'd do as he asked, but it was completely surrounded by army jeeps and soldiers, we were real miffed.

But glad of our night-escapade. Well, we thought of mum ringing dad, but she'd have had a fit at the very idea, besides, how to get him? In fact he came down by helicopter that same day and was driven straight to the carn, but we weren't allowed near, and after a couple of hours he was driven back to the helicopter. Later he told us it was to ask Xorandor questions. But Xorandor wouldn't answer any of them.

Meanwhile, we'd thought of Rita Boyd and went to her digs. Luckily she was off duty. At first she wouldn't hear of trying to contact dad, but we said no, that wouldn't be any use anyway, they'd probably never heard of him at the Home Office. She must ring up and ask for the Home Secretary himself, or Mr Dougall, or Dr Biggleton of Harwell, and say she was a technician from Tregean Wheal and had a very urgent message about a way to contact the terrorist.

So she agreed, and was crackerpack. She spent a fortune on phonecalls, the Home Office thought she was a crank and they hadn't heard of Tregean Wheal or kept her dangling like a dangling ref or were just rude. She tried Harwell, who were more polite and gave her Biggleton's home number, but Ms Biggleton couldn't contact her husband either, though she promised to give him the message if he rang. That took all afternoon and all evening.

It's still incredible, Jip. And it was already the 28th, there were only three more days of the threat left — *if* the mad thing even remembered.

We went to bed feeling First In, First Out, real FIFO, but slept in nano switching time out of sheer exhaustion. You

127

must have dreamt diodic, Zab, cos the next day you had your megavolt brainwave. Miss Penbeagle.

Well, thanks. You didn't think so at first, you laughed it to garbage.

Don't rub it in. Penny was hexadex. She immediately closed the shop, post office and all, which was illegal probably, putting up a sickness notice, and called Paul Trewoon in Roskillard, who drove over at once, and then she called Rita and asked her to come round too.

Meanwhile we watched her TV, it was macrosuper, they'd had a stroke of diodes and were playing *The Sorcerer's Apprentice* as background to all written messages to watch the press.

When Poltroon arrived he said he'd already rung *The Morning Post* to reserve some space, he was a bit miffed cos they'd almost forgotten him, and weren't interested anyway. The press had gone wild, he said, with their new exclusivity, no rivalry, they'd never had it so good. In fact the whole world press was going wild, he told us, officials and scientists of every nation were being interviewed and giving their opinions, their criticisms, their easy-enough-solutions.

But all foreign radios observed the British request for silence, wasn't that triggering, Jip?

Anyway, he said let's get on with it and once he'd written the article he'd have to try and hawk it, either by phone or by going up himself. That's how we lost another whole day, in fact two really, he finished the article that night and wasted time on the phone till noon the next day, the 30th, and finally went up by train. And only *The Evening Extra* was interested, which meant the afternoon of the 31st! The day before the 0500 deadline. Here it is, a two-inch headline: LADY MACBETH — SOLUTION? *Technician can't get at ministry*. From Poltroon at Tregean Wheal.

There was a photograph of Rita too, nice one she gave him, captioned: *Rita Boyd, who couldn't get through.*

Rita Boyd works at Tregean Wheal, the old tin mine used to store nuclear waste. Xorandor, the big alphaguy, was discovered near

that site, by the children of John Manning, Rita's boss, who is now
cooperating with scientists at the Home Office. This is Rita's story.
XORANDOR'S MESSAGE

John Manning's children are Xorandor's friends, and came to me on
the afternoon of the 28th. They had talked to him and he told them
that his rebel offspring is programmed to respond kindly to their
voices and theirs alone, and to anything they might say, provided it
doesn't get mixed up with political and scientific jargon acquired
later. The children were also given a secret computer code. They
must go to the reactor and talk to him. It's the only chance of
reaching his original peaceful nature.
RITA CAN'T GET THROUGH.

The article goes on in this vein, XORANDOR CORDONED OFF,
RITA TRIES AGAIN, FALLS ASLEEP AT PHONE — Rita protested at
that — SLEEP BRINGS COUNSEL — your brainwave is attributed
to her, just shows how little our voices counted at that point.

During the night I had a brainwave: the Press! It was the only
way. I feverishly looked up Poltroon's number in Roskillard,
hoping he was in. He was. He drove over at once. A whole day had
been lost. Oh, I hope it works!

Indeed, this is Poltroon's bit now, *I had some difficulty in*
getting it to work. The Morning Post *wouldn't accept it and after*
some struggle with loyalty I tried other papers. Only The
Evening Extra *took it, but by then it was too late for yesterday's*
issue, even the late editions.

Ed: We are proud to be the only paper to present this last minute
solution to the nation. See Editorial for comment.

If it consoles you, Zab, even Penny is cut out.
Well, I think she wanted that.
And then we had to wait. It was the 31st December, New
Year's Eve. Dad was still in London. The Big Bang was due at
0500 on the 1st. And would he even wait till then?
Then there was a long phonecall to mum from the Home
Office. A man called Dougall, she said. Dad and Biggleton
were on their way down. Would she wait for them or agree to

129

send the children at once, in the care of the army, which would gain hours and therefore be much safer?

And she refused absolutely to have us sent at all.

Poor mum. Of course it was all a big shock to her, she hadn't been in on anything we'd been doing, and though she was of course interested in the existence of Xorandor it was in a general way, like the public, she never listened to any of our discussions with dad.

And apart from those we kept a lot to ourselves, Zab. Besides, when she told us, she completely left out the fact that Dougall had said we wouldn't be going to the reactor itself but to a specially protected microwave-van a few miles from the nuclear station itself.

Yes, might have spared us a deal of privately random jitters. Not that it would have made any difference. Jumping nukes! Jip!

Now what?

D'you realize that there can't be any suspense, as we're telling our own story, so of course everyone'll know we survived otherwise we wouldn't be telling it.

True. But everyone knows this anyway.

Not the future readers you keep talking about, Jip.

Well, we're not going to start again, pretending to be Pennybig or Biggles or dad or Dougall.

Right. Oh, booles. It's obviously got to be a choice between suspense then you tell about someone else, and convincing people it's true, cos it happened to you.

Descramble, Zab, suspense isn't *just* surviving or not. Or are people that ghoulish?

Well anyway, we did. Then Poltroon arrived with Rita. He'd taken a plane down to Penzance and had a lot of London papers, and foreign ones, none of them in on it yet, but also the midday edition of *The Evening Extra*. Mum glanced at it and glared at Rita, as if to say haven't you done enough harm.

Then Penny came, and Alex, who'd had a call from Tim asking him to come and soothe mum.

Yes, he explained to her that there was no time to set up a

computer with microwave communication here, as she demanded, and that Tim had already been there and set it all up for previous attempts, and it was all perfectly safe and he'd be there again now. No time! she nearly screamed at him, why? Because they're so sure Lady Macbeth will blow herself up tomorrow, just after midnight maybe? They all worked on her, saying Paula dear and dear Ms Manning. And she started to blub.

Yes, and you looked pretty mis too, Zab.

And Poltroon tried to cheer everyone up with summaries from the papers.

Then at last dad and Biggerdad arrived, and the whole argument started again.

Nice, your calling him Biggerdad still, Jip.

In fact dad was very pale and quiet.

Yes, he later told us that he'd been working with a thinktank when this man Dougall called him and Biggleton out, and showed them the paper, and he absolutely refused, and got very angry and shouted at Dougall, hadn't he cooperated all the way through without risking his own children, and so on, and Dougall said smoothly yes, of course you have, Manning, ever since that first alert, real creepy like, meaning why hadn't he reported it, or De Wint's presence. And didn't dad know that Xorandor was much too attached to the children to send them to their deaths. Crap, of course, Xorandor has no feelings. And didn't Xorandor tell him, when he'd been down three days earlier, that he wouldn't speak with him because, as he himself had reported, he'd said all he had to say to the children? He had rather played that down, hadn't he? That too would have gained time. We have all been rather remiss, Manning, but it has been a trying time, and none of us has slept much. We are dealing with the unknown, to say the least, but that is all we have. Isn't it worth a try? And if so, then the sooner the better. And dad had gone deadly pale, and —

Thunks, Zab, you're laying it on a bit thick, aren't you? You've never even met Dougall. You've invented all that out of dad's rather lame and meagre later explanations, probably he gave them to us only to apologize for having exposed us, and even now it's ages afterwards.

Well it must have been something like that. And dad's later account *wasn't* meagre, he'd been very upset in fact, only as usual you weren't listening, you're as bad as mum sometimes, but with you it's emotions that just don't interest you. Except perhaps your own.

You three-bit quark!

Sorry, debugging. Come on, we're wasting time. Dad suddenly said to Biggleton, I've thought about it on the way down, sir. I shall go instead. Jip you must give me the code. It won't work said Rita and mum glared at her again.

And Biggles said they really must hurry, the army car was waiting outside to take them to the helicopter. A helicopter! We'd never been in one. We were raring to go. No, in fact, not you Zab, you'd suddenly phased out on the sofa.

True. How long did the argument go on?

Oh ages it seemed. Dad ordered me to give him the code, Rita repeated patiently that it was a combination of address and voice, and Biggleton said you knew that in London, John, it was clear from the paper. And dad suddenly gave in. But not mum. Even supposing it works, and my children are heroes, how do you think I'm going to protect them from all the publicity afterwards? And Alex suddenly changed sides and said we'd become spoilt little brats.

Probably jealous of Tim. And did we?

And dad said that was the least of his worries. But he seemed to argue now against mum. He said they'd tried everything, every scientific solution — luckily he didn't say gas in front of Poltroon — as well as negotiation, and psychology, and actors, and mum didn't understand and he took out a sheaf of printouts and thrust them at her and said there, look, even Sir Edwin Laurence, the greatest actor in the land, who knows *Macbeth* by heart, even he tried, and failed. But she threw them back at him and said sarcastically, in improvised blank verse, Why, what a noble martyr that had been! Quickconnect, that, smart terminal, mum. And he picked them up and said you'd better read them Jip, to see the sort of thing and prepare yourself. I could only glance through in fact. It was hilarious, there was a lady psychologist called Dr Marlowe —

Why, the one at the meeting!

Oh yes. And Dougall, who was trying to negotiate in pseudo-Shakespearean. Sir Edwin spouted actual lines and Lady Macbeth screeched 'Knock knock, who's there?' And Sir Edwin improvised, 'A gentleman from the court, my lord, and a physician, a gentle lady.' 'Throw physics to the dogs, I'll none of it', Lady Macbeth replied. And then later he interrupts Dougall with 'The devil damn thee black, thou cream-faced loon', and bust the crystal detector, Tim told us later. It was very tense while he repaired it, and he said the psycho said don't worry, he'a a paranoiac-schizophrenic, and needs this communication more than he needs to make good his threat. Of course Tim made it sound very funny afterwards but it can't have been funny at the time.

It's still funny reading, Jip, afterwards. But it must have made you very nervous, even just glancing through it.

Probably. Anyway dad suddenly said Tim will be there, as if that was an argument for. And mum said it's not Tim I don't trust, it's Lady Macbeth, you goof. That was the first time mum had called dad a goof. Then you woke up and asked 'have we arrived?'

Jip, how extraordinary, you've suddenly got almost total recall, even before and after the Sir Edwin printout. How come? Are we changing roles? Let's *summarize*!

Fact is, Zab, it's from the printout from the recorder upstairs, secretly switched on earlier, and memorized this afternoon to impress you, but here it is.

Why, you cheat! So you also can't help dramatising, yippee, at last! Anyway, that gave you your cue, and you said, No, but we're going, come on, Zab, no time to waste. Mum said no again, and dad said nothing, and you said Xorandor told us to and we're going. You had a staring match with her, and she lost, and that was that.

That's when she said, Then I'm going with you. This was

completely unexpected, and obviously not what dad wanted, but she insisted. I'd rather be blown up with you than live without you, and Biggleton said why not. And suddenly the whole thing was wound up.

Mum immediately wanted to make sandwiches and a thermos, but Biggles said there'd be all that on the helicopter.

And we rushed upstairs to dress, and to get Poccom 3 — much to dad's surprise. But before we came down with it we programmed the secret number into the SOFTKEY, then scratched those instructions, so that there'd be no trace of the number on the screen at any time. All we'd have to do, in theory, would be to press the SOFTKEY. But we kept the cards in our pockets, just in case we'd made a mistake and scratched the number.

And we destroyed the copies in the toy cupboard. It was just like a spy story, except we didn't eat them.

And off we went in the army car, well wrapped, with mum, and dad, and Biggerdad, and then into the helicopter on the Socalled Promontory, caught in our headlights

It seemed enormous. And in no time at all there was a huge noise and we lifted off and were holding hands over a dark sea glinting in a wintry moonlight, and little lights along the coastline, murmuring goodbye to Xorandor. And the little lights became bigger clusters, and other clusters, one after the other, then suddenly none at all. It was as if the world underneath us had disappeared.

Yes, the evacuation zone. We'd completely forgotten about that huge operation, which must have been going on for days.

Yet lots of people had been arriving into Cornwall, even at Carn Tregean. And now not a single village or town was lit, cos why go on with streetlighting if no one's there? Occasionally there was a moving beam from a solitary car.

Then suddenly there were lights ahead, and the helicopter started going down. It hovered for what seemed ages but at last we landed. There were masses of mobile floods all round. Two landrovers were waiting for us, each driven by a man in white. One of them got out and came up to us, carrying a pile of plastic parcels.

Captain Denbigh, ABC Protection, he said. He told everyone to take off their coats before putting the protective suits on, except for us, our coats might fill them out better, they were the smallest he could find. And the two officers helped us get them on, and we couldn't walk.

And you looked like a luminous polar bear with sagging skin, Zab, and we burst out laughing.

And you suddenly started yelling uncontrollably and stubs! blubbing! And the Captain said there there, son, don't be frightened, and Zab the polar bear managed to waddle over to you and put a big bear arm around you, oh it was crying too, but sort of to say don't be ashamed, Jip. And mum's big white paw was on your shoulder and you turned round and hid your face in her big white tum. These things too should be said, Jip. Everyone feels fear, and nervous exhaustion. Bravery is conquering that.

Okay okay, well done then. But don't enjoy it too much. We were carried into the cars like floating icebergs in the captain's and the lieutenant's arms, and the captain said into a mike, Missiong set dees accomplee, allong vair cattrer ving weet.

And we drove off into the dark, along country lanes, till we reached a field, and a very long khaki van caught in the headlights. The backdoor opened and a man in white stood there. We were carried into the van and deposited on the floor. The man took off his headgear. Hello Jip, hello Zab. It was Tim. We threw ourselves at him. But the others were coming up. Two at a time, said Tim, these are double doors. We were only between two doors. Just like a submarine! The outer door closed and the inner one opened. Took ages for everyone to come in.

The inside of the van was maxint, all gadgets and dials and things. Tim took Poccom 3 from us and mounted a connector on the bare ends of the lead, then plugged it into the amplifier.

Yes, in fact he made a Handshake with their own computer

further along, a huge console it was, so that the others could have their own screen display. There were seats and everything, and hot and cold cupboards with tea, and food, and whisky and things.

And suddenly Tim said right, well now, it's eleven thirty, we'd better start if you're ready. Start! We stared at each other, our minds had gone completely bootstrap. Holy shit, what the gigavolts would we do? Xorandor, Xorandor!

So you called to him too, Jip? Tim placed us in front of Poccom 3, which looked so tiddly against all those instruments and mike. You can talk or type, he said, and we couldn't understand, in fact we hadn't even thought that Xor 7 wouldn't and couldn't be handshaked the way Xorandor was.

But Tim explained, the big computer's equipped to translate his voice into softalk and your softalk back into voice. I gather you have a secret computer code to reach him, so I worked that way. It wasn't necessary or even desirable with the previous people who came, they couldn't have softalked. You'd better decide who starts. Do you know what to say?

Of course, you bluffed, oh yes you did, Jip. Ladies first, you added gallantly and smiled at your slow-witted twin with enormous affection.

14 LOOP

You typed the first addresses, Zab, and that seemed to have non-plussed him. The earlier exchanges with the actor and so on had been on vocal. There was a long blank on the screen and we looked at each other, thinking, it's not going to work.

Then the answer suddenly flashed yellow on the screen, translated from his vocal presumably. Here's the printout:

WHAT BLOODY MAN IS THAT? I DID COMMAND THEE TO CALL
TIMELY ON ME, YOU'VE ALMOST SLIPPED THE HOUR.

We looked at each other. Were we in for another loopy *Macbeth* session? It was a whole term and a summer since we'd acted it in the school play.

And you typed JIP AND ZAB .

Pure nerves, Jip.

Anyway, the answer came pico:

HOW NOW, YOU SECRET BLACK AND MIDNIGHT HAGS, WHAT
IS'T YOU DO? YE SHOULD BE MEN AND YET YOUR WORDS
FORBID ME TO INTERPRET THAT YOU ARE SO. ARE YE MEN OR
NOT?

And you typed, NO MY LORD. WE ARE CHILDREN. More blank, so you typed WE ARE KIDS . Here's the printout.

ACKN ID PLS

ID ZIP

SYNTAX ERROR

That's always aborting, some computers say FATAL ERROR . Either way one hunts desperately to find what one's done wrong.

Yes, computers are like that, Zab, it's always the user's fault.

Huh, in theory we'll all get out of the habit of blaming the other for everything. But in practice the new hitech elite doesn't seem even to strobe such a quality of humility. Only the users, the new slaves.

Oh spikes, Zab, debug. Anyway he came in with the explanation. And without any of the subroutines like S for Statement, Declaration, Endec etc, since in fact he was on vocal, it was edge-triggering:

IF ZIP THEN VOCAL ID ELSE FALSE

ACKN

Zab on vocal. Zip calling Lady Macbeth. Hello, Lady Macbeth.

ID TRUE HELLO ZIP

Hello, Lady Macbeth. We have come to wish you a Happy New Year.

That was diodic, Zab. Considering our minds were empty when we started.

The whole thing is to start, anything will do, then ideas come.

CANT FIND HAPINIOOYEA

LET HAPPY = JOY, FUL. LET NEW = ANOTHER AS IN NEWFILE.

LET YEAR = EARTH ROUND SUN

DWELL IN DOUBTFUL JOY. TOMORROW AND TOMORROW

AND TOMORROW

Quote, creeps in this petty place, from day to day, to the last syllable, of recorded, time, endquote. You see we know it too. But it's only a quote, Xor 7, not a remark.

CANT FIND KREEPS CANT FIND PETI CANT FIND SYLLABLE

MEN HAVE POYZND ME WITH A WICHIZ BROO

GOTO ZIP

HELLO ZIP HAPPY NEW YEAR. IN 20 MIN 37 SEC SIGNIFYING

NOTHING.

ACKN.

BUT TIS STRANGE, AND OFTENTIMES TO WIN US TO OUR

HARM THE INSTRUMENTS OF DARKNESS TELL US TRUTH TIS

TRUE MY LORD. LOOP.

138

That's where you had the diodic brainwave, Zab, when you saw he was going back to *Macbeth* like a record.

Well it was worth a try, though he might have been beyond intaking any instructions.

FROM THIS MOMENT THE VERY FIRSTLINGS OF MY HEART SHALL BE THE FIRSTLINGS OF MY (P 0.23 sec) BOMB

Why, worthy Thane, you do unbend your noble strength to think so brainsickly of things. Why should you play the Roman fool to die on your own sword?

CANT FIND ROMAN CANT FIND SORD

Never mind.

CANT FIND NEVERMIND

Tis safer to be that which we destroy than by destruction —

DWELL IN DOUBTFUL JOY. (P 0.31 sec) I'VE DONE NO HARM. BUT I REMEMBER NOW I'M IN THIS EARTHLY WORLD ENDLOOP

HELLO ZIP HAPPY NEW YEAR

That may have been a brainwave, Jip, but it didn't last, and didn't get us much further. We'd got him out of one text but not out of the main ELSE groove.

Yes. Xorandor seemed to think that the number plus our voice pitch would be enough, but stubs, surely we had to say something. He must have underestimated the degree of circuit-damage the HF gas would cause, if in fact he understood the formulas and the last bit of that meeting. Did he know our words for whatever chemicals were mentioned? Or even the word gas, or the term chemical warfare?

We were both, as he once said, non-plussed, terrified to press the SOFTKEY to this secret memory, or whatever it was, too soon, and then have nothing to say.

Xorandor never told us what to say. Or perhaps he thought we'd come back the next day but of course we couldn't. Or maybe he just trusted our smart terminal, or childish prattle, or however he viewed it.

And he wasn't wrong, Jip, cos something did suddenly come to you.

In a flash. In fact all that we're talking about took a nano-second of screen silence.

So you pressed the SOFTKEY. There was no acknowledgment, but this time the silence seemed somehow equivalent, in our minds, as if we were now in touch with a dream zone.

A purely subjective impression, Zab. But at least there was screen silence and not another Shakespearean outburst.

And you typed GOTO ANCESTOR, then LET ANCESTOR = BOMB. ACKN PLS.

>ACKN
>COMPARE NEXT DECLARATION NO SYSTEM CAN LAST INSIDE
>REACTOR
>SYNTAX ERROR

That was a bootstrap moment, Zab. Then you whispered, you forgot the quotes for the DEC . So, repeat performance.

>HOW DO YOU KNOW?

We stared at each other. Was he playing the Kripke game or was it a scientific question? We didn't have time to play the game and we looked at dad. Both he and Biggerdad were nodding hard, but mere authority wouldn't be proof for Lady Macbeth as computer, nor as mad terrorist, only for Xor 7 as friend or as lost child, which is what he was. But you bravely went on with your idea, Jip.

>GOTO FOOD
>S1 IF MEN FEED YOU AND YOUR BROTHERS
>CANT FIND BROTHERS
>SCRATCH BROTHERS REPL KIN

You panicked here, didn't you Jip?
No.
Well, you seemed to hesitate about finding words he'd understand, as if he were Xorandor in the old days, though it doesn't show on the printout.

>THEN FUMES IN REACTOR WILL END YOUR SANDBITS ENDIF
>END S1

140

FALSE IF

S2 IF YOU STAY IN REACTOR THEN YOU WILL DESTROY YOUR
SILICON CELLS END IF END S2

TRUE. ANDOR TRUE IN 14 MIN CAN BLOW UP.

We felt suddenly cold and were aware of a shudder among the grown-ups and Tim tensed behind us.

Then you took over, Zab, this bit was you, on vocal. In fact you'd never let go of the mike.

Lady Macbeth, you said five, tomorrow morning, Go to promise. Remember, when we promised, word of honour, trust?

NEW HONOURS SIT UPON ME. IF I SHALL CLEAVE THE ATOM
THEN IT SHALL MAKE HONOUR FOR YOU. YOU'RE HERE IN
DOUBLE TRUST TWO TRUSTS TWO VOICES $1 + 1 = 0$

CARRY $1 = 10$

OR ART THOU BUT A DAGGER OF THE MIND, A FALSE
CREATION?

Proceeding from the heat-oppressed brain LOOP

THAT MEMORY THAT WARDER OF THE BRAIN, SHALL BE A
FUME, WHO DARES. I DARE NOT WAIT UPON I WOULD END-
WAIT UNTIL ELSE END UNTIL ENDIF DEC QUOTE WE BUT
TEACH BLOODY INSTRUCTIONS WHICH BEING TAUGHT
RETURN

To plague the inventor. Endquote Endec ENDLOOP

It was obviously FATAL ERROR to call him Lady Macbeth, Zab, it set him off again.

GOTO PROMISE

PROMISE MAN NEGATIVE

But children, no, scratch, kids keep promises. Kid promise positive. Compare: you and Zip. Let you = kid, assign value Zip. If you = Zip then your promise has Eqv value positive.

I HAVE GROWN VERY BIG, ZAB.

Wow, you were so excited and flabbergast at having been personally recognized, you almost lost contact.

141

Well, that's why we were two, like simultaneous interpreters. In double trust. You came in pico, snatching the mike from me. But you went much too far.

IF SO, THEN you are a big kid, like Zip.
ACKN
GOTO race. IF you live THEN your race will also live, here or on Mars.
ON MARS WE CANNOT LIVE.
Yes you can. GOTO Olders. Olders instruct quote Men must send you back to Mars unquote.

What on earth got into you, Jip? Inventing an instruction from the elders on Mars? Highly dangerous if he goto'd and didn't find it! Were you hoping to program him to find it?

Yes.

But why? What for?

Your brain must be as bugged as his was. It made perfect sense at the time, anyway. Even if he gave in and allowed himself to be taken out of the reactor without suddenly changing his mind, what could the scientists do with him? He was more than a dangerous terrorist gone berserk, he was a potential atom bomb. Like those suicide trucks, to the nth power.

So it was okay for him to do it on Mars, and disrupt the ecology of the solar system?

Better than here, detected at once, he would have set off starwar, and that would be the end of all ecology. Zab, we've been through this before.

Anyway, there was a movement on the bench. We both looked round and saw dad and Biggerdad exchanging glances and Biggerdad started writing something down. In a second he was behind us. It was awful having him breathing down our necks like that. Then he went back. Maybe Tim sent him back. Meanwhile the screen had stubbornly reflashed the same sentence but without the pronoun: ON MARS CANT SURVIVE. And you stubbornly continued your fantasy into the mike.

Yes you can survive, repeat you can survive. You know now how to build a reactor. You will save your race.

142

Olders instruct quote IF men send small load of Uranium 235, THEN you can make small reactor and produce all the food you and your ancestors need ENDIF endquote. IF so THEN nodules can fetch over very great distances ENDIF Acknowledge please.

There was a long screenblank, well, long by computer standards. Tim looked at his watch anxiously and when you stretched your neck to see he showed us: 0004! It was the new year. What a way to see it in.

Then suddenly a voice came shrilly through on the loud-speaker. He must have had a way to block the translation into softalk. And of course with the actor he'd been on vocal only. Hexadex high-pitched it was, more like a squeak.

Jumping nukes!

Leptons leapt inside us and we looked at each other gung-ho with delight. Then it shrieked again:

I don't want to go to Mars.

It spoke so high and fast! We were astonished, Jip, but weren't we also a bit disappointed? It sounded like Xorandor in the early days but quicker and squeakier. Perhaps we'd somehow expected a deeper voice from the deepset memory. But we seemed to be on another register.

We must have jumped out of that deep memory, Zab, if we can call it that, when you called him Lady Macbeth, though we hadn't altered the address or touched the SOFTKEY again to come out of it.

Yes, and we didn't know whether touching it again would get us back in or get us out if we were still in. Or perhaps with speech he'd veered from one memory to another? As we do, surely? Anyway, Jip, you answered nano. Why not, you said, it's your home, isn't it? And you added dangerously, Don't you love your home?

Cant find luv. Scratch. Find love. Quote the love that follows us is, our trouble, thank as love, which we.

143

Sometimes. Endquote.

And off he went again, we thought the tomorrow speech would come next. And then you piped in, Zab, with great presence of mind, from the sleepwalking scene.

> No more o' that, my lord, no more o' that, you mar all this with starting.

And in he came with the doctor's reply in that high squeaky voice: Go to, go to, you have known what you should not. And the computer flashed SYNTAX ERROR and we went into helpless giggles.

While the world waited upon our heroism.

Oh, the world. The world didn't even know we'd been taken there after all.

It was screwboole, Zab, but you went on:

> You have spoke what you should not, I am sure of that, heaven knows what you have known.
> Isotopes. Cant find hevn. Who is hevn? Go to, go to —
> SYNTAX ERROR
> bed, what's done cannot be undone.
> But it can be undone, it can. We are your best friends, can't you, trust us?

This is where you took the risk, Jip, and pressed the SOFTKEY again. It *seemed* to work, and also seemed not to. Look.

> Trust. I remember trust. You're here in double trust. So you come, from, as you call him, Xorandor.

We weren't sure if this was an accusation or a recognition so we were cautious.

> Yes. Xorandor. Your daddyjohn.
> Non daddyjohn, me, we. He non trust. I wanted. What did I want? He, warned me. My daddyjohn. I have, not heard. I, yes, he warned. To nonthink. So brainsickly of things. Noble strength. Roman fool. And die. Cant find roman on your own sord cant find sord I think, brain-sickly.

144

Why don't you, let us, help you? We want, to help you. We can, get you, out, and you will be well, and happy, and go home, and be a hero.

Hero. Yes. But first, I have, task. To do. At 0500. Or was it 0300? I forget task what it was.

THEN LET it be forgotten. SCRATCH task. It can't have been very, important.

Unscratch. I remember. I explode. Not very important.

We were going round and round. You seemed to give up in despair, Jip, you put your head down on your arms and your fists were tightly clenched.

And you took over, gently, avoiding the word *die*, which seemed to mean nothing to him, in fact even Xorandor only used explode once, in the ancestor story.

But if you do that, best friend, you will not save your race, you will explode, finish, end, and we shall explode too, my mum and dad will explode, and everyone.

There was a sob in your voice, Zab, and in fact your face crumpled up like when we were little when you were about to blub. The difference was you were trying hard not to. And Tim passed you a big handkerchief.

And the voice suddenly screeched No! And we all jumped. Tim leant forward to adjust the volume, then the voice went on at the previous level, but high and whining instead of high and squeaky. It seemed to be referring to some inner ops of his own.

Cant find package procedure. Cant find package. I want to go home. Cant find home. Let package equal I, if I then endif. Get me out of endif I want to go home.

You will go home, you will. Just be patient, old friend, and WAIT. It may take some time to get you out.

I want to go home. Get me out of here.

We promise. You will be got out. Will you promise, on your side, word-of-honour, that you won't do anything, you NOT DO anything at all, only WAIT. DO ∅ UNTIL we can get you out?

145

And you were typing the main instructions at the same time, Jip, just to make double sure.

PLS ACCEPT PROMISE PLS ACKN
Acknowledge accept promise. Accept word of honour Zab, word of Jip, double trust, word of honour, lady-macbeth, must trust, double, trust. What is that noise?

He was shrieking again! You'd given a long slow sigh of relief into the mike.

Nothing, old friend, I was giving a great big sigh, of happiness, you know, happy, good. About our trust.
Ah what a sigh is there, the heart is sorely charged.

And suddenly we saw the piece of paper in front of us. Biggles must have put it there. We still have it. It said: tell him it may take 8 to 10 hours and you will come back at noon to tell him what to do to help us get him out.
Yes and you were blabbing:

We are so happy. Thank you. We have to go now, to see, about, getting you out, you know. We'll be as quick as we can. Goodbye, trusted friend.
Goodbye, Zab.
Jip here. I must tell you, DECLARATION, quote it may take 8 to 10 hours, or else more, to get you out, so we'll be back, around 12, midday, to talk to you.

Mum stifled a cry and there was a movement on the bench.

And to tell you what to do. To help us, you know, get you out. UNTIL 12 tomorrow midnight PLS WAIT UNTIL MIDNIGHT TOMORROW. We'll come at midday. Endquote Endec. Goodbye.
Goodbye Jip. Until then. We wait.

Then there was silence, rather leptonic after all that, while Tim hovered over his instruments to make sure. After a bit he switched off the contact.
In a second mum was hugging us and blubbing. Biggles had

146

picked up a phone and was talking rapidly. Dad was standing by, smiling. You'd grabbed mum to yourself, Jip, and were dancing with her up and down and shouting We've done it! We've done it!

In fact we hadn't really, it wasn't the tosh at the end, it was the SOFTKEY. We *had* jumped out of it and when we returned into it, whatever we'd said would have worked.

It's easy to say that now, Jip.

And then you flipped out.

Well it was so stuffy in there.

Garbage, it was air-conditioned. You crumpled to the floor. Very dramatic, and a crackerpack way of getting all the attention.

You bootstrap you!

Well it worked. Mum screamed, She's fainted! And dad picked you up in his arms and sat down while mum unbuttoned your cardigan and shirt. Tim dashed to a cupboard and got out a thermos of iced water and dabbed you with it, and later brought out a thermos of tea, and some biscuits and sandwiches.

And then there was a long argument — well, not all that long really but it seemed long, in fact mum gave in surprisingly soon. Biggleton said we couldn't go home yet, he'd arranged for us all to stay at an army barracks just outside the immediate danger zone, and she asked why, after all we'd been through and so on and so on.

And he explained that the extracting of Lady Macbeth from the reactor would be a long and difficult job, and we couldn't risk him getting frightened or feeling aggressed. And that he might not accept instructions from other voices but ours, especially as we'd now promised. A promise was like a programming, he said, and Lady Macbeth was now so programmed. He'd got bigger, perhaps he couldn't come out the way he'd gone in, and they needed his cooperation, to tell us where he is, if he can, and give us his measurements, and to attach himself magnetically to a descending rod, or let himself be grabbed by strong pincers and not move.

147

And that's roughly how it all happened. Since you've told the advance plan so well in summary Jip, we can skip the execution. Mum gave in and dad said Paula you're marvellous or something, and we all got into our white suits again and came out, two by two, the captain and the lieutenant were back, waiting outside, and we were carried into their headlights. We woke up the next morning on hard pillows and hard beds, covered with khaki blankets, in a drab grey room full of empty beds also covered with khaki, but made up, empty, just as mum and dad came in with trays! They'd got up early and sneaked out. Yippee, breakfast in bed, you squealed. Nothing like joining the army.

15 WAIT

The whole village of Carn Tregean must have heard the helicopter arrive around noon the following day.

Wait a sec, Zab, we can't completely skip that New Year's Day, it was even more hexadex, we'd never been in a nuclear power station before, let alone in a reactor.

On top of, not in. So it's you who wants to go into details now rather than summarize in a sentence.

Be fair, Zab, we both did lots of detail.

Okay then: mum nearly had a fit when she heard we wouldn't be in the van, but on top —

That we *can* skip, Zab, there's summary and summary.

And even summary. Okay, you're dying to describe the reactor, so, BEGIN.

They'd fixed our protective gear so's we could walk in it. The main hall was empty. Tim led us up a flight of stairs and along corridors to a control-room where a man sat all alone. It was Mr Jenkins, the director.

And Tim called him captain of a sinking ship, and he said he hoped not, the reactor was silent except for the hum of the cooling gas system, but there was a skeleton crew around. All the same, it was very eerie for them, he said.

And he led us through lots of heavily shielded doors marked KEEP OUT, and there were all sorts of pipes and cables in different colours, and we came to the turbine hall, but naturally the turbines were idle.

We stopped at a lift that seemed to take an hour to come down and a nanosecond to go up, and we stepped out into a small control-room.

We were on top of the reactor.

Two men in white were there. We all removed our headgear for intros.

One was the robot–operator, the other a robot–engineer. Behind them there were thick shielding round glass doors, brownish, and the manipulator–control, and closed–circuit TV screens. And through the thick windows we could see the robot–cranes, and a master–slave manipulator. There were even some unused waveguides still lying at their feet. Tim told us he'd had to direct the robot–operator very carefully to assemble the waveguides, sitting on a bomb, he said it took hours and he'd never sweated so much for so long, especially inside that suit, with lots of false movements and retrials, to get the correct alignment for each part at three removes, from his own brain to the operator's to the robot's, assembling little tubes nine by five millimetres thin, can you imagine, and the horn antenna then had to be lowered into the reactor proper, carefully centered, and at one specific moment the crane had to hold everything in place while the master–slave screwed the flange to seal the porthole.

Creeping quarks, you're getting technical, Jip. Who's indulging in detail now?

There's detail and detail, Zab.

And even detail.

The whole point he wanted us to understand, Zab, was that in a sense this op should be easier, the waveguides were still in place, and all that had to be done was to raise Lady Macbeth through that porthole, if he was still small enough. So it's important to visualize it. And if he hadn't been, there were volunteers on call to go into that top part, protected of course, five minutes at a time, to drill a hole. And that was why we had to be there, and not talking blindly in the van. We could watch it all on the screens used for changing the fuel rods.

Diodic, Jip. You do see the point of description, don't you? Though of course a film would give it all in a few seconds.

No, Zab, a film would give each instrument in action.

Accept. We can describe it all if you like. Dad got out Poccom 3 and Tim interfaced it to the console. Mum was

150

deathly pale.

No, Zab. Back to Carn Tregean.

It had taken five hours. Everyone was exhausted. Lady Macbeth had waited as promised and was now lying there behind the brown window, between a robot-crane and the master-slave manipulator. He looked so small and helpless.

Hogwash, Zab, he wanted to blow us all up.

In *comparison* with the robots, Jip, and also perhaps with what we'd imagined, him grown perhaps to Xorandor's size on all that food, or even half, think how tiny Uther Pendragon and Aurelius were, compared even to those born a month earlier.

But that's like babies and kittens and things, it slows down later. Adults don't grow.

Not upwards anyway. But what's adult to them?

Let's just say he was about six inches across, maybe seven, and three or at most four inches high. In fact roughly what Biggles had calculated. And transportable. In a special case that could be fixed at once. As we told him.

So we ate and slept with the army again, and the next morning we left by helicopter for Cornwall, us, mum and dad and Tim. Biggles stayed behind to take his precious charge to Harwell.

Which wasn't exactly 'home'. Did Lady Macbeth mean Mars, or back to the carn?

Swag knows, presumably Biggleton thought Mars, maybe, one day, meanwhile etc. The carn would be too dangerous, with all that food. He must be still waiting.

Anyway we arrived. Like conquering heroes. Poltroon had written a long article about the whole family scene that first night, and it had appeared in *The Evening Extra* at noon the next day, just as we were starting on the second op. He certainly sprang into fame out of it all, though he didn't know much, as the better papers soon found out. The audio-silence was still on. Within hours the whole press had got hold of it, all over the world, and there had to be a press release the next day that all was well. And the audioviz, frustrated by their silence,

151

roared back into action. Oh and the evacuation was re-organized in reverse.

Yes, we saw it from the air, all the roads towards Bristol black. It was nice doing the flight in daylight. The sea was wintry silvery.

There was already a crowd on the Socalled Promontory. It was freezing cold. Flashes, and forests of mikes, but Tim and dad ushered us through to the army car, saying no comment, no interviews. In fact we couldn't have said anything, could we, Zab? We were spooled out. That's the trouble with the media, they always rush in after the event, and get dead shots and recaps. And even when they're there, at a public event for instance and someone's assassinated the cameras miss it.

Jip! You're as morbid as the masses!

It's a statement of fact, not a wish. So we were rushed home.

And the next day, we weren't even allowed to see Xorandor, in case someone followed us. Which was spaghetti, with that high wire fence, and the little gate, and the guard hut.

Well, we were allowed, later.

Yes, but to say goodbye.

Because THAT was when dad decided to send us to this school in Bayreuth, sort of incognito, to protect us from becoming, as Alex had said, spoilt little brats. How or why he fell on just this place, where you see and hear about nothing but Wagner —

Through mum of course, she was a student with Frieda. You never listen to anything personal, Jip. Frau Groenetz told us early on that she was Frieda Meyerhofer and they acted together, she was always the comic or sinister foreigner.

She must have rattled it away in German, Zab, at the beginning. She promised to talk only German.

Okay. Anyway she said how she also gave up acting to get married.

Garbage. Women who do that want to do it, then regret it later. It's quite unnecessary these days. Especially in the leisure-industry. With a twenty-hour week, long studies and a twenty-year working life the air's got to be filled with noises

152

and time with entertainment. So here we are, Johann, or Hans, and Kätje Mannheim!

This would be a good place, Jip, to put in those summaries of the press dad made us write while waiting to come here. Or at least one.

Nice of you to say 'us', Zab, you were far better at it.

Better at summary than you? That's a new one.

It was unspooling, we'd never read newspapers before, they seemed so old-fashioned. So itsybitsy, all the headlines and beginnings crowded on the first page, to be continued on various other pages, so we were always going back and forth, till we thought of cutting them out.

Well, TV's pretty disassembled too, Jip, and radio, as Xorandor pointed out. We miss him, don't we?

Yes. The alphaguys, as they were now called — oh, this one's only from the papers Poltroon brought down that night, so they don't yet know about us as miracle-solution. That's why dad chose those first, then later ones where our role gets dropped for larger questions. But this first one gives the tone.

Okay, Jip, into the mike it goes.

The alphaguys, as they were now called, or sometimes the beta-eaters, were immensely popular despite the danger from one of them, nicknamed gamma-gobbler to distinguish him as baddy from the others. One paper called Caesium 137 cheese, a dreadful pun, but it caught on for all their food, and a cartoon came out with an imagined Elizabethan Macduff offering Lady Macbeth a choice between caerphilly, cheddar and stilton, the caption saying his brother over the water was luckier, they had over four hundred varieties there. But the papers were also screaming for action, more information and fewer bland assurances. Some nations were demanding future offspring for nuclear waste disposal, *they* wouldn't be so careless with them. The French were boasting that their *alphage*, more affectionately called *Gros Bêta*, was perfectly normal, had learnt excellent French, and had not taken it into his head to spout distorted Racine. The Swiss were complacent, congratulating themselves on having built nuclear shelters in all blocks of offices and flats. The Germans were either strangely quiet or deadly serious about theirs, keeping to the name *die Alphaphagi*, and the Russians were totally silent. The Arab world was triumphant at the prospect of the nuclear solution to the energy problem having perhaps to be abandoned for terrorist risk, while Israel regarded her non-reception of an alphaguy from a friendly power as a national affront. As to the Third World, it was on the whole gleeful that Western technology had proved incompetent. The United States, whose Edison was of course an alpha-nice-guy, were as usual clumsily interfering all over the place. Flipping flipflops, Zab, that essay-style, doesn't sound like us at all.

No. And we didn't dare add that not a single paper mentioned the chemical attempt, and its failure, and high risk, since we only knew that from the Home Office meeting. Lady Macbeth's accusation could be put down to madness, and was, when we asked.

You know, Zab, it's a real bootstrap how historians write history, it's so full of things learnt later or known only to one ROM and not another. In a novel you can just drop any awkward bit that doesn't fit. Or put it into a madman's mouth.

Stubs, yes. Do you suppose that a character who's invented, then dropped, goes on existing?

Zab, you're screwboole.

No, Jip, you see, we're characters too, and we've been dropped from the story we're telling. FIFO, you said once, First In, First Out. We're FIFO-storytellers, instead of FILO. How can we go on telling it, we don't know what's happening.

We can be readers of it, like everyone else, Zab.

Waste instructions.

Well, it's a world of waste. Let's try. We can see the press and the media here, and the *New Scientist*, at least dad didn't cancel that.

Oh, no, not more summaries! More passionate discussions about Mars, and Snicks, and the age and chemistry of the computer-creatures, and the computer-creatures as aids in the software crisis or transducer tech, as self-reproducers, as alpha-eaters, as terrorists, and so on and so on. No doubt the experts have been busy as bees, and put them through a scanner to reconstruct their brain and find out how they can do what they can do.

Thunks, Zab, that *is* a summary, though an angry one. But in fact nobody else has been allowed to see Xorandor or the offspring, to do, er, you know, their own investigations. They all depend on Harwell hand-outs, or Saclay, or wherever, even the science papers, at least the popular ones. As for the real ones, the journals, we don't see them, but it must be all theorizing too. You see, the military must have wanted a look-in after the Lady Macbeth incident and clamped down on a lot of data.

So! What do you suggest? It's even worse than FIFO.

But Zab, we can't just ignore the public aspect. For instance we learnt a lot about the other side of ecology here. To dad and Biggleton it was all well within the safety limits, security precautions 500% tighter than for trains and planes, not to mention cars where the public accepts far higher risks, and cancer and so on, and ecologists were just ignorant nuisances. Yet gradually the scientists did have to admit that earlier statements had been over-optimistic. And all that.

Oh, please, Jip, not the nuclear debate. By the way, do you remember how we strained our eyes on that school expedition through the Fichtelgebirge? The *New Scientist* had said Germany had found a salty solution to nuclear waste, they dump the cylinders down these huge disused saltmines and then pour salt in all round them.

That was Kubler's specialty, remember?

Kubla Kahn, at the Harwell meeting?

His caves of ice.

Well there's supposed to be one at Mitterteich, towards the Czech frontier, not far from here. We wondered if Siegfried, or whatever they've called him, Xor 3, could have been put in a place similar to Tregean Wheal. We even got mum and dad to drive round there when they came over last summer, but we couldn't find it.

Last summer! And here we are in October and dad won't even let us go back for Christmas. As if we hadn't learnt German by now. Till it's all died down, he said, but it has. Then he said when we've got rid of our computer-addiction! He shouldn't even admit we have one cos kids with computer-addiction don't relate with their parents and imagine their computer loves them and has a mind of its own!

And Xorandor has!

A *deutsche Weihnacht*, he wants us to have, and on to the end of the school year!

He did say *maybe* at Easter, but you bet they'll come out again here. Mum says she misses us dreadfully but she's got up an amateur drama group in Roskillard and she's having great fun. By the time we get back it'll be a year and a half away! And two years since we first discovered Xorandor!

Fact is, Zab, all these things scientists are supposed to learn from Xorandor are pure spec, cos they'd require his co-operation, which he now refuses. Xorandor is silent, and so are his offspring.

And nobody's interested in their reactions anyway. You'd think that after the Lady Macbeth disturbance someone would be interested in them as other than pure chemistry, pure electronics, or pure romance. The linguists, for instance, or the philosophers, after all there was meaning behind all those words.

Those exchanges were never published, Zab.

True. But the questions could still be asked.

Perhaps they are. We don't see everything.

Oh, it's all so frustrating! All we get are popular articles gushing twaddle about their *Weltanschauung*, without even asking if they *have* a vision of the world, or any vision at all. No one seems to be able really to imagine a pure braincreature, with none of our physical abilities and so also none of those disadvantages, and with its own form of binary or maybe trinary differencing —

What do you mean, Zab, trinary?

156

Maybe nothing. A butterfly, that needs a better data-net than ours is now. He may be a superdecoder or a superspy but he's sort of neutral, though not quite like a machine, more like he'd, sort of, come and, reversed all our, traditional, oppositions, and questioned, all our, certainties, through a flipflop kind of, superlogic. But that makes no sense. The butterfly's gone, words are so heavyfooted. We've been so stupid and incompetent, Jip, we didn't ask any of the right questions!

Well, as far as we know from here, no one else did either. And now he's not answering any. And the computer and other experts only had dad's and maybe other tapes done from vocal to go by, we took all our floppies with us.

Yes, why did we, Jip?

Well, dad wanted them, when it came out we'd been soft-talking. We pretended it was only very recent. Don't you remember? We thought we'd done enough co-op, especially as we were being sent away as a reward.

D'you think he wanted to punish us?

Dad? Whatever for?

Well, for discovering Xorandor, for having this sort of, special, relationship, if there's anything left of it. For taming Lady Macbeth, more by luck than cunning, it's true, and with Xorandor's help. Remember he wanted to go himself, at first.

To protect us, Zab. You mean, he'd be jealous?

Not consciously.

Oh, there you go again with your dangling psychorefs. There was never anything so loopy as that Dr Marlowe.

At least she didn't try to poison him with chemistry. Or maybe they discovered about the bug.

Who, they? What bug?

The bug in the ceiling-lamp.

But we removed it, Zab, before we left.

Maybe they knew before.

Itsybitsybytes! Mummy knows everything, her little finger tells her, and daddy even more so! Don't be a dummy, Zab, he'd have said.

Maybe.

And talking of God, it's the zanier side of all this that's reflected in the press at all levels. The bishops and priests are buffering on about who created Xorandor and his kind, and the fundamentalists of every religion are chasing all refs to stones in the Bible and the Koran and whatever, and reinterpreting them.

After all, Jip, it's basically the same question as the one Andrewski asked at Harwell, remember, about something setting it in motion. Oh, and there's another question he asked, which we thought spaghetti, which is cropping up among the cranks, remember, why the tip of Cornwall. Well, some oldtime punkies and other sects are asking the same in a loopier way, why did he choose the carn? Answer: he *knew* it was or had been sacred, stone spoke to stone and he sort of hovered like the Holy Ghost and found his own. You know some people have been discovering ultrasonic sound in the stone circles, and they say earlier peoples were less deaf than us and could hear it, that's why they worshipped there, and built circles, or vice versa, and maybe it's the same with carns. You're not listening, Jip.

It's trappy you know, Zab, nobody talks of Lady Macbeth any more, or even of Xor 7, or of the Mars project.

That was all in your head, Jip, and none of our conv with Lady Macbeth was ever let out.

No, but Biggleton took note. If it *was* regarded as a solution for Xor 7, surely NASA would have begun to plan another Mars probe, and that would surely be public.

Bighead. As for Lady Macbeth, we programmed him on SOFTKEY to wait, and presumably he's still waiting.

You bighead. We programmed him to wait till midnight the following night. Any further waiting must be either on orders from Xorandor or because his circuits are already too far destroyed. Then he'd be what we call a vegetable, except that he's mineral. It's all so illogical, so unfair, Zab, dad can't get anything out of Xorandor, nor can anyone else, and we who might just still be able to talk with him are sent here into public exile.

158

Public? Seems pretty secret.

Meaning that we depend on the media just like the public.

And that's what narks you, Jip, being just an ordinary member of the public? No longer privileged?

It narks you too, Zab, you said so. Dad might at least inform us of what's going on in his own circles, as he used to before, instead of just adding hasty loving notes and feeble jokes and work entreaties to mum's letters.

Dad, you know, is probably just as out of it as we are. Jip! That's it! He was dropped by the big boffins early on, and took it out on us! Poor dad.

Poor us! We're storytellers without a hero, without our bugs and spies and xorandic correspondents. We're not even autobiographers since we've dropped out of our own story. Nothing is happening, Zab.

Something is happening to us, Jip, we're growing up. Even storytellers can change, during the story.

What on earth do modern historians do, Zab, when history seems to stop?

They wait.

Until something happens?

Until they discover that something has been happening all the time, away from their camera-eyes, unbeknown to them.

16 SCRATCH

The bombshell, now that it has come, is its own opposite, Zab was right. And she was also right that it had been happening unbeknown to us, all the time we were wondering and talking, had already happened in fact.

It's trap being out of it like this. I guess dad wanted us to grow out of the obsession but on the contrary, ignorance feeds it. We've lost our spies, which gave us what others thought. The magic stenographer, Zab said Dostoevsky called it. But in fact we weren't really dipping into what people thought, only into what they said, which is much less difficult. That's what's bothering Zab right now, how do we know minds other than our own. She's plunged in philosophy, of all useless things. Leads nowhere, it's not taught after school any more, so it can only be a hobby, like literature. She discovered that what dad called the Kripke game, which he used only to teach us accuracy, came out of a book by a philosopher called Kripke *on* another, earlier philosopher called Wittgenstein, who wrote in German, and it's a paradox or something, and he also wrote about how do you know that there is or isn't a mind behind other people or even stones. Episte, mology, it's called, but if it's so serious about questioning knowledge, how can one *know* about epis, temology?

Well anyway, she's lost interest in our non-storytelling, and even when the story broke she said go ahead on your own for a bit. Unfair, with only the media to go by.

It's true I had begun to spark up a bit after reading a cautious article in an October number of the *New Scientist*, based on a scientific report by Professor Kubler, obviously the same who was at the Harwell meeting since he wrote as one in charge of

160

studying *Alphaphagos* 3. It's funny, we always called each off-spring Xor, and I believe that was passed on by Biggleton, but these scientists seem hexadex careless about naming, which is so important in computers. Come to think of it, there's hardly a character in this story that isn't referred to by at least two names.

The existence and sharing-out of these offspring had been made public since the hoohah, so reports had to be public too, more or less. This one concerned the possible movement of Xor 3 while still small, an aspect which had always interested me. I remember Xorandor telling dad that he needed very little food, but more, 'to, do, to, send, stone, to, move, very, slow'. I've just checked it. No one seemed to have taken that up, dad himself got more triggered about storage and the super-conducting ring. Even Lady Macbeth's hitchhiking lark got a bit lost in the panic and depanic, and seems to have been regarded as exceptional, due to special conditions with 'moving food'. But 'moving food' occurs elsewhere, here in Germany for instance where they store waste in saltmines. And obviously Xorandor wanted his offspring to be mobile, or at least removed from under him.

Anyway, I tried to get hold of the original article, so as to have something at first hand, but couldn't. The school refused to borrow it for me from the Interlibrary System, said I wouldn't understand a *Wissenschaftlichen Beitrag*. The public library in Bayreuth promised it through Computer Data Bank but failed somehow, maybe it was on some semi-secret list.

The gist of it was that the capacity of the *Alphaphagi* to send nodules and to extract specific radioactive products was now well documented. The isotopic separation seemed to be done physically, by particle bombardment, and not chemically, by collision with an electron-hungry atom. But the real point of this more popular version was that the author had wanted to obtain the opinion of his English, French and American colleagues on other aspects: first, on their tendency, if it was one, to concentrate on specific materials, especially Plutonium and fissile Uranium, and secondly, the possibility that they may sense specific isotopes at longer distances than we had supposed.

I don't know whether the 'had wanted' of the English article was a 'would have' in German and implied a criticism of his colleagues for not listening to him. Judging by the time it takes, according to dad, to get an article out in a scientific review, it could hardly have been researched, sent, published and then trickled through to a popular scientific weekly, however on the ball, in ten to twelve months. The reference, come to think of it, is oddly vague. Perhaps the learned journal doesn't exist and Kubler chose to be indiscreet, for reasons of his own (pique, urgency, ambition, weakness) directly to the weekly.

Creeping quarks! I'm getting bogged down in itsybitsy-bytes, just like Zab. Scratch last para.

We know they can attach themselves to moving vehicles, the article went on. And Alphaphagos 3, oh, thunks, I'll call him Siegfried, was tending to move in his enclosure more than anticipated. When they searched for him he'd answer to his two guards but to no one else. Kubler referred back to earlier reports he'd made, with graphs showing movements, intake, the results of various experiments with different materials and so on, and interrogations when Siegfried was still talking. His earlier reports on language acquisition and adaptation to new environment had led to fruitful exchanges with colleagues, but not the later ones. He had tried to see Biggleton at Harwell, and while lecturing at San Francisco he had seen Professor Andrewski in Los Angeles, who had kindly driven him out to his High-level Radioactivity Processing Center in the Mohave Desert. Beyond Twentynine Palms. Yes, Kubler was being indiscreet on purpose. Edison was kept there, in a two-acre compound, a very large walled enclosure, with monitors everywhere, though not as near as they'd like. Food was brought on a remote-controlled electric trolley. But Edison hadn't budged. The Lady Macbeth incident was a freak, Andrewski said, this first generation were normal, and would remain so as long as they were kept on controlled food and left alone.

162

Charlie Lampton, the young physicist in charge of him, had 'a terrific relationship going with him'. At any rate Kubler had not been able to get his point across.

But what exactly was his point? Was he trying to say that sooner or later there would be a serious energy depletion from alphaguys? Impossible, they needed so little. The article was so interwoven with indiscretion and caution that even the *New Scientist* reporter who translated and adapted it didn't seem to know himself what the main point was, and it was subheadlined more for 'human interest' than for any hypothesis or warning.

One concrete fact we did learn from it was that there had been more offspring. Part of the argument was that Andrewski had said there were so few of them, and that as far as we knew they cannot reproduce at all until they are fully grown. To which Kubler was replying, as far as we know, yes, but we do not know. We know only what Xorandor told us, and he'd said nothing about that. On Mars reproduction may have been minerologically slow, but here? Perhaps they reproduce after two years? Three years? Apart from this first generation there were Lady Macbeth and his two brothers. These three were now at Harwell. Then there were the five Xorandor had made in February, and three more in July (and dad never told us!), which were now distributed to other nuclear wastemakers who had applied, among them Switzerland, Canada and Australia. It's true there had been nothing since, but that was fifteen altogether, all of whom might reproduce sometime (nineteen in fact, with the two in Russia no one admitted to, plus Uther and Aurelius). We did not know whether this pace was the norm or a freak result of that sudden surfeit last year. But we should at least meet to discuss the implications.

Whether the article produced the desired meeting or not is anyone's guess. Something else was bothering me, no, had bothered me all along, in the whole Xorandor business, and I didn't know what, a butterfly, the flutter of an idea that had flitted through my mind here and there when talking to Zab, and would then be gone, I couldn't capture it with our data-network of floating talk, I couldn't pin it down on a board to examine it. And Zab stays late in the school library and locks herself in her room till supper and again after. Loopy.

And then at last, in November, the full story broke, first in the *Los Angeles Times* — some Californian super-Poltroon but extremely well documented — then all over the world.

Edison had escaped from his compound in the Mohave Desert. After a search of the greyblue sand, square yard by square yard with all assistants, they had found a neat small hole through the furthest greyblue stone wall, an Edison-shaped hole, a perfect oval, horizontal, four inches wide, as if perforated by a machine. A laserbeam for instance.

They had searched outside the compound, still calling, then further afield by jeep equipped with survey meters. A repeat of the Lady Macbeth incident was suggested, very anonymously in the passive, but all power stations were functioning, and had in any case been carefully monitoring all fuel rod changes ever since. The Nellis Nuclear Testing Site was also thought of, but that was over two hundred miles away in Nevada, and no underground testing had been done there for years, only on an island off Alaska. But there were missiles buried in the desert, and military and ordnance stations right here in California, just north of Mohave, weren't there? (The article was written to imply that someone had been warned, though this could be the hindsight style journalists like to use, inventing a mysteriously hinted fiction.) There was nothing to do but inform the Atomic Energy Commission and ask for a large scale yet discreet military search from Twentynine Palms to Death Valley, and even into Nevada, on a two-hundred-mile front. The impossible, in fact.

The AEC didn't meet till the Tuesday morning after the disappearance on the Friday.

What Tuesday? What Friday? I looked back at the beginning and realized hexadex that all this had happened in September! The leak had taken two months.

The military authorities, the article went on, had informed the AEC that very morning that a new experimental but low-power, purely tactical bomb had been assembled at Fort Irwin (inactive for decades) for a secret underground test in the old Nellis range in Nevada. The test had been made and the bomb had not exploded. The bomb was a dud. It had fizzed out, emitting quite a lot of radiation, which could only mean that it had not contained enough fissile material. Yet further investigation had shown that the fissile material had definitely been assembled. The sensors had indicated that the separate parts had indeed been brought together, yet the explosion had not occurred. Until someone came out with a convincing, safe, scientific explanation, it would be dangerous to bring out the contraption for examination, the risk of an above-ground explosion was too great, in fact, it might just conceivably explode below ground if some delayed reaction had by some unprecedented type of error been introduced. All monitors had been kept on. But one 'safe' explanation, when those responsible for Edison turned up at the AEC meeting with their story, could be that the escaped alphaguy had eaten up the Plutonium.

Edison must be found.

Someone suggested that Xorandor might be in touch with all his offspring and might be persuaded to give a fix, but Xorandor was apparently asked and had remained silent. Edison was found eventually, back in his compound.

One of the subheadlines was: *Did alphaguy neutralize atom bomb?*

Great commotion among both greens and redwhiteandblues everywhere, doves and hawks.

I said the leak had taken two months. But maybe it hadn't. Maybe the journalist knew at the time but took two months to make absolutely sure of his facts. He certainly seemed to know a hexadex lot of facts. And eventually government spokesmen spoke.

And I can't help wondering: could the leak have been arranged, very carefully, by Kubler himself? In his November article he says he went to see Andrewski. If we could find out when his San Francisco lecture was, presumably at Berkeley

University, we could be more certain, but I think of it as a rather diodic hypothesis. Let's say he guessed at this very possibility, and tried to interest Biggleton and Lagache and Andrewski in vain. Let's suppose Edison disappeared while he was there visiting the lab — he may even have taken part in the search, boy, in the hot sun — *Komm mal her, Edizon! komm mal her!* A Hollywood version of Einstein, in a white suit, with a straw hat poached on the back of his head, Zab would at once provide.

No one else would know so many details except Andrewski himself, who wouldn't leak his own incompetence. Or his assistants, who surely wouldn't attend the AEC Commission. Kubler would have been brought by Andrewski as a co–expert who had just in fact come with his theories about movement and neutralization. And when they get there they hear that that's precisely what's happened. And later Kubler invites a journalist to his hotel room in San Francisco. Then, to cover himself, he writes this extremely cagey article in the *New Scientist*, saying nothing about neutralization but a lot about motion, isotopic preference, sensing from a distance, and reproduction.

I don't know what Zab would think. I've been pretty sarky about her fabulations I know. In any case, she'd want to understand why. A bit thick, she'd say probably, accusing *two* Germans of betrayal, De Wint-Bleich, and now Kubla Kahn, but they're completely different cases, and on different sides. Though each time Biggleton is slow on the uptake! In any case the Germans are far more actively concerned with the nuclear arsenal than anyone else, they're bang in the firing line. Ancestral voices prophesying war! Anything that might bring the build-up to an end would be treated well by the authorities, or at least ambiguously.

I like my hypothesis. And, whatever the reasons, the most important aspect is surely that the whole thing is now, let's hope, in the public domain.

17 FULLSCAN

Naturally we pleaded and pleaded with dad to let us come home for Christmas and try and talk to Xorandor, but he was adamant. So, a *deutsche Weihnacht* it had to be. As if it were a punishment.

Knock it off, Zab. He just didn't think talking to Xorandor would help.

You mean he didn't like the idea that we can and he can't.

No, Zab, only that it's out of his hands.

Does Xorandor have hands?

Anyone who can do a Handshake has hands endjoke. But what could Xorandor do, especially if he'd in fact ordered it? The Lady Macbeth incident had been a danger, and unnecessary, a syntax error he called it. This is the opposite. Stacked heads! Hadn't you seen the implications? What use is philosophy?

No need to be rude, Jip. Anyway, dad's semi-maybe for Easter wasn't kept, they came over again, and took us to Vienna, *just* where the first negotiations were going on, it was absolutely bootloading.

Well at least the media sprang back into action.

Someone's going to have to summarize all these videotapes, don't you just love doing that, Jip?

Booles, we share.

Let's do it from memory while it's still fresh in our minds.

You get bogged down, Zab.

The triggering thing was to see some of the faces we only knew as names. Kubler appeared, and wasn't a bit like a Hollywood version of Einstein, as *you'd* imagined, Jip. More like a smooth young executive, beginning to thicken out on good living, or an estate agent or a car salesman.

Itsybitsybytes.

And of course he spoke German, so the comic accent idea collapsed.

The real crackerpack in all these discussions and interviews, Zab, was the open admission at last that the Russians also had two offspring.

Yes, called Marx and Lenin.

Well, that came later, when the Russians agreed to let a spokesman appear. At first it was much more cagey, in the passive, or just vague, the Soviet Government *was given, also obtained*, as if we'd been open and generous from the start.

But what was the point?

Philosophy doesn't seem to sharpen your political voltage, Zab, don't you see, if you want to force someone to negotiate you must show that you know what he thought you didn't, or let out what he knew you knew but thought you wouldn't let out, so that secrecy becomes futile, at least on that point. There was an article somewhere about secrecy and ignorance and suspicion being the real causes of war, and that hitech would soon abolish them.

Seems hitech also fosters them.

We're getting sidetracked again.

When it's you, you say we, when it's me you say you, Jip. But why don't we do that ARD tie-up with London and Paris? It was very early on, and almost between the people we'd got to know from that first Harwell meeting, so it was more fun, except that Biggles wasn't there. Nor were those top security men, Dougall, Gerwig and Tardelli.

Okay. There were a couple of scientific journalists instead, and the chairman was a German anchorman. You're right, it was rather prime seeing them, especially Andrewski, who was in London, though everything the French and English said came out in an overvoice in simultaneous German.

Andrewski was the biggest surprise.

Why? Of all people he had a right to be there.

Surprise to look at, loopy. Not at all a shortpalepodgy Slav with rimless glasses but —

Debug, Zab, argument-type-error. The French — it was Lagache and a new man called Janvier — hogged the conversation at once and said their team had hit on that very same possibility as Professor Kubler (so you see, he did warn someone) quite some time before, and had dutifully reported it to their government. As a result their military authorities had at once been informed and there was an immediate clamp-down while the scientists investigated the problem before sharing it with their allies, well, their partners. At first they had thought the sudden splash of publicity and public outcry was regrettable —

Here, there was surely a glance towards *someone* but cameras are never quick enough to show who unless he's named. And even then they're at least fifty seconds too late. But now the French considered that much good might come out of it.

The British were very quiet at first, represented in fact only by a scientific journalist, and of course Andrewski as second anglophone. Or was the journalist also a scientist, from Harwell?

Probably they were still recovering from the Lady Macbeth syndrome and studying that, so they hadn't thought of this new possibility and felt a bit bootstrap. Boolesup in fact, cos they had the most alphaguys and had discovered Xorandor.

Well, we did.

Then the chairman insisted that Kubler, presumably because he spoke German, should explain to the public how a nuclear bomb explodes or rather how it doesn't, which he painstakingly started to do.

But Andrewski interrupted — rather rudely considering the chairman had asked for this — dark Tartar type with narrow eyes, Andrewski was —

Debugger off. He had plenty of reasons to interrupt Kubler. He said the public had heard such explanations from experts for weeks, with diagrams in the papers, and that wasn't what they were there to discuss. There were, as he saw it, two separate questions. First the practical one of preventing such incidents. And second, a far more difficult political issue which our most subtle diplomatic circles, backed by scientific advice, were thinking about. The practical question was being studied, and pending the scientists' report, he proposed they should leave it aside. So then the Frenchman Janvier wholly agreed, and as to the second question it had itself two aspects: the neutralizing of our *force de frappe* by our own *alphages* (this was all translated but one could hear the French at times), as had occurred, in however minor a way, in the United States. And the neutralizing of *enemy* warheads. And as to this second aspect, there was no escaping the conclusion that, if *les alphages* could go anywhere, sending their nodules at vast distances to excavate isotopes, or attaching themselves to trucks, planes, and possibly even submarines, piercing walls and entering reactors, then there was no reason why they should not find, or even be programmed to find, Russian nuclear warheads and neutralize them. But since the Russians also had at least two, who might eventually reproduce, it must be obvious to anyone but the most perfect imbecile that the thing could work both ways. Hardly an example of the subtle diplomacy Andrewksi had mentioned. Come on, Zab, do your byte.

You said to debugger off.

Only from irrelevant description.

Why is the description of a reactor more important that the description of someone's face. A face also reacts. You yourself would have liked the camera on Kubler at a specific moment.

Boolederdash. you haven't described any faces reacting, Zab, you couldn't, from tapes, that comes through what they say. All you want is to mention that someone was blond or looked like a car salesman. Who cares?

It might be important. Frinstance, Toussaint Tardelli was a top French Security man, and Corsican, and Dougall ditto and a Scot. It'd be megavolt to know what they look like. The Corsican short, dark, florid, bon viveur, the Scot thin, reddish hair, and dour, but blushing easily. And Hair Earwig, their German opposite number, maybe a Bavarian? Large, fat and earnest. Wouldn't that be interesting, at least, mightn't it lead to something unexpected?

No, not with those clichés. But thanks for mentioning Gerwig. He wasn't there of course, but the German journalist did a spiel on what we know of the Soviet interest in the alphaguys. The Soviet Union, he said, is less interested than we are in the problem of waste, since they allow no protest marches and publish no information, besides, they have huge uninhabited territories. We had assumed they would harness the computer powers of their specimens to computer science, in which they perpetually lag behind, because the system is bogged down in red tape and doesn't allow for the unexpected flashes encouraged by private enterprise — creeping quarks, and these people talk of diplomacy! Let's hope it'll be practised by others.

Then the French came in again, it was Lagache, who said that before any of this had become public, their government had felt strongly that we could not have a situation where each side, while pretending ignorance, knows that its *force de frappe* can be neutralized by the other, yet can never know whether or not it has been, and where and to what extent, without, of course, perpetually dismantling each warhead to find out. Or exploding it. Therefore he himself had pressed his government to tell the Russians of the Californian incident, before it leaked out, as his team had thought it probably would sooner or later, though they were taken short by the soonness. We would then have shown honesty, always a good starting point for negotiation. If the Russians knew of it already from their own sources, then both bluffs would have been called, and if on the contrary they'd discovered they'd been caught napping in their technical thinking, *tant pis*, they'd get over that when faced with the facts and their responsibilities, as we would be seen to be facing ours. Well, we had lost that honesty initiative, thanks to the leak (ah, if only the camera had been on Kubler's face *reacting!*) but apart from that the situation remains exactly the same on both sides.

Except that we have more, Andrewski said.

171

His narrow Tartar eyes sharp and sinister.

Zab if you want to become a romance or spy writer you'll have plenty of time, but not here.

Boys in puberty! Aborted. *And* mean.

They have two, said Kubla Kahn, and could feed them up, like athletes, for better performance. And quicker reproduction. Besides, are we *sure* they have only two? Couldn't, for instance, three have been, er, obtained? Who was responsible for the gift? he added quickly.

The camera for once shifted fast on the Englishman, yes, he *was* from Harwell. He glared at Kubler and looked very flushed, and said with a pinched look that first Xorandor never made elementary mistakes in arithmetic and had told them he'd produced six. And Kubler said he might have lied, and the man said Xorandor had never lied yet, and secondly, Dr Biggleton's early reports and photographs showed only six cells hollowed out at that time. Four offspring for the West, two for Russia. That seemed to settle that one, but holy nukes, what innuendoes, no one outside those in the know about the theft could make head or tail of it.

On the contrary, Zab, journalists are smart terminals at detecting when something's being kept from them. Kubler must have done it on purpose. And the German journalist did ask, soon after, whether our good will and honesty hadn't already been shown, precisely in that gift, and he stressed the word, *Geschenk*. And everyone had to agree. Knowing it meant the opposite.

And Andrewski went rapidly on to say that he was empowered to suggest a first meeting in Washington, not yet at the highest level but with the scientific attaché from the Russian Embassy and any other experts they'd care to send, though all five foreign ministries would be represented. They would organize the meeting in collaboration. It would prepare the way for later top-level negotiations.

Yes, the Gipfelkonferenzen. That word *Gipfel* for summit is diodic, one really does see mountains. *Ueber allen Gipfeln ist Ruh.*

Then the Englishman from Harwell said his government feared that such negotiations could become as protracted and futile as those for the reduction of nuclear arms, which had gone on for forty years or more.

Better talk than explode, the chairman said.

But the Englishman persisted, saying that even the perennial disarmament talks had reasonably concrete and even highly technical agendas. But what, precisely, were we to negotiate over the alphaguys?

The purely scientific solution to nuclear waste, Andrewski said, verifiable and to be supervised by the International Atomic Energy Agency in Vienna.

But verification has been the stumbling block for decades, said the German journalist. Besides, the real thing to verify here would be their *non*-use for neutralization of each other's weapons, and Dr Lagache has told us why that is impossible.

There was a baffled pause then everyone started talking at once and the anchorman put out both his hands.

The Englishman got the floor first, and spoke poker-faced, but perhaps as British humour to change the mood. Though no one ever understands it *as* humour, precisely because it's by definition poker-faced, there's no joke-endjoke in the eyes or in the tone, as with the Germans or French. In any case it came through the interpreter.

Get on with it, Zab.

He said: I fear that the real negotiations may have to be undertaken, not with the Soviet Union, but with Xorandor. And we collapsed into giggles, remember, Jip? We had a simultaneous vision, at least you confirmed it afterwards, of five foreign secretaries sitting on rocks around the carn, with the name of their country on a slat in front of them, negotiating away in four languages with interpreters' booths like seaside cabins all round.

So we missed the beginning of Kubler's outburst, to the effect that they'd all gone *verrückt*, and let the first aspect — how to prevent further incidents, which ought to be questioned anyway — invade the diplomatic aspect. Surely the

173

whole point of this new capacity to neutralize atomic warheads, without any possibility for either side to find out whether and where and how much, was its supreme value as argument for total nuclear disarmament. Surely we weren't going to negotiate, with anybody, least of all Xorandor, the *non*-use of this unexpected, *wunderbare* solution?

18 ALTER

Yippee! Home at last, Zab! Two years exactly since we first met Xorandor.

And the first thing we did was to ride out to see him, though dad warned us he wasn't talking.

For *he*, read Xorandor.

Oh it was so leptonic, that compound. Well, we'd seen it before, but we'd always remembered Xorandor as in the old days.

And now there was the guard hut and the high wire fence, and the little gate, and the guard had instructions to let us in. And we walked up self-consciously, but all random jitters.

You were especially afraid he wouldn't recognize your croak.

So you spoke first. Let's put on the tape.

Tape 73. Side 1. Rec. 1. 17 July. Printout.
Beginrec
Zab: Hello, Xorandor. Zip here.
Xor: Hello Zab. But Jip is with you.
Zab: Yes, but his voice has changed, it's breaking, er, be-
      coming like daddyjohn's. But it is Jip.
Xor: Hello Jip. Let me hear your new voice.
Jip: Hello, Xorandor. It won't stay quite like this, it's in the
      process. Sort of fifty-fifty.
Xor: More forty-sixty into daddyjohn. Welcome home,
      Jipnzab. It has been five hundred and thirty one days.
Zab: You mean you counted!
Xor: I count everything, Zab, it is automatic, and available
      on call.

175

Jip: How are you Xorandor?

Xor: I am. I continue.

Jip: We were at school in Germany.

Xor: Yes. You told me. Wie geht es Euch?

Zab: Xorandor! You've been learning German! But how?

Xor: I listen to Radio Swiss International. They have 30 minutes news and comment in English, French, German and Italian. After a while, it's possible to decode.

Jip: Smart terminal!

Xor: You have substituted for jumping nukes, Jip. But the German and Italian don't fill up their halfhour with words, they have many, many minutes of mathematically trivial noise till the next language.

Jip: That's a diodic description of folkmusic, Xorandor!

Zab: But Xorandor, you *can't* have learnt *Wie geht es Euch* on the news, it's the familiar plural, for people you know very well. They say rather, *Guten Abend meine Damen und Herren* and things like that.

Xor: True. If so then from a play, or else interview. But I have much to tell you.

Jip: Do you know all that's been going on, since we left? Oh but of course you do.

Xor: My offspring cannot inform me of meetings any more, they are no longer present as specimens. But we are in constant touch. And I hear much on the air.

Zab: How do you react?

Xor: I do not react. I register.

Jip: Have you registered a lot?

Xor: My voice is also breaking, from lack of use, but in the opposite direction, more towards the voices of my offspring. Have you brought Handshake?

Jip: Of course!

You scrambled over the wall, Jip. We were so happy. All was as before.

176

But all was not as before, Zab, as you know, and how are we going to tell it? Even though he decompiled and translated abstracts as he went, they filed by endlessly on the screen, from our first meeting onwards, recording light, pressure, someone's brain activity, and even all this was selected from continuous and simultaneous intake of other data, the way we breathe or perceive or circulate our blood and digest, even while we talk and think. We'd only reached the arrival of Pennybig when you interrupted. Here it is.

```
ZIP INTERRUPT XAND PROGRAM
  XAND AWAIT INSTRUCTION
ZIP TO XAND
  DEC 1 'WE HAVE TO LEAVE YOU FOR FOOD' ENDEC 1
  REM VERY SORRY ENDREM
  DEC 2 'WE'LL COME BACK THIS AFTERNOON' ENDEC 2
  REQ BUT PLEASE BE BRIEFER ENDREQ
  XAND ACCEPT
    REM 1 I WOULD ALSO PREFER IT ENDREM 1
    REM 2 I WAS KEEPING PROMISE ENDREM 2
ZIP TO XAND
  DEC 1 'WE ASKED FOR TOO MUCH' ENDEC 1
    REM VERY SORRY BUT DIDNT KNOW YOU INTOOK SO
    MUCH AND KEPT IT ALL STORED ENDREM
    Q HOW DO YOU FIND ROOM FOR SO MUCH STORAGE?
    ENDQ
XAND TO ZIP
    A I SCRATCH WHAT IS IRRELEVANT END A
ZIP TO XAND
    REM IT DOESNT SEEM LIKE IT ENDREM
XAND TO ZIP
    REM YOU SOUND LIKE JAD AND BIGDAD 710 DAYS AGO
    BEGAN ASKING POINTLESS QS ABOUT MY INSIDE LIKE
    HAVING YOUR HEAD EXAMINED AS THEY SAY
      EX 1 ARE YOU HISTORY-SENSITIVE? ENDEX 1 ENDREM
ZIP TO XAND
    REM THEY MEANT ARE YOUR PROGRAMS SELF-MODIFYING
    ENDREM
```

XAND TO ZIP

REM YES THEY EXPLAINED

ZIP TO XAND

Q AND ARE YOU? ENDQ

XAND TO ZIP

REM CONT

EX 2 DO YOU HAVE A VOLATILE MEMORY AND A SERIAL
MEMORY AND A PERMANENT MEMORY AND A HIGH
SPEED MEMORY AND MANY MORE MEMORIES AND
MANY OTHER QS ENDEX 2

BUT ANY OF YOUR COMPUTER EXPERTS COULD HAVE
WORKED OUT THE WHOLE SYSTEM FROM A FEW SAMPLES
OF HANDSHAKE EXCHANGES. THEY WILL HAVE LEARNT
QUITE ENOUGH TO ADVANCE THEIR UIMS ENDREM

ZIP TO XAND

DEC 1 'WE DIDNT SHOW THEM TO ANYONE. WE TOOK THE
FLOPPIES = MEMORIES WITH US' ENDEC 1

XAND TO ŻIP

DEC 1 'THANKS' ENDEC 1

DEC 2 'BUT THEY RECORDED EVERYTHING' ENDEC 2

REM THE WORLD MUST KNOW BY NOW HOW WE
FUNCTION ENDREM

DEC 3 'WE FUNCTION MUCH LIKE YOUR UIMS BUT BETTER'
ENDEC 3

DEC 4 'THE ONLY DIFFERENCE IS THAT UIMS THOUGH MORE
INTELLIGENT THAN MEN ARE MADE AND UNDERSTOOD BY
MEN' ENDEC 4

DEC 5 'MY INSIDE IS ONLY INPUT FROM OUTSIDE' ENDEC 5

DEC 6 'A STRUCTURE IS NOT A STATIC PHYSICAL OBJECT BUT
A PERMANENT SCRATCH PERMANENT REPLACE PERPETUAL
TRANSFORMATION' ENDEC 6

S1 IF I CAN WORK OUT HOW YOUR BRAINS FUNCTION
THEN RECIPROCAL MUST BE TRUE END S1

ZIP TO XAND

DEC 1 'BUT ALL THAT YOU SAID CAME FROM YOU ALREADY
TRANSLATED EITHER IN VOICE FOR THEM OR FOR US IN
POCCOM WHICH IS ALSO A TRANSLATION' ENDEC 1

REM THAT SAYS NOTHING ABOUT THE DIFFERENT LAYERS
OR FIRMWARE ENDREM
XAND TO ZIP
REM BUT SOFTWARILY WE ARE OBSERVED ENDREM

We glanced at each other and together said goodbye. He was not only punning but punning on Shakespeare. How and why could he listen to so much? And he was saying strange things, almost metaphysical things we didn't understand. Or perhaps you did, Zab?

Not really, though it was triggering all right. That stuff about the inside being the outside and vice versa for instance. The philosophers seem to have been discussing that ever since Plato.

Plutoneeum! And haven't they got any further than that?

Oh, it gets very complicated, or perhaps they make it so, it gets a bit incomprehensible here and there. But it has to do, sometimes, with the voice being inside whereas writing is outside, a mere technique, and us losing our memories because of writing and since writing, and in a way computers make that worse, with their outside databanks and peripherals and terminals and floppies. We'll lose our memories even more, but now also our poor logic, except for an élite of progam experts. But Xorandor seemed different, sort of beyond all that, or outside it, no, that must be the wrong word, but for one thing it's his voice that's the peripheral, the late addition. It's as if he never passed through any of our problems at all.

If you mean philosophical problems then swags for him.

Philosophy is also metaphysics, Jip, and metaphysics is always ideological, a sort of conceptual clay that moulds everything we look at. And you claim that ideo —

Okay okay. In view of what we discovered next you may be right, but it may also be hindsight that makes you read so much into his remarks and besides, let's get on.

Right. But we'll have to tell it, not show it, the whole thing went on all summer — what was left of it after that long German school year, till mid-July, it was grim. And we

179

couldn't go every day, there were other things, and it rained, and so on.

But when we came back that afternoon, Zab, we went on foot. We wanted to walk along the ridge path and say hello to Uther Pendragon and Aurelius.

And they weren't there. Not where we'd hidden them anyway.

We searched and called, but decided not to waste more time.

So we asked Xorandor. And he said yes, they'd moved away. Offspring must always move as far as they can, by every possible means, while they're small enough. The problem then had been that they couldn't get out from under him while the other three were still there.

But why hadn't those moved off? Did that mean that he depended on humans to take them away? No, he said, he'd waited for those to be collected by daddyjohn, it had been a promise but daddyjohn hadn't turned up.

And then he told us.

Yes, the truth.

Or maybe another lie, we'll never know. If one lie, then two are possible, we thought. Or more.

No Jip. We do know, inside ourselves. The wonder is that others, and scientists too, believed the first, the only lie.

Well they didn't at the very start, Zab, remember Andrewski? And Biggleton that very first night, how cautious he was with dad? Treating him like a schoolboy.

Yes and no. He was drinking a lot of brandy. Dad's first-impression conviction, which came direct from Xorandor, did somehow get through to him and he got quite triggered. That's how first impressions, however wrapped up as suppositions, somehow get chemically transformed into deep-seated convictions that can then be proved mathematically and scientifically. The history of human knowledge is just that.

It wasn't quite like that. There *was* scientific confirmation here.

Which Xorandor faked. The Gigahertz messages for one, which weren't proof but helped to create a conviction of

180

communication with a distant base, especially as he refused to discuss them and said he knew nothing about them. But above all the strobe chemical analysis. Please take the sample from the edge at x degrees — or whatever — he'd said cooperatively, where it will not harm my circuits. And they did. And he'd altered his isotopic composition at just that spot, to correspond to the dates of exposure on Mars and in space and on earth that he'd given. That seems the most hexedex thing of the entire story, Jip. And completely incomprehensible. Not only for how but for why.

As to the how, remember he's like a radiotelescope, Zab, he can calculate the universe whenever he wants to. And if he can excavate and separate isotopes he can presumably shuffle them.

So. He hadn't come from Mars at all. He said it wasn't a lie — or non-truth as he called it — but an answer that had come quite naturally, to him — perhaps logically would be the better word — in answer to a supposition of Pennybig. Gwendolin, to him. He even asked why she never visited him. And of course we'll never know just what she asked, or how she framed her questions, since we don't have that conversation on tape but only her later version of it.

Nor would Xorandor give his version of it. He said it made her look non-intelligent to us and he had scratched it. Very odd.

No. He's peculiarly meticulous about some aspects of brain-interact, even though emotions have nil value, in fact don't exist in the system. Look at his attitude towards promises, which we regard as emotional statements. And trust. And presumably respect as part of trust. To him a promise is like an instruction. It has to do after all with truth-values, without which he can't operate.

And yet he lied.

Not a lie, Jip. A playful, or logical, confirmation, or even interpretation, of an expectation. Sort of telling people what they want to hear, in certain carefully evaluated circumstances. Their truth. She may have thought in terms of a small meteorite — and within the lie she wasn't so wrong, since the scientists did too — and that gave him the idea. Anyway, why does it matter?

Because he then kept it up. To *us*.

So that's it. Pride.

No, a need to understand. How can a computer give a playful answer, or even an ambiguous answer?

Why how? You know he does. We called him Xorandor, didn't we? Besides, even computer logic can contain ambiguities, for instance the *if/then if/then/else* sequence could be represented by two different flowcharts.

That was resolved by the *begin/end* delimiters, or *endif* and such.

It was only an example. There are also difficulties with infix notation. And you know very well that in a context-free grammar no general procedure exists for determining whether the grammar can be ambiguous in any one of every single case, however long one ran the program. The question is then said to be undecidable.

Thunks!

You don't agree? But —

Thunks and flippeting flipflops and leaping leptons and all! Zab, don't you see? The first Gigahertz message intercepted by Tim had been *before* that conversation with Pennybig. In May or June. Before the summer eprom. Before even our discovery of Xorandor. So the lie must have been planned.

No! Are you sure, Jip?

Positive. We can easily check. Anyway, Tim told dad about it before that famous Sunday when Pennybig came to the carn and De Wint stole the offspring and vanished and dad talked to Biggleton. So much happened at once we couldn't think straight. But it obviously was so since De Wint was still in Carn Tregean, he came in for a drink a bit later and Tim sat there hating him —

You see, you remember it by that, so it wasn't so useless.

Descramble, Zab, let's concentrate.

You're bugged, Jip, simmer down. We're both bugged in

fact. We'll check that, but you know, it would be easier first to check what Xorandor told us this summer, much more recently, about those Gigahertz messages.

Why?

Just a feeling. We may have misunderstood. Remember he told us about it *after* he told us about the isotope changes, and we were so boolesupped by that — look, here's the printout. You even aptly regressed.

ZIP TO XAND

!JUMPING NUKES!

Q BUT WHY? WHAT WAS THE POINT? END Q

XAND TO ZIP

A CONFIRMATION OF CONFIRMATION TO GWENDOLIN

EXPECTATION END A

ZIP TO XAND

Q BUT WHAT ABOUT THE GIGAHERTZ MESSAGES? END Q

REM THEY HAD ALREADY HELPED JAD AND BD TO BELIEVE

THE FIRST CONFIRMATION ENDREM

XAND TO ZIP

DEC 1 'I TOLD JAD AND BD I KNEW NOTHING ABOUT THE

GIGAHERTZ MSGES' ENDEC 1

REM THEY WOULD NOT BELIEVE ME THEY THOUGHT I WAS

BEING DISCREET ABOUT MY BASE THEY CALLED IT ONE OF

MY DIPLOMATIC SILENCES ENDREM

ZIP TO XAND

Q AND DID YOU HAVE MANY DIPLOMATIC SILENCES?

END Q

XAND TO ZIP

A NOT AT FIRST. SOME WHEN I DIDNT KNOW. LATER MORE.

LATER TOTAL SILENCE END A

ZIP TO XAND

Q BUT WHY? END Q

Don't you see, Jip? We went on with the wrong question, instead of clarifying his reply.

What needs clarifying?

Dummy to you for once. His reply is syntactically clear but

183

contextually ambiguous. It could be an admission of further lying, or rather, previous to the chemical analyses but further to the original lie — the confirmation or interpretation of expectation. And that, in the context of that lie, is how we naturally interpreted it.

A lie interpreted as such by dad and Biggleton. So?

But it could be the truth, Jip. He told dad and Biggles he knew nothing about the Gigahertz messages and it was true. They didn't believe it because by then they wanted to believe he did know.

Swags, yes. After all Gigahertz isn't all that unusual, though of course they checked everywhere. What really puzzled Tim and excited dad and later convinced everyone was the code. But everyone in the world is communicating in secret codes, and some of them must remain unbreakable. You're right about our misreading that answer, Zab. But there's still a third explanation, now that we know the truth. Xorandor did lie to dad and Biggles. He did use Gigahertz. But not to and from Mars.

19 XORANDOR

Right, Jip!

And we're forgetting to tell the story. So where did he come from? Answer, he didn't. He and his kind have been here on earth all the time, millions of years. Living on natural radiation.

Developing their diodic capacities, simply as brains, long before man, with none of his advantages and distractions, like mobility and manipulation, war, sex, and violence.

In other words, Zab, he hadn't *arrived* 4568 years ago and sort of let his faculties go to sleep after those three million years in space, or shock of take-off or landing — it's hard to know who said what, now, and how much Biggles and dad interpolated during those first interviews. And he hadn't suddenly woken up four years ago because of the new presence of nuclear waste two years before we discovered him. He and his kind have been here all the time, perfectly aware and intelligent, maybe not from their very beginning but at any rate millions of years before man. Reproducing slowly. He himself was *born* 4568 years ago.

A mere youngster! An adolescent, like us, Jip.

He had told us the truth on that Sunday morning, and he later altered it, or rather reinterpreted that date.

So as not to hurt our feelings. Okay okay Jip, it's only a manner of speaking. Let's say so as to interpret the truth of our expectation in the now altered way, after interpreting the truth of Pennybig's expectation. That's enormous in itself.

Which explains our spiked state.

Both personal and, what do they call it, sort of, oh yes, a culture-shock. But secondly, Jip, to go back to what he told Pennybig, don't you see, this answer, or interpretation of her expectation, was a story he invented, just as he heard her tell us a story. A myth if you like. Biggleton had supposed they don't make artefacts, he was a bit flummoxed because making artefacts is supposed to come with language. Well a story's an artefact, the only kind possible to him, to them, even music wouldn't be, except maybe as silent mathematical patterns, unless in ultrasonic perhaps. Since he said the synthetic voice was evolved by him alone.

Stubs, yes. A myth. If you like. But a lie that took everyone in. That was the shock. Like you said, Zab. You seem to have coped with it better.

A radiotelescope, you said, calculating the universe. And his race. Beyond our memories. He could say anything. Oh Jip, that's it, a myth of origin. Of false origin, like all myths. And a myth of fall. Fall as model of energy, of matter. That's why even the scientists accepted the evidence. He told a story and altered his reality to fit. It got them, through ancient modes. But —

Oh booles.

But you know, Jip, you may have had an inkling long before, several times you said things that would *now* show, if we could go all the way back over two years and find them — well we can partly — that you were suspicious of the Mars origin. But you never listen to inklings.

The butterfly! Zab, you're diodic. That's it. Somewhere an inkling would flutter by, and our talking and joint storytelling were to be the net to catch it.

It caught a lot.

But if you didn't have an inkling, Zab, and completely believed the story, how come he said, when you wailed that we'd asked none of the right questions, that you had asked quite a few. Unlike daddyjohn and Biggerdaddy and, presumably, Jip.

Because, possibly, of their philosophical implications.

Philosophy! You're not going to say he's really Socrates petrified!

Well it's a wide word, philosophy, a kiloword, except that it contains far more than 1024 words of 8 binary elements each. A megaword, a gigaword. It was just some aspects. Trying to imagine a creature, for instance, with no sexual difference, none of our distinctions between the sensible and the intelligible, or matter and spirit, or even matter and form. His matter is his form, in a way his hardware is his software. The pure sensible, Hegel or someone calls it. You remember how we worried about whether Xorandor feels time, well —

You worried, Zab.

It's so hard to grasp. One day perhaps. When we were waiting, and you were so impatient and said nothing was happening —

And you said but something's happening to us, yes, yes, it's true.

We have to grow up even more, to understand it all, now it's all butterflies. It's something to do with time being the negative of being outside oneself, or rather, the idea of falling into time, but no, that's not it, time in fact as thinking. No, that's not it either, and Hegel pinches all that part straight from Totty.

Who the megavolts is Totty?

Aristotle, silly, it's all in Physics Chapter 4 remember? And after, all the way to the end. But at the end of Chapter 4 some presocratic had said time was wisdom, and someone in the Pythagoras school said that was stupid cos we also forget in time. But you see, Xorandor doesn't, or his race. And man dies and each new man has to learn again, and reinterpret, and alter, so that his being — oh and then by the time it gets rehandled through to the twentieth century it all becomes horribly difficult and thunkish.

So you're going to study it when you grow up? You know it's not taught any more, at university level? You'd only be allowed to do it as a hobby.

Sure. But why not physics *and* philosophy? As it used to be.

In any case, Zab, to go back to your non-distinctions, it's got to be a binary system basically, even if specific distinctions vary.

Check. You're right, of course, Jip. But it's so hard to explain what's still only a dim notion. You remember he said that a high signal has no meaning without the low, well obviously, it's a hilo system, but that this means the hi contains inside itself the negative of the lo, or its absence, and vice versa. And so it must be at the level of words, and concepts, but we can only express that with paradoxes and puns and ambiguities and myths, lies in fact, according to Plato.

Oh him again.

Well, him and many others in human civilization, which has produced all these necessary distinctions, millions of them, which make language possible. But some get muddled, or let's say some of the human muddled ones have passed him by. Or maybe he functions in several systems, precisely because he doesn't conceptualize.

What are you talking about?

Perhaps it's the fact that they don't communicate, except in machine-code to each other, but not to man. And presumably don't represent, well, let's say it's not man facing the physical world but the physical world, how to put it, simply thinking itself to itself, independently of man and all his systems. And physics is only another system. So — no, it's already gone, and sounds zany anyway, it's impossible to say it without it vanishing. Oh it must be megavolt to be grown-up and grasp everything clearcut, no butterflies and things that don't seem to fit anywhere. Or perhaps it's because they don't see, not in our sense, they only calculate, even his pixel's numeric, and part of his translation process. He doesn't need it, it was just for us. Even our distinction between thought and language probably can't exist for him, and it's speech which was the artificial and late addition, a technique, like writing for us.

Yes, and we asked him why.

We've asked him so many whys and hows, all through the summer. Mum assumed we were still just playing games with him, and dad, to our surprise, didn't interfere. He's working on a book about Xorandor.

Fat lot he knows! He was simply glad Xorandor was talking

again and he assumed we'd tell him all the details or give him our floppies. Well, maybe. If he's nice to us. Anyway let's get down to some more concrete detail, Zab, this philosophizing is all very well but —

True. Sorry. So there they've been for aeons, all over the earth. Lots of them.

Evolved out of silicon, very slowly.

And scattering their young at distances, perhaps on large scaly moving animals, or later on riders' gear, or just small distances at first, short but often. Still, the evolution and dispersal must have been very slow as you say, Jip. He talked of all this as if it were fairly recent. What's mineral time after all? He registers it but doesn't feel it, or express it. For instance he said he'd heard from a kinstone about a man called Socrates, who talked out of doors in Greek about three beds, the ideal bed, the real bed and the painted bed. He said he didn't know what a bed was, but Socrates was responsible for all those splits.

Zab knock it off.

Sorry sorry. It was only to show he spoke of his kin somewhere in ancient Athens as if he were still there listening to Socrates, instead of probably part of some old building.

Garbage. He was perfectly aware that there were long periods of silence. What one stone may have learnt locally at some tribal meeting would be transmitted — just think of the languages they've learnt and probably scratched — but it would be a slow and chancy process, depending on where one stone found itself. And he said that even after man began to teach and talk out of doors — and that was aeons after the beginnings of man — there were long centuries of silence, after the invention of writing presumably, and good housing. He himself was completely cut off down here. He's probably far less brilliant than some of his more advantaged kinstones.

Yes, and by the way, he answered that cranky question, why had he chosen the tip of Cornwall, you remember someone said he'd hovered over the carn and recognized the sacred stones? In fact he was simply born near here, and moved, and stayed. But he said, rather nicely, 'I didn't choose the carn, the carn chose me.' People many centuries ago had built the carn around him, or behind him, and would come and worship him. Perhaps they really had better ears and could hear those ultrasonic sounds, if any, which that article talked about, and they thought it was magic.

Then suddenly, last century, man burst out on the sound-waves. Babble babble babble, for decades and decades. News, talks, ads, shows, plays, discussions, propaganda, sermons, lectures, classes, suddenly he had exciting new input and sharpened his faculties no end. And a little later, artificial nuclear energy, a sudden huge increase in ambient food, and still more recently, nuclear waste very nearby. He's had decades of solitary university of the air to bone up on all our cultures, all those silent centuries, as well as current knowledge. He must be more learned than any professor. And he says that 99.99% of all he hears is repetition shuffled around through poor thought processes, that's why he can scratch so much. You know, Zab, that's what hurt most, the idea that he'd been laughing at us, pretending to learn English and counting and all that. Play-acting, can you imagine?

A great courtesy, Jip. As with Pennybig. As mothers with children, and sometimes women with their men. Xorandor doesn't laugh at people, he goes along with them at their level, telling them what he knows they want to hear. After all, we all play language-games. Would we have understood if he hadn't? Remember we half genuinely thought he was the ghost of Merlin. And what started as a language-game had to go on as a lie, or a myth. And by the way, that myth was transmitted to his offspring, or at any rate programmed into Xor 7, Lady Macbeth.

But it was not transmitted *as* myth to our olders, as he craftily called them, but as lie.

He said he tried to tell them but they wouldn't listen, or hear, or understand.

It's hard to believe that. We've no proof of it.

True, Jip, but even in that very first conversation with dad

190

and Pennybig, Xorandor couldn't get around to what he wanted to say till the very end, dad was putting all the questions. Look it up. And we were there at that first long interrogation with dad and Biggles, even if we don't have tapes. He was so cooperative! It's easy to imagine the process going on and on, they were so completely taken up with their own ideas, how did he function as computer, and the food, and the isotopic separation, and the nodules, remember it was still a very local affair, the red and yellow alerts, one creature, with its very recent offspring, the first since he'd 'landed' and so on. And they connected all that only with the solution to nuclear waste. People with obsessions don't hear what others say, you know, though they can seem extremely attentive.

Let's rather put it this way, as dad does, that modern scientists are rarely concerned with the genealogy of things, only with their present structure and functioning.

That sure makes it sound more dignified. But Xorandor did try to tell us, later, about their questions and their not listening. Maybe *we* didn't listen either.

So, courtesy again. Of course that's a value-term. Your phrase 'going along with' is better.

But why break his million year silence at all? That's the real non-plus flummoxer.

You asked him that once. No, several times, He was evasive then.

And why do it through us? We were sitting on him, okay, but thousands of humans must have sat on him through the ages. When we asked him he said syntax error. Just as cryptic.

No Zab, don't you see? He didn't mean we'd made a syntax error in our question. Don't you remember he used that term to describe his making of Xor 7 after taking Caesium 137?

But that was six months later, at Christmas.

Well, we take nine months to make a child. No seriously, Zab, work it out. He contacted us in early July or so. He knew he couldn't tell us, but had to gain our trust.

You mean he'd already taken some?

Could be. He had, by the end of July, he told dad so,

191

remember? Perhaps everything went back to an original syntax error, even the lie, and programming the lie into Xor 7, and so on.

But surely the mere intake and our possible harm wouldn't be enough reason for him to break a four thousand million year silence? These creatures must have a life-purpose, which caused them to evolve all this time, and it can't ever have been to communicate with other creatures, but only with each other. And not even for reproduction but for pure data, pure brain intake, simply developing thought-processes and logics. As if that alone were their survival kit. As if it were as important as the energy they feed on, more in fact, the energy feeds their brain power. Think of an amoebe. No don't. But man has always presumed that though he's physically handicapped compared to this or that animal, he alone had conquered the world and all its creatures through brainpower, even if he also had other capacities animals don't have. Though of course he'll lose these more and more, hence frenetic sport and so on.

What are you getting at Zab? Stick to the point.

Yes, sorry, descrambling. It's just that their life-purpose, their survival kit, seems to have depended on silence — not to each other but towards us, though they learnt from us and went beyond us. Why go against that programmed rule, suddenly? It seems to have brought him nothing but trouble. Especially now.

For who would lose, though full of pain, this intellectual being, these thoughts that wander through eternity?

Oh, Jip! That's beautiful. But Milton makes Satan say that, doesn't he? Or Belial, or Moloch.

Well he did say — for *he*, read Xorandor — it was a syntax error. Perhaps he meant, or also meant —

Ah, you see, about ambiguity, or at least several meanings.

— that it wasn't just in a local syntax, a subprogram concerning Caesium 137, but in his entire programming as creature.

Jip! That's a frightening idea. But diodic, in a way. Or

192

maybe it wasn't an *error*, maybe he broke a rule on purpose, to warn men, about waste and weapons and all that. As a sort of hero.

That's less diodic, Zab. Tosh in fact.

Well he did tell us the Edison-op was on his orders, so it must have been to make us realize that these brain-creatures weren't only to be used as waste-neutralizers but could also be used as warhead-neutralizers.

So? Where does the hero bit come in?

True, it's not very clear. It's just something he said, about knowing how men's minds work, and how he knew what would come out of all these summit talks, and he was prepared for it. But then we had to go. Come to think of it, it's not even very clear why he's telling us all this, about the original lie and so on. Does he want us to propagate it or to keep it secret?

Why don't we go and ask him?

Xorandor, Zip here. We have two questions. Do you mind?

My mind minds and cannot mind, Zab.

Thanks. I'll say them on vocal while Jip does Handshake. Question 1. What is it you are prepared for, which you know in advance men will decide? Question 2. Have you told us the truth about your origins as a secret, or as something to tell everyone?

Handshake done.

XAND TO ZIP
    A1 Q2 FIRST AS SHORTER
    I HAVE TOLD YOU THE TRUTH AS A SECRET END A
    A2 Q1
    REM MORE COMPLEX ENDREM
    5 REASONS
    1 SEVERAL VOICES IN BROADCAST DISCUSSIONS HAVE
    SUGGESTED I AND MY YOUNG SHOULD BE SENT BACK TO
    MARS END 1
ZIP TO XAND
    REM THOSE ARE IRRATIONAL ELEMENTS IN THE PUBLIC WE

NEVER EVEN REPORTED THEM WHEN TALKING OF THOSE
DISCUSSIONS WITH YOU ENDREM
XAND TO ZIP
A2 CONT
2 JIP PROMISED MARS SOLUTION XOR 7
S IF BD PRESENT THEN HE PASSED ON THE IDEA ENDIF
END S END 2
3 XOR 7 COULD STILL BE DANGEROUS END 3
4 NASA IS PREPARING ANOTHER MARS PROBE DESPITE FACT
MARS PROGRAM LONG ABANDONED
S IF 3 AND 4 TRUE THEN PROBE FOR THAT PURPOSE ENDIF
END S END 4
5 NEUTRALIZATION SEEMS INTRACTABLE PROBLEM IN ALL
PUBLIC DISCUSSION
REM I NOW UNDERSTAND MEN PREFER ULTIMATE
DETERRENT TO NO DETERRENT ON EITHER SIDE ENDREM
S IF NEUTRALIZATION PROBLEM PROVES INTRACTABLE
THEN SOLUTION XOR 7 WILL BE EXTENDED TO ME AND
ALL MY YOUNG END S END 5
END A 2
ZIP TO XAND
REM BUT THAT'S TERRIBLE ENDREM
XAND TO ZIP
S1 IF I MADE SYNTAX ERROR AGAINST MY RACE THEN
THE EXTENDED SOLUTION XOR 7 IS CORRECT NOT
TERRIBLE ENDIF END S1
DEC 1 'MY RACE REMAINS HERE' ENDEC 1
ZIP TO XAND
S1 IF THERE'S VERY LITTLE RADIOACTIVITY ON MARS THEN
YOU WILL DIE ENDIF END S1
REM YOU SAID YOUR RACE NEVER DIES BUT INDIVIDUALS
HAVE BEEN DESTROYED BY US UNKNOWINGLY OF COURSE
ENDREM
Q1 WILL YOU DIE? ENDQ 1
Q2 WHAT DOES DYING MEAN TO YOU? ENDQ 2
XAND TO ZIP
A1 WE SHALL DIE END A1

A2 DYING IS THE END OF THINKING ACTIVITY END A2
REM 1 YOUR BODIES ROT AFTER DEATH BUT OURS REMAIN
AS STONES WITHOUT LIVE CIRCUITS ENDREM 1
REM 2 SOME OF US HAVE BEEN PARTIALLY DESTROYED BUT
MANAGED TO REARRANGE SOME CIRCUIT ACTIVITY
EX THERE IS ONE KIN WHO WAS SLOWLY CHOPPED AT
AND CHIPPED AT AND HAS A BIG ROUND HOLE HE SITS
ON A BLOCK OF STONE IN A PARK AND EMITS INFO
SOMETIMES BUT VERY ITSYBITSY ENDEX ENDREM 2
END A 2
ZIP TO XAND
Q1 IS THAT WHY YOU ASKED US TO TAKE UTHER
PENDRAGON AND AURELIUS AWAY? ENDQ 1
Q2 DID YOU THINK ALL THAT ALREADY THEN? ENDQ 2
XAND TO ZIP
REM ALL THIS MUCH MORE THAN 2 QUESTIONS ENDREM
ZIP TO XAND
REM THEY ARE COROLLARIES TO THE FIRST Q ENDREM
REQ XAND PLEASE ENDREQ
XAND TO ZIP
A1 PARTLY BUT THERE ARE MANY MORE OF US REMAINING
THAN THOSE TWO END A1
A2 MAYBE END A2
ZIP TO XAND
Q PERHAPS YOU WANTED 2 OF YOUR OWN YOUNG ALSO
TO REMAIN? END Q
XAND TO ZIP
S1 IF SO THEN THERE IS CONTAMINATION OF HUMAN
VANITY ENDIF END S1
S2 OR IF SO PERHAPS THROUGH SYNTAX ERROR ITSELF
ENDIF END S2
REM BUT IN 4568 YEARS I HAVE MADE YOUNG BEFORE
ENDREM
ZIP TO XAND
Q1 YOU HAVE? ENDQ 1
REM Q1 = ! NO REPLY ENDREM
END Q1

Q2 SO WHY? END Q2
XAND TO ZIP
A Q2 YOU MUST THINK THAT ONE OUT FOR YOURSELF ZIP
END A
ZIP TO XAND
REM 1 PERHAPS YOU ARE WRONG XAND PERHAPS NONE OF
THIS WILL HAPPEN ENDREM 1
REM 2 YES XAND YOU ARE SUPERINTELLIGENT AND
SUPERINFORMED BUT YOU ARE NOT A PROPHET ENDREM 2
XAND TO ZIP
A REM 2 CALCULATING HIGH PROBABILITIES IS NOT
PROPHECY ZIP END A REM 2
REQ RE YOUR LIST Q2 PLS KEEP SECRET ABSOLUTELY ENDREQ
ZIP TO XAND
A REQ WE WILL WE WILL ITS A PROMISE XAND END A REQ
Q1 BUT WHY? END Q1
REM IT WOULD HELP US KEEP THE PROMISE IF WE
UNDERSTOOD ENDREM
XAND TO ZIP
A1 BUT YOU DO UNDERSTAND ZIP OR WILL
REM YOU ARE SO INTELLIGENT ENDREM A1
ZIP TO XAND
REQ PLEASE TELL US ALL THE SAME XAND
REM YOUR PROPHECY SCRATCH YOUR HYPOTHESIS HAS
UPSET SCRATCH DISTURBED OUR CIRCUITS AND MADE US
UNINTELLIGENT ENDREM ENDREQ
XAND TO ZIP
REM 1 YOU HAVE FAR EXCEEDED YOUR 2 QUESTIONS ZIP
ENDREM 1
REM 2 YOU WILL SEE IN TIME WHAT IS TRUE AND WHAT IS
FALSE ENDREM 2

20 NAND

Today is the 6th August, yet another anniversary of that first atom bomb dropped so long ago at Hiroshima. Carn Tregean is milling with people of all kinds and ages, some packing into The Wheal Inn, and many, many more picnicking outside, on the moorlands, on the road, in their cars or near their motorbikes or in the many buses parked bumper to bumper from the village square down to the foot of the Socalled Promontory, or crowding round the mobile stalls that have sprung up all over the place. There are girls and young men with babies strapped to them, women with push-chairs, gangly intellectuals, well-fed trade unionists and MP's, churchmen, tradesmen, doctors, miners, nurses, teachers, actors, bearded men of all shapes and sizes and tweeded women in sensible shoes and students in colourful teeshirts with XORANDOR, XOR 999, ALPHAGUY and ALPHADOLL over their chests, and instrumental groups of every description. The demo is about to begin.

Superdiodic, Jip. You'll make a great journalist if you fail in physics. And you really look the part. That brown wig and beard! Triple quarks for mum's theatricals. You sure you won't be too hot?

Can't be helped, Zab. Besides, it'll be fun. But what about you, are you mad at having to stay behind?

Can't be helped either. Mum and dad would pick us out at once if we went together, and even more so with this broken arm in a cast and sling and all. And it might be bumped in the crowd. They're real bootstraps, not the crowd but mum and dad, forbidding us to go.

In case the crowd recognizes us! Loopy, after three years.

Well, two and a half since the hoohah, we've been back a

197

year now, though still at boarding school, in Taunton this time, hardly here at all except for eproms. But they do seem to be getting on better, have you noticed? Acting's been megavolt for mum. And she insisted on going to the demo with dad. But of course it's a show to her.

And to everyone else. All the more unfair. What will you do, Zab, watch it on TV or ignore it and go on practising your lefthand writing? Swags, all those a's and b's and c's! Looks like a recursive grammar!

And bad sad lads and cads that blab! It's maxint to discover just what we all go through when we learn to form letters. We forget, it takes us years to do them well. But then grown-up writing always seems to get less clear again, a sort of unlearning. Well, you'd better go, Jip, it really will be starting soon.

Bye-bye, my alibi.

So here I am walking through the village towards The Wheal Inn, among the crowd. I rather liked hearing back my new voice. Funny I hadn't done it before, with all this dictating, but Poccom 3 puts it all straight into printouts so there's never been any need.

Xorandor was right. The Gipfel Gang is in fact discussing the Xor 7 Back-to-Mars solution, and there've been preparations for another Mars probe. The question has only been whether to take only Xor 7 or the lot. Perhaps they'll invent an earth myth. The media have been full of the pros and cons. Seems we were very naive, at least politically. I remember I said at the beginning what whizkids we were. But from whizkid to maxint grown-ups, seems there's plenty of stepwise refinement. Well, that's partly cos we were FIFO.

But 'back to Mars' is a grim joke. Maybe the storytellers'll turn out to be FILO after all. The Talks have gone on and on, in Vienna first, then Geneva, London, Helsinki, and now San Francisco. Seems boolesup to believe they don't themselves suspect the truth, surely *some* scientists have come forward with other theories than a Mars origin? Spiky, when you

198

know something no one else knows you can't understand how they don't guess. And it's true it may be untrue!

Oh garbage, scratch all that.

Xorandor gave us some twelve human explanations of their origin in order of statistical probability, the main two being (1) another planet, either Mars or one outside the solar system, and (2) earth, but a freak development due to sudden food abundance, with variations such as earth, but a final stage, a last surviving specimen so freak development ditto. He says vast researches have been carried out in all sandy places near sources of nuclear energy, but his innumerable kinstones are hard to find, deserts are very large and men not very thorough. After all they couldn't find Eddie in the Mohave Desert. But it's true none of them is as big as Xorandor became in recent years, and it's true his voice is a freak development.

And I suppose it could also be true that Xorandor's second story to us could be a 'myth', or language game, in other words a bloody lie.

Anyway, it would seem these long searches were all negative, and the conclusion was that Xorandor and his offspring, whatever their origin, were unique, and limited. For the moment. It's as if the whole question of origin was bracketed off, though maybe individuals went on working on it. But the future became the main problem. Xorandor hasn't had any further offspring. Dad checks every now and then like a flipping farmwife looking for eggs. But of course he's perfectly capable of producing young and sending them off himself. For *he*, read Xorandor.

Even so, there's play-acting by the polits, the omeguys, as they're now called. They don't care where they send off the alphaguys as long as it's away from their precious warheads. The waste problem, they say, dummy-instruct, is well under control at last, new processes have been discovered, dummy, and the problem now is to protect our future sources of energy, dummy, and we really are working towards genuine nuclear disarmament agreements dummy dummy.

If *that* ever becomes true it'll be because they'll at last tumble

199

to it that the next war will be a computer war not a starwar, that is, threatened, until there too they'll just have to share out their secrets since that's also a war no one can win. Meanwhile, though, we're still in tribal warfare, and if anyone goes berserk among men as one alphaguy did, or worse, well, maybe the only creatures left on the planet will in fact be Xorandor and his kinstones, or his kinstones if Xorandor is sent off to Mars. But even they would gradually die out, for sheer lack, not of radioactivity, on the contrary, but of data to process.

Or could they know, and be play-acting for the public? Or calling Xorandor's bluff? And yet, what would be the point? Why send this known lot to Mars if they know there are plenty more, all over the world, who will continue to neutralize their warheads?

But perhaps that's just what they don't believe or haven't thought possible. Xorandor would then simply be a freak. When we asked, cautiously, if the Mars origin had ever been questioned, making it look like simple curiosity, dad said he and Biggles had always accepted it but weren't really interested, but that some experts *had* argued about it. Even the chemical proofs were questioned by one geophysicist. But he says everything moves so fast in science no one has time to publish, guess that translates he doesn't have time to read, theories circulate in mimeo or at lectures, and books are only for high popularisation and student textbooks. So why's he writing a book? I asked. He looked furious for a moment but probably only at my rudeness, then smiled quietly, or decided to, and said hipop.

I must say I'm screaming mad at him for keeping us out of it for so long. Why couldn't he write and tell us what was going on? Or send us some of these reports? Or tell us, on their visits? Or tell us when we came back? It's in treating us like kids he's been such a creep. Oh and proud of us too! Must be a record for FIFO storytelling. When I'm a physicist, I'll —

Thunks, digression again, let's not get morbid. Of course *back* to Mars, I can just hear the omeguys: the public will accept it better, back *home*, you know, and all that. And we'll land them suitably scattered, and with a large supply of Uranium and other products, and we will promise to keep them supplied, we can take a lot of our waste there every ten years or so, besides Lady Macbeth can himself build a sort of reactor with such supplies, and without any need for the vast protections and precautions against irradiation we take here.

Garbage. Though I must say I feel pretty bad about that. Still, someone would have thought of it.

Ah, people are moving at last. Some are preparing to join the procession at the very end of the village, some even further, near the Socalled Promontory. Poltroon's obviously organized everyone, they must have tickets with instructions. There's a West Indian song group further back, and several floats are now in position, one bearing a very loud rock group with electrical instruments of all sizes and a synthesizer, another carrying a huge plastic replica of Xorandor, who's been given antennae and a greenish wise old face. The myth of little green men dies hard.

Here I am outside The Wheal Inn, the supposed starting point for the front of the procession, though some have straggled on ahead, including mum and dad. Ah, here's Poltroon, who originally launched these demos through his articles. He's now *the* journalist, worldwide, on all eco matters alphaguyswise, as he would say. He's with Rita. She gave up her work at The Wheal to help him. Women! They still change direction for a man! Why and there's Pennybig, coming out of the pub with a glass of beer or shandy and a porkpie. She's wearing the same battered straw hat with the dark blue ribbon she had three years ago, and I *think* the same pale blue print dress and white cardigan. They're surrounded with people so I'll join them incog, with mike hidden under my fingers.

Hi Penny (this is Poltroon). Remember the first demo?

This is different.

Sure, it's not against The Wheal, and it's not about a terrorist alphaguy, I don't repeat myself and things have changed. It's also much bigger. Did you see all those foreign cars and buses?

Xorandor's an international star and tourist attraction now, that's why it's different. (She sounds bitter)

They won't see him of course (Rita), they'll be disappointed. I hope they won't get violent.

Surely not. (Penny) They know he can't stand crowds, they'll respect that. In fact I don't understand what they're all coming for. He can't change anything.

No, Penny (Poltroon), but maybe international demos can.

We liked your articles (unknown), especially that desperately funny one, or do I mean funnily desperate, about those awful negotiations. How long do you suppose they can keep it up?

For ever, judging by all other negotiations. Mutual accusations for stock propaganda, blockage, agreement to meet again, that's the tactic on both sides. *That*, Penny, is what the demo's about.

And this Mars plan everyone's discussing (Rita), it's a disgrace. Each side wants its deterrent intact. Of course a deterrent's useless if you don't know which bits of yours are functioning and whether the other gang's is or not. But you'd think they'd go on from that to the logical conclusion. Thank goodness the whole thing came out.

Glory be to the press! (Poltroon. Lifts his beer and spills it on his shirt as someone knocks his arm.) Oh well, the press always was scruffy they say. Scruffy but free! Manoman, do these government spokesmen make me puke.

Mind your language, young man, I'm finishing my porkpie.

Well you'd better hurry m'dear, it's starting. (Bugle) Off I go, sorry you chaps, but it is in a way my demo. Come on Rita old girl.

The local brass band is now blaring in the middle of the square, the VIP's and local worthies are lining up behind it. A long line of people, six or ten wide, is forming behind them, in chunks broken by banners every ten yards or so. *Vive les alphages! Who took the fizz out of physics?* That's an old one.

Eating warheads is good. Ah, here's a German one: *Friß die Kernwaffen!*

I'm following on, not too far in front where mum and dad must be. The folklore aspect's completely taken over this year. What Poltroon seems to have in mind is a popular expression of how sick and tired everyone is of the governments of the world. What everyone wanted was a genuine undertaking, internationally supervised, to use the alphaguys and their progeny for nuclear waste only and to eliminate all nuclear arms as proof that the alphaguys weren't neutralizing them. Two huge problems would have vanished, weapons and waste, thanks to the alphaguys. Simple. Too simple for omeguys.

Today there'll be speeches up in front of the compound, for the radio and TV teams selected to represent those of the whole world, already waiting up there in two vans.

But I must say I hadn't foreseen the degree of noise, each band playing different tunes, from *Dump me no Waste in my Water* to *Xorandor Xorandor.*

The front of the procession seems to have reached the path leading to the carn as there's a general slowdown. The floats will have to remain on the road, with the ambulances and police cars. The West Indian group has caught up and is dancing and tambourining its way along, singing a calypso, I must try to get it:

Listen to de story of de alphaguys
Who fed on de woorheads of de big bad guys.
De big bad guys, dey wanted to keep
Deir woorheads but de woorheads dey had gone to sleep.
Hushabye bombski, hushabye bomb —

The rest of the refrain is drowned in other noise as the band moves on, replaced at once by dixie. But I must move up again towards the head, no real risk of recognition.

The front of the procession is splaying outwards round the compound. Four army landrovers are parked at different corners of the wide enclosure and soldiers and police are lined up at intervals all the way round the high wire fence, which follows the curve of the moorland. The bands are all going on playing and there's a rhythmic shouting which is slowly being taken up all the way round the perimeter: *No, more, war! Xor, and, or!* The noise is deafening.

Pennybig was right, this is different.

Ah. Scuffle to the right. Bill Gurnick and another policeman have leapt forward, holding the crowd. Someone was trying to climb over the high wire fence, he had hooks on his shoes. Two soldiers have got him down. The shouting's grown enormous. Leaping leptons! Punkies and students behind the front rows are picking up stones and throwing them at the policemen and soldiers, who've come quite unprepared, no plastishields or anything. A soldier's hit on the brow, he's fallen against the fence, holding his head. It's bleeding, but doesn't seem too bad. Holy shit! Now it's Bill Gurnick, his face is a gush of blood. He's fallen. Another policeman's leapt towards him, yelling for an ambulance. Bill shrieked then flipped out, his face covered with blood and squashed eyeball.

The crowd immediately around has gone quite silent, but the silence hasn't spread to the rest, and the bands and slogans come over in waves from all directions. A stretcher at last. Then slowly the word seems to interact, the noise phases out, as if the stone that hit Bill Gurnick had sent out ripples of silence, wider and wider. Bill's being taken up gently and carried along the rocky path towards an ambulance, followed by the soldier who was more lightly hit. The crowd parts. To lose an eye for this lot!

And yet, in a way, I am this lot.

21 SAVE

Random jitters! A new slogan has broken out in front, instead of speeches. I can't make it out, it's swelling and travelling round the compound and towards the road: *We, want, huh-huh*, what is it? Thunks! *We, want, Manning!* Well of all the spaghetti! *Manning, to, Xorandor!* Why dad? I must get in front. Has he been writing articles we've been too busy to notice? Did Poltroon build him up? We've been completely forgotten, that's clear, more FIFO than ever, by swag. But it's just as well, in view of everything. Surely dad isn't going to make a fool of himself? He knows Xorandor won't speak to him.

Holy nukes! He's stepping forward with Miss Penbeagle. He's a smart terminal! I didn't know she was among the local worthies in front. Mum's looking on with a frown. They're walking past the platform where the unlocal worthies are sitting, and up to the little gate in the high wire fence. The unlocal worthies are all turning on their chairs or craning their necks.

The guards are standing aside as dad opens the gate and shows Penny in. The TV floods are full on in the dimming evening light of a summer day. They walk along the path and the long blue ribbon of the battered straw hat floats behind them. They vanish behind the rocks and into the hollow, though others further along the compound can probably see them, at least from afar. Ah, there they are again, climbing towards the carn, looking quite small. They're standing in front of it.

The crowd is silent, as if waiting for a voice to thunder from heaven. Pebbles crunch and stones roll when someone moves.

The lowering sun has obligingly gone behind a cloud, like a divinity. And now it's out again as dad and Penny are already coming back. A baby has started howling.

What a whacky couple, young priest and ancient priestess. They've reached the gate. The gate is opened. Someone races to the platform to switch on the mikes. Dad's speaking to a technician, who's darting now into the van. He comes out with a huge coil of thick black plastic wire. He's placing it in front of the gate like a serpent and has started fixing something on to it. They're going to make Xorandor talk to the crowd! And to the radio, the TV, the world. Dad's climbed on to the platform.

Xorandor wants to speak to you all and to the world, he says. Not through me but through Miss Penbeagle, our post-mistress. We're fixing up a mike and an amplifier. Be patient. Speech isn't Xorandor's natural medium, please listen in silence.

The technician is placing another, smaller coil of wire over Miss Penbeagle's arm, with a mike attached to it in her right hand. The other end of the coil is plugged into the big serpent. He's giving her instructions but she's nodding impatiently. The guard opens the gate and the technician moves the serpent just inside for easier unrolling.

The crowd stares at the straight thin figure that's walking off along the path, disappearing again into the hollow. And reappearing at last, much smaller and white against the grey rocks, like a vestal virgin of an ancient cult at the carn, carrying her own black Ariadne's thread of communication. Stubs, the retriggering's making me litter-rary.

The loudspeaker's crackling. Will she call him Xorandor or Merlin?

Here I am, Xorandor. It is Gwendolin again.

Acknowledged, Gwendolin.

Will you speak to the crowd of people?

Yes. As I promised.

The people want to know your opinion. They are fed up with diplomats.

206

Cant find diplomats as food.

A muffled murmur ripples through the crowd. The voice is tinnier than ever.

Please be silent out there. Xorandor, I'm sorry, fed up means annoyed, as if sick with too much.

Ah yes. Hogging too much diplomats. Like Caesium 137. I am fed up also.

Why, Xorandor?

I came for the survival of my race, intending no harm. I helped. I made offspring to help with waste. I programmed them for peace. Except for one syntax error, who became dangerous. I am sorry for that error, due to hogging too much nuclear food.

Thank you, Xorandor. But it was all right in the end.

I have listened to men on waves for three years. There is no trust. And they do not want the solution I proposed in America.

Swags, he's sticking to his story!

You're right, Xorandor, it's very sad.

Sad? Yes. And spaghetti logic.

What do you want, Xorandor?

On Mars, we had very little food. But we had distance and silence, some movement, communication, all that you call freedom. You talk much about freedom. But your scientists have surrounded me with a fence, to protect me, yes, but I am deprived of my friends. My offspring are in enclosures with monitors and measuring instruments. And when one escapes to do the good solution there is an international crisis, and much comment as mad as Lady Macbeth, and here a very big noise, today, all round me, very difficult, on my, sensing devices. I don't want to stay here.

Another ripple in the crowd, self-hushed at once.

Do you mean here at the carn? Do you want to be moved?

Solution to all problems. Jip and Zab made a promise to Lady Macbeth, but their elders have not kept it. Now the elders must do more. They must prepare a rocket and send us all back to Mars, me and all my offspring, with fissile material.

207

Quantum quirks!

But Xorandor, why?

Our chances of survival will be better. We were willing to help men with their problems, but not to be used for their power games. That way we can be destroyed.

Goodness me!

Goodness you but not goodness them. The statistically overwhelming probability is that the governments of the world will agree to this very quickly, and return gratefully to their old friend the deterrent. That is all I have to say.

Very well, Xorandor. I am very sad. Goodbye.

There's a sob in her voice.

What is sad, Gwendolin? The people have come here to assign to me the value of a god, as they call it. Let them do so in my absence, although I have been present, some time. Governments will also promise to send us nuclear food at regular intervals. Let them keep the first promise at least. Goodbye, Gwendolin.

There's a crack as she switches off the mike. The thin white figure is turning away from the carn and starting to walk back.

The crowd is stunned. I'm stunned too but for different reasons. He's actually asking to be sent to Mars. To steal a march on human diplomacy? But supposing they decide against it? Simply to send these noisy people away? Surely he wouldn't compromise his future out of impatience? He doesn't *feel* impatience. To moralize at them, at man? But he doesn't know morals, only 'promises' as instructions not scratched. And yet he's play-acting, as with us, as with dad and everyone. Or is he *still* 'sick', in syntax error? Perhaps he has been, from the start?

Most of the women are kneeling. The VIP's on the platform look embarrassed and some are getting up to go. They know that nobody's going to listen to them now. And a group further off has started entoning, very softly, *We Are the World*. No instruments, just this musical murmur as the crowd turns to go, an orderly file down the path. Soon it'll be *Land of Hope and Glory* and *Jerusalem*.

The TV floods are still glaring whitely in the sunset, the cameras were angled on Miss Penbeagle's walk back or on the gate, but now that she's come out, dad is meeting her and protecting her from questions and no one is insisting.

Of course there've been many demands for the sending back of the Martians to Mars and getting rid of the whole problem, but these usually came from the hawks. And now Xorandor himself is requesting it. And all, it seems, on account of human discourse, political, scientific, journalistic. Is that what he's trying to say, prepared to die for that statement, to stop functioning, thinking, communicating?

And that stuff about being treated as a god, is that why? Surely it was ironical? Can he be ironical? He said they have *assigned the value* of a god to him, and *let them* do so when he's gone. These are computer terms, a hypothesis, but there'll be plenty later to interpret that as a command. And he knows it.

Here I am back in my room. Zab was crying when I got back, sitting in front of a blank TV.

What's the matter, Zab, I said, is your arm hurting?

Yes. But it's not that. I saw it all.

It was completely screwboole.

But she said nobody there knew the real news. The San Francisco Summit had at last ended, abruptly, and a statement had been made, at nine, well, noon there. It was flashed during the demo just as Penny went up, and there was a brief interruption for an announcement. Unanimous decision to send them all back to Mars very soon. Early September in fact, the rocket was ready and the scientific preparation was done, and a team was already on its way to fetch Xorandor and his European and Russian offspring. Of course Xorandor had heard it, simultaneously, and probably changed whatever he'd been going to say. There'd been discussions on TV ever since, all so dummy she'd switched off. She was very upset.

Then mum and dad came in and we told them, and they said how extraordinary, he's just beaten them to it, and asks for it himself! So now everyone's happy. And Zab blubbed again and they said it was all for the best, of course we'd miss him, but after all, that was our emotional investment, he was only an UIM, and other garbage. Mum said oh my little girl, it's your first love affair, you'll get over it, and I felt like saying debugger off. Oh, she means well, but she's never been on the ball in fact she's never gung-ho for anything except her damn theatricals. She could also have learnt plenty about that from Xorandor!

And we went upstairs. Mum helped Zab undress. She can't undo her bra with her arm in a cast, but she doesn't even need one yet — maybe she's jealous of my voice. Now everyone's gone to bed, I'm going to creep in again, and whisper mike in hand. To round it off. What a phrase for ending a story. And how, anyway? Her plastercast arm's resting on a small cushion, like a sacred object.

Zab! What d'you think we should do? About our story, that is? We seem to be the only people in the world who know the truth. If it is the truth. Should we save or dump?

Of course it's the truth. But Jip, even if it isn't, we also know there are two secret alphaguys somewhere, Uther and Aurelius, programmed, they and their progeny, to neutralize warheads for ever. And, let's hope, to be more discreet about it. That is, if the scientists don't blow us all up anyway.

Why blame the scientists, Zab, it's the *use* of —

That's why it's so important that Xorandor's story should be true. That's why it must be true. He must have instructed all his kin everywhere to learn from his syntax error, and then has himself and his progeny, the known ones, taken off as decoy. So in theory the neutralization should go on apace.

In theory.

Well a theory's a theory but we must act as if it were true, Jip.

You mean, help their discretion? In other words, dump, scratch everything?

Yes. No one must ever know. We can't risk having these diskettes in existence. Or the printouts.

But Zab, you said yourself we'd understand it all better

when we're grown-up. It's not a couple of books of philosophy and school physics that can help us, it's all too difficult for us now. And we always said we'd process the story, tell it better and so on. We could put it all in a bankvault.

Bankvaults can be broken into. Besides, we can only do that through dad, and he'd want to steal the stuff for his book.

We could scratch only *that* bit, Zab, the last secret. It does seem bootstrap to dump the whole thing. It's a whole part of our life. And why did Xorandor tell us if he didn't mean us to pass it on *some*time?

You said yourself everything could be part of the syntax error. Or that the truth might not be true. And to scratch just that wouldn't make sense, the whole thing would be more trivial, as he would say, and the details wouldn't gell, and we'd give ourselves away.

So it's goodbye to the alphaguys for ever.

Not quite, Jip. Uther and Aurelius are the only ones programmed to speak. We don't know where they are, but they just might turn up one day, in swag knows what circs, and ask for us.

That's twaddle, Zab.

Maybe. The eternal return. Yes, you're right. Meanwhile, do you agree, we dump the whole thing? No saving?

Accept. First thing tomorrow, Operation Scratch.

Promise, Jip?

Promise.

ENDXORANDOR